The arrivals lounge at Alicante Airport was its usual chaotic summer self. People stood six deep behind a barrier at the opposite end of the walkway from the sliding doors that held everyone's attention. As each wave of tourists and home comers emerged, their faces were scanned and clues about where they had flown from sought. Flight status boards were checked and rechecked in anticipation of the appearance of friends and family, as the baggage handlers struggled behind the scenes to load and unload the enormous volume of traffic experienced at this time of year. As the gateway to the Costa Blanca, Alicante was pushed to the limit by those from colder northern climes seeking solace in the hot Mediterranean sun.

At the rear of the expectant gathering stood a tall broad shouldered man in the livery of a chauffeur. A peaked cap and mirrored sunglasses covered much of his face and he paid no attention to those around him. His gaze was firmly fixed on the sliding doors and those emerging from them. Although he had never seen the people he was waiting for, he knew what to look for. A man of twenty-three and his sister aged twenty-one. Daddy was rich and therefore they would not be hauling their own luggage. Others did that for them. As those around him jostled for a better view, his intimidating presence seemed to emit a force field that kept them at bay. When the two young people came into view, he knew instantly they were who he had been waiting for.

The young man was tall and thin with foppish curly black hair. He was good-looking and wore a creased, but clearly expensive, white suit, and his air

1

of arrogance was unmistakable. The girl was a Spanish beauty, with straight black silky hair falling almost to her waist. Her complexion was flawless and her make-up immaculate, suggesting that she was used to the attention of the press, while her svelte figure showed off the designer clothes exactly as intended. They too were granted the personal space denied to the shorts and t-shirted family groups with their chaotic collection of unlikely luggage. The newly arrived siblings scanned the sea of faces for their champion who would take them somewhere more exclusive.

Pedro responded by holding high a banner with 'Los Alvés' clearly printed, black on white. The young woman smiled and waved in acknowledgement while her brother merely redirected the porter pushing a trolley with far too much baggage for two people. The chauffeur indicated that they exit to their right and he met them as they found the open space beyond the remaining greeters.

"Mr and Miss Alvés, your father has sent me to collect you."

"Where is Juan, the usual driver?" Sergio asked.

Despite his lofty demeanour, the only son of one of the wealthiest businessmen in Spain felt uncomfortable with anything that wasn't familiar in what he considered his home environment.

"Juan is unwell, sir," Pedro replied. "The car is waiting just outside the door."

This time it was he who guided the resigned looking porter struggling with the overloaded trolley. As they emerged into the hot late afternoon sunshine, it hit them like a slap on the face.

"Back to temperate weather and civilization," Sergio commented sarcastically. It was a little disguised fact that he hated the hot Mediterranean summers, preferring the cooler, less-predictable ambience of London or Paris.

They were here at the insistence of their father, he who held the strings to the purse that allowed them the lavish lifestyle they normally led. Their grandmother's eightieth birthday was indeed a notable event but Sergio doubted that the old girl had enough of her wits about her to notice who was and wasn't in attendance. This trip was all about appeasing his father and making sure that the gravy train stayed firmly on the track.

The chauffeur opened the rear left door of the long elegant vehicle and held it while the brother and sister got in.

"One moment," he said, indicating that he would take care of the bags and the tip for the porter.

Sergio took the cut-glass decanter from the Tantalus and poured himself a cognac. He brandished it at Carmen but she waved away his offer and continued to observe their driver managing the porter. The chauffeur gave the porter a small denomination note and the porter looked between the giver and the gift. He realised that his gratuity was non-negotiable and retreated to the shade for a cigarette, muttering beneath his breath about 'hired lackeys'.

The driver proceeded to the front of the Limousine and opened the door, but didn't get in. He picked up what looked like a small deodorant spray and opened the right-hand passenger door. Sergio was about to complain but never got the chance. As he looked up from his drink, the chauffeur sprayed the contents of the canister into his face while covering his own nose and mouth with the handkerchief he held in his left hand. Sergio instantly dropped unconscious into his seat.

Carmen grasped the handle of her door but it didn't move. As she turned to complain, she met the same fate as her brother. Pedro checked that their seat belts were properly secured before closing the door and taking a few deep breaths of fresh air in order to offset any effect the spray may have had on him. Happy that the public part of his mission had gone exactly to plan, he settled in the driver's seat and drove serenely away from the airport.

He chose a petrol station not ten kilometres from the arrival's lounge as the place to make sure that his prizes would not slip away from him. This was a place where people with hire cars would stop to repack their holiday luggage and check to make sure that someone had actually picked up the red bag. It had an expansive parking area and he chose the most remote corner, far from the shop and CCTV cameras. He looked around to make sure that no one was watching him before he took his own holdall from the boot and removed the items he required; duct tape, rope, and two soft black scarves.

He started with the tape around the wrists, thighs, and ankles of his two passengers. He had much practice in this form of bondage and he completed the task effortlessly. The rope was tied in a knot he had learnt in a prison in Equatorial Guinea, and despite ten years having passed since being shown this elaborate configuration, he was pleased that it appeared to work perfectly. Finally, he tied the scarves around the heads of his victims, covering their eyes. He took off the chauffeur's cap and jacket and threw then into the boot beside his holdall before returning to the driver's seat.

It was Sergio who woke first. The darkness didn't make sense; he was in Alicante, wasn't he? As he tried to bring his hands up to his face to make the darkness go away, he realised that they were tied together in front of him. His legs were the same. What the hell was going on? He remembered the airport and the strange chauffeur. As he mentally worked through his actions in order to rule out drugs related confusion, he could still taste the cognac in his mouth and so knew that this wasn't in his imagination.

The spray; the driver had sprayed something in his face and that was the last thing he could remember. He could hear the purr of the five-litre engine and suspected that he was still in the Limousine. He tried to move and felt something tighten around his neck.

"What's going on?" he demanded to know.

He heard a click as the driver switched on an intercom.

"You have been kidnapped. Your arms and legs are tethered but other than that, and the blindfold, you are unharmed."

"What's around my neck?"

"That's just a little something to stop you being a nuisance. It is a rather ingenious knot, tied around your neck and that of your sister. If you sit still, it will remain slack, but if you move, it will tighten around your sister's neck. When she awakens I would advise you to tell her about this, otherwise she may panic and choke you."

Despite the air conditioning working perfectly, Sergio began to sweat heavily. He reached out with his legs and found something soft and giving, which he assumed was his sister. He gently nudged her a few times, and was rewarded with a soft throat clearing noise as Carmen regained consciousness.

"Carmen, Carmen, can you hear me?"

Carmen sat bolt upright in panic as she tried to move her arms and legs and couldn't. The blindfold confused her and she heard a guttural sound as Sergio strained to warn her about the rope around their necks. He struggled to breathe as the devious knot did its job.

Pedro looked in the rear-view mirror and sighed as he saw what was unfolding in the back seat. Sergio's gasps had further panicked Carmen, and this cycle could only end one way unless he intervened. He looked beyond the back seat to make sure that it was clear for him to stop at the side of the narrow road. Sergio was beginning to turn blue and fall forward unto the floor of the luxury car, and this was now tightening the noose around his sister's neck.

Pedro quickly got out of the static car, opened the back door, and released the tension on the knot. As he prized the gasping young man back into his seat, he held his sister in place to prevent a recurrence of the unfortunate but professionally pleasing action.

"Carmen, listen to me. It is important that you sit still. Every time you move, the noose around Sergio's neck will tighten. His panic caused your rope to tighten too. He will be ok in a few minutes but it is vital that you sit still."

Carmen's instinct was to cry, and she followed it. Her brother heaved air into his oxygen starved lungs as Pedro supported his shoulders.

"You will be alright. No more drama and that goes for the pair of you."

Sergio's powers of recovery were better that Pedro had imaged, as his bound hands were whipped up at pace and smashed the driver in the face. Caught completely by surprise he fell back into the road, hitting his head on the car door in transit. He wiped the blood from his split lip and looked at it before attempting to stand.

"I knew you were going to be a little shit the moment I set eyes on you," he said as he strode to the holdall in the boot.

He returned with a knife. This was no ordinary knife, it was a special knife. The Fairbairn–Sykes fighting knife was that preferred by the British Royal Marines and one that Pedro had come to love over the years. With two razor sharp edges, this knife allowed the bearer that extra second when it counted, orientation being no problem. He pulled the blindfold from Sergio's eyes so that he could see what was happening; the psychological effect of torture outweighing the actual damage done. Pedro restrained the young man with a heavy knee on his chest before raising the knife in front of his face. This move had the desired effect as Sergio's eyes opened wider than ever before and as they focused on the evil looking weapon centimetres from his face. The chauffeur knew exactly what he was doing as he drew the razor sharp knife across the throat of the petrified passenger.

"What's going on?" Carmen insisted on knowing, but neither man replied.

Her brother was too frightened to breathe, let alone speak, and their captor, with a wide, manic grin on his face, was enjoying the moment. Pedro knew how little pressure he had to apply in order to generate what seemed like a lot of blood. He let it run down the glistening blade before lifting it theatrically in front of his victim's face once more. Sergio, now in a state of terror, tried to move but the older man's weight was too much for him.

"It's a scratch, no more, but take it as a warning. Do we have an understanding?"

The man holding the knife smiled as though he were offering afternoon tea. Sergio, now shaking and white with fear, nodded feebly.

"Good. Let's get on with our journey."

With this, he lifted his knee from Sergio's chest and replaced his blindfold.

Carmen asked if he was all right and he gasped something unintelligible. At this moment, Sergio felt small and very alone. Only twelve hours ago, he was the life and soul of the hottest party in Las Ramblas in Barcelona. He knew that a number of his guests were there, not out of friendship, but because of who he was. This wasn't important; when he threw a party, everybody who was anybody wanted to be there. Now he felt like a nobody, a small pathetic figure who wanted to cry. There was an element of guilt and shame about his previous boorish, bratty behaviour when compared to his complete helplessness at this moment and this didn't make him feel any better. He was glad that Carmen didn't see the tears he could hold back no longer. They travelled on in silence.

At Alicante Airport, Juan the chauffeur was beginning to panic. As normal, he had been there thirty minutes before the flight was due to land and stood in a prominent place at the very front of the crowd in arrivals. He knew that he looked like a cigar Indian with his placard but that was exactly what he was paid to do. The waves of arriving passengers came and went with no sight of Sergio and Carmen. He double-checked the details in his phone to confirm that he had the correct flight, and being correct didn't make him feel any better. There seemed little point in waiting there any longer, so he made his way to the Iberia desk and asked them to check the passenger manifest for the Alvés siblings.

The clerk seemed less than willing to divulge passenger information so he moderated his questions to accommodate what she was allowed to disclose.

"Yes, a Mr S Alvés and a Miss C Alvés were booked on an Iberia flight today. I have no record of them boarding in Barcelona. They tell us nothing."

"Did they perhaps take an earlier flight, or even a later one?"

The clerk tapped at her keyboard while peering suspiciously over her glasses at the chauffeur. She had taken an instant dislike to him and wasn't making a good job of hiding it. Juan tried smiling but this didn't help.

"I have no record of them boarding in Barcelona," she repeated.

"Did they or didn't they get on an Iberia plane?" Juan was getting exasperated.

"I cannot check every passenger manifest. All I can tell you is that they didn't board the flight you asked about, sir."

"Did they get off the bloody plane then?"

"I'm sorry, sir. If you insist on taking that tone, I'll have no option but to call for security."

Juan held his hands up in a gesture of appeasement, realising that he had encountered an unmovable object. He thanked the clerk for her help, although neither felt any sincerity in his statement.

His next move was to scour the airport in a state of growing panic. He knew of Sergio's blatant disregard for schedules and other people's sensitivities and went to the most likely place to find him, the first-class bar. His uniform meant that he entered unchallenged and several suited sippers looked at him in anticipation of their transport having turned up. The result was disappointment for both parties. Juan had little choice but to call his boss and their father.

Fernando Alvés was a busy man who didn't like interruptions to his schedule and Juan knew this all too well. He would only consider taking this route when all other options had been exhausted, and in this case, he felt that he had no choice. If something had happened to his precious children, Juan wanted as much distance as possible between himself and whatever problem might have arisen.

He had been with Fernando Alvés for eight years now and admired him immensely. Fernando Alvés had suffered some heavy knocks in his business dealings but always came back fighting, giving better than he got. The daughter, Carmen, had always been a sweet, well-mannered girl who treated Juan like part of the family. However, the same couldn't be said for Sergio. On many an occasion Juan would happily have throttled the 'supercilious little prick', as he called him in confidence with other members of the household domestic staff, and this was allowable as it was a view held by most. Above all else, Juan loved his well-paid job and wanted to keep it. Fernando's Alvés' PA put him through to his office.

"Sir, it's Juan. Could there have been some kind of mix up about the arrival time for Sergio and Carmen this afternoon?"

"What do you mean 'mix up'? All you have to do is pick them up and bring them home. Is there a problem?"

"They haven't arrived, sir."

"Have you checked with the desk?"

Juan decided that he would answer the question asked without revealing the awkward details of his encounter with the airline clerk.

"They don't have any record of them boarding the plane in Barcelona, sir."

"Wait there until I call you. They have probably missed their flight. They'll most likely be on the next one. I'll call them and get back to you."

The phone went dead and Juan returned it to his pocket. He checked the flight status board, saw he had at least an hour until the next arrival from Barcelona, and took the opportunity to get a cup of coffee.

"I hope someone has got a gun to his head," he thought as he drank his overpriced mocha. This wasn't too far away from the truth.

As they continued their silent vigil in the rear of the Limousine, Carmen gave a small squeal when her mobile vibrated in her coat pocket. She was in a trance like state as she considered the probable outcomes to their situation. This was always a possibility when you have a rich father, and he had carefully guarded them against such an occurrence since they were children. But, when they left their private schools with elaborate security for the freedom of university life, there was little he could do to keep them safe. She chose the Sorbonne in Paris where she was an unknown entity. She knew that her studies were no more than an indulgence by her parents, as they expected no more from her than to marry well and produce grandchildren. Sergio, who never mastered languages, only got as far as Madrid and followed the business studies route that was expected of the man who would one day be the head of Alvés.com.

On the security side, their study years were untouched by those from the dark side, though Sergio needed bailing out when he incurred a large gambling debt, his markers being held by a powerful underworld figure. Fernando Alvés pulled some strings, and with his even more powerful friends, money was exchanged and Sergio threatened with disinheritance if there was the slightest hint of a recurrence.

Now they had virtually volunteered themselves into the back of a car with a stranger, blindfolded and bound, without checking with their father and heading to God knows where. She knew who was calling and why.

"That will be my father,' she said stoically in hope that the importance of her father would influence the kidnapper and he would perhaps reconsider his options.

The driver looked at her in the mirror.

"Is he looking for his naughty children?"

She didn't answer. She turned to where she knew her brother sat.

"It'll be all right now, Sergio. Father knows we are missing and he will have every policeman in Valencia looking for us by nightfall."

There was no response from Sergio and Carmen was worried about him.

"Are you ok?"

"Yes", was all he hissed in reply. Her brother could be a brat at times.

When they felt the vehicle slow and come to a halt, they wondered if their journey had come to an end. They heard the driver get out and waited for their doors to be opened. They weren't. At the pay phone, Pedro found a sheet of paper in his pocket and dialled the number. A garbled voice answered. This was the man he knew only as 'The Fixer'. The Colonel had been quite specific about no real names being used. For Pedro, this wasn't an issue as he had used so many names over the years that he had almost forgotten what his birth name really was.

On every job, he would study the given identity documents and drill his new life history such that this is what he would reveal under serious interrogation. The Fixer opened the line without speaking.

"I've got them."

"Were there any problems?"

"No problems. What do you want me to do now?"

"Take this number and call their father. He is a businessman called Fernando Alvés. Tell him that you have them and that a ransom will be demanded at a later date. Take them to the location you have prepared and wait for my instructions. Do you understand?"

"I understand. Give me the number."

The distorted voice dictated the number of the father of his captives.

"Call me tomorrow for your instructions" was all he said before he cut the line.

Pedro, having worked with many unsavoury characters in his professional life, knew the value of anonymity. The Colonel had told him that the Fixer was the paymaster and the money was guaranteed. He had already received €50,000 up front, and that was as much of a reference as he needed. He dialled the given number and asked to speak to Fernando Alvés.

An officious sounding woman answered and was reluctant to connect him without a name.

"It's about his children, Sergio and Carmen. It is very important."

"Just one moment, I'll see if he is available."

Twenty seconds later, a man's voice replaced that of the officious woman.

"Fernando Alvés. You have something important to tell me about my children?"

He said this more in the manner of a demand than a question. Pedro thought that this was a man who was used to getting what he wanted.

"I have Sergio and Carmen. They are safe for now. You will receive a ransom demand in due course, but for now it is imperative that you do not contact the police. If I as much as suspect that you have talked to them, I will start to remove body parts and return your offspring piece by piece."

"Who the hell is this? You can't threaten me. Do you know who I am? I have contacts all the way up to the government."

"That's quite enough of the self importance. You have got a bit of a temper, Fernando Alvés. If we are to do business, I suggest that you address your manners. Anyway, I've got things to do and I'll be in touch."

"When?"

"When the time is right Fernando, and not one moment before. Remember, any hint of police involvement and I will get very nervous indeed."

Pedro returned the handset into the cradle and enjoyed the satisfying click followed by the loud purring sound that it made.

The same purring far from satisfied Fernando Alvés, and he cursed as he heard the caller hang up. He clenched his fists in rage, more at his own helplessness than the plight of his children He informed his PA that he was finishing for the day, and when she pointed out that he had two further appointments that afternoon, she received an abrupt rebuke for her professionalism. When he left his office stating that he would not be questioned, she knew that the mysterious call had something to do with his change of demeanour. This was so unlike him; he was always in control.

Today, he wasn't in control and Pedro smiled to himself in this knowledge as he started the Limousine for the final leg of their journey.

Only two weeks before, Pedro had received the call from the Colonel.

"I have a job for you, Pedro" he began.

Pedro recognised the voice instantly and hoped that it would be a return to the front line. The Colonel had previously told him that it was be unlikely that he would be offered another contract in Africa because of his age, but this didn't stop Pedro hoping above all else that he could return to military action for one last time. Africa was in his blood.

He had been a soldier all of his life and it was all he knew. His initial loyalties were national, then international and finally, purely mercenary, but he always gave one hundred percent for whatever flag he was fighting under. Once he was much sought after but now was the day of a younger man. God knows he had given enough blood, sweat and tears in his time, but the Colonel, trying to let a faithful servant down gently, only passed him what he called 'private commissions' these days. Pedro knew that this was another 'private'.

"Good to hear from you Colonel" he lied. "I hope you called to tell me the contractor in Libreville has reconsidered the training job?"

Colonel Klaus Meerkerk, expected this question and ignored it.

"I have a very lucrative private commission for you Pedro. Something you might enjoy and will make your approaching retirement a whole lot easier."

The very fact the Colonel mentioned retirement made it very clear to Pedro that his usefulness to the Colonel's organization was nearing an end. Private

Military Companies, or PMCs as they were called in order to give an air of respectability to mercenary soldiering, were a lucrative business. However, the Balkans, the Middle East, and the Arab Spring had produced an abundant supply of seasoned younger soldiers who were familiar with modern weapons and tactics, and all too willing to side with a cause bolstered by gold and blood diamonds in darkest Africa. Pedro had once been that younger man and found it hard to accept that he had survived to an age where he could no longer compete with the new blood. Nonetheless, the Colonel still rated him highly enough to pass work his way, work that carried his personal guarantee of success.

"I'm listening, Colonel."

"You are to abduct two people from Alicante Airport and take them to safe house that you will have prepared. You will then contact your paymaster, 'the Fixer'. He will give instructions to you directly."

Pedro recalled the botched kidnapping he had carried out five years before in Barcelona. He had gone freelance on that job and it didn't end well. The family refused to pay the ransom, so he started to torture the victim, recorded every painful moment on video, and sent it to them. Their resistance broke on seeing the brutality being meted out but that wasn't the only thing to break. His victim could take no more and hanged himself with a shredded towel. Pedro fled the scene and called to tell the now distraught family where they could find the body. He hoped that this had gone unnoticed by the people who mattered to him.

"When is this to happen?"

18

"In two weeks."

"Where is the safe house?"

"All of the details will be in the envelope that is waiting in your post box."

Pedro silently cursed the Colonel for his arrogant assumption that he would accept the mission. He would have done his research and known that Pedro was currently 'between jobs'.

"How much?"

"Fifty up front and another fifty on completion."

One hundred thousand Euros would certainly help his financial situation. He had been less than prudent over the years with money, and on more than one occasion needed to flee a scenario without being able to take his prize with him. He had to take this job. He wanted to take this job.

"I will make sure that the Fixer is satisfied, sir."

"I know you will, Pedro. One last thing."

"Anything you want, Colonel."

"No fuck ups like Barcelona."

He knew. Pedro had done that job on his own. He had never breathed a word about it to anyone, but the Colonel knew. How? He was tempted to ask but thought better of it. Colonel Klaus Meerkerk had contacts everywhere.

"There will be no mistakes, I guarantee you, sir."

"Good luck, Pedro."

Fifteen minutes later, he was collecting the parcel from his post box in town. He had never informed The Flying Dutchman PMC of his whereabouts, having given only a phone number, but the Colonel knew exactly where he was. Pedro also knew things, like the fact that the Flying Dutchman was actually a

South African: however, he would never dare to divulge this. The parcel was a standard A4 bubble-wrap envelope and he could tell by touch that it contained a set of keys. He waited until he was seated in his car before opening it.

The heavy bundle of keys fell onto his lap as he pulled out the papers containing the details he needed. The brief was on paper with no header, produced on a standard computer printer, completely untraceable. It told him to proceed to the location identified on the map attached. The one to ten thousand scale map identified a building in what Pedro considered the middle of nowhere. He had to make the building secure and, if necessary, soundproof. Two cells were to be organised for the victims and equipment was to be available for recording video footage of their pleas for the ransom to be paid. A Limousine was to be procured and the plates changed. A chauffeur's uniform would be necessary for the pick up at the time given. This was not to be purchased from the same place that the Limo was hired from. He was to play the role of a temporary replacement for a chauffeur called Juan who was unwell.

A further sheet gave details of the victims: a Sergio Alvés, twenty-three, and his younger sister, Carmen, twenty-one. It included a brief history of their short adult lives but no photographs. The Fixer was adamant that Pedro took the two young people without appearing in anyway familiar with them.

The last item in the envelope was a banker's draft for fifty thousand Euros.

Pedro followed the instructions to the letter, all too aware that the Colonel might have someone watching him. He took the Limousine on a week's hire from a company run by a British ex-pat in Malaga. He could tell in an instant that this man was no stranger to the police, so would ask no questions. They shook on their deal with a cash payment under a name that both knew to be false.

The secret location was a large building in a remote valley that took some time to find. The landscape was barren and mountainous and it was all too clear why so many movies set in the deserts of Mid-West America and Mexico had actually been filmed in Spain. Over the millennia, water had carved the landscape into a fascinating array of channels and layers separated by inhospitable plateaus and surrounded by steep intimidating mountains.

The water, like the people who depended upon it had long gone leaving their homes to crumble under the hot summer sun. The dirt track leading to the safe house hadn't been used in years and would need a bit of work to fill the worst of the potholes before he would attempt to drive a Limousine down it.

The building was on two levels and had been built for someone very important in this region. There was no way of telling how long it had been empty but the deterioration of the facade indicated that at least a decade had passed since any maintenance had been carried out. The lock on the front door needed several applications of lubricating oil before it ceded to the wishes of the key, and when it eventually opened, it revealed a place that was frozen in time.

It was as if the previous owners had left without packing. The reception desk had in and out-trays with unopened mail lying under a layer of dust. A cup sat on the desk as though the user had just popped out for a moment. The whole place looked as though it had been evacuated for a fire exercise and the occupants forgot to return. This building had been abandoned in a hurry.

As Pedro picked his way through the corridors, it soon became apparent that this had been a clinic or some kind of hospital. Six rooms were clearly identified as wards, and names of the doctors and nurses adorned the doors to the offices. Hospital beds still sat in the wards and the linen needed to cover them lay on shelves in an adjoining room. More disturbingly, the hospital owned two gurneys, indicating that it probably wasn't a rest home. The straps pointed to the fact that the residents occasionally needed restraining, and this was a bonus that Pedro hadn't anticipated.

He was relatively satisfied that this afternoon's abduction of the Alvés pair had been carried out without drawing undue attention. They were initially compliant, and now they were too scared to cause him problems, which is exactly where he wanted them. The remaining part of the transit to the safe house was carried out in complete silence. When he stopped the car in front of their destination, it was Carmen who spoke.

"Is this just about the money?"

Pedro considered the question before answering.

"Yes, I've been paid to kidnap you and your brother. I don't know you and have no interest in your lives. To me, you are merely names on a sheet of paper. There is nothing complicated about our relationship: I will demand a ransom and your father will pay it. After that, we will never see each other again."

Carmen felt reassured by his purely financial take on her and Sergio's abduction and began to relax into what now seemed an adventure. However, reality wasn't too far away, and made itself known all too soon. The driver got out of the car and she heard him struggle with a door that required kicking and swearing at several times before grudgingly opening. The driver won the battle but it did little for his sense of humour.

"Out" he spat as he opened the car door beside Carmen.

She waved her strapped wrists to show that she wasn't comfortable in launching herself blindly at a doorway she couldn't see. Pedro looked around to confirm that there were no prying eyes before he removed her blindfold. She blinked to focus as the bright afternoon sun burnt her eyes, and looked across the back seat of the car to see her brother, who seemed to be asleep. She was shocked when she saw the blood that had now dried on the front of his formerly pristine white shirt and had obviously come from his throat. She looked at the man who had just removed her blindfold and he reassured her that Sergio was in no pain.

"Merely a bit of theatre to stop him being a nuisance."

The remnants of his intemperance the night before seemed to have triumphed over his current plight as he continued to sleep. Her next focus was on the man she had assumed was a chauffeur. Her captor was a tall, heavily built man with an expressionless face.

His accent betrayed him as Spanish but the language he used was of an internationally accepted military standard: no wasted words, no ambiguity.

He helped her as she made it unsteadily to her feet and suggested that she took a moment to adjust. She winced as he produced an evil looking knife and was relieved when he cut the tape around her thighs and ankles.

"I have no intention of carrying you."

She was pleased to hear that. He then repeated the process with Sergio, who he woke with a kick. She dashed towards her brother and Pedro made no effort to stop her. She clutched him to her and sobbed as she spoke.

"Sergio, are you ok?"

He sheepishly looked at Pedro before answering. The chauffeur remained impassive.

"I'm ok. The bastard only cut my throat enough to make it bleed, a lot of blood but no real damage. Isn't that right, driver?"

The word 'driver' was said with such utter contempt that Pedro clenched his fist ready for use. He grabbed Sergio by the scruff of the neck and launched him towards to beckoning doorway.

"Gobby little shite," was as eloquent as Pedro could muster.

Carmen, realising that there was no percentage in resisting the will of the chauffeur, followed them into the building. Her brother was led into a side room and she followed. The chauffeur propelled Sergio into the room and turned to stop her.

"Next door," he said in a firm manner.

He pointed at the spacious room that she knew was to be her home for the immediate future and complied. Heavy beds had been pushed against one wall, with only one made up for use. Pedro indicated that this was hers.

"Make yourself comfortable. I will bring you food in half an hour. There is no reason for you to worry. We will make a video for your father, he will pay, and I will release you. It doesn't have to be any more complicated than that."

Carmen, at that moment, felt reassured. The thing that bothered her was that their captor had clearly said that he had been paid to kidnap them, and therefore he wasn't the brains behind the operation. What if the man pulling the strings wanted something more? What might it be? Those questions could wait. She was hungry and told the man who said his name was Pedro.

"Sandwiches tonight, love: cheese and ham. I haven't had time to cook, too busy kidnapping silly little rich kids from the airport."

She forced a smile and made her bed comfortable. Twenty minutes later, Pedro brought her a tray of the promised fare, which she wolfed down with the soft drink, unknowingly laced with a strong sedative. In the adjacent room, her brother followed suit with the same result.

When they awoke several hours later, they were securely pinned on gurneys. Their limbs, firmly tethered by leather straps, were prevented from moving like those of so many others over the decades. As she came to, Carmen detected a smell that was familiar but not instantly identifiable. It soon became apparent that the smell was that of blood.

Carmen had no way of confirming her suspicions, as she was incapable of moving her head. It was only when Sergio was wheeled in beside her that she saw the red smirch across his face and bare chest.

"Oh my God," she gasped as she looked at her bloodstained brother.

Pedro put her out of her misery.

"It's pig's blood. You are also covered in it. This is just a little stagecraft for your father's benefit."

As he spoke, he scanned the room with a video camera and slowed as he concentrated on the soiled siblings. He zoomed in on Sergio's throat to give credence to the blood he had liberally applied. Sergio realised what he was doing and called out that it was only a scratch. Pedro told him of the futility of his valiant gesture.

"I am going to record a lot of footage and carefully edit it before sending. What I send will be exactly what I decide is appropriate. Over the next few days, you will each read several prepared statements. I will decide which will be used depending on how the scenario develops."

"What if we refuse to co-operate?"

Pedro smirked at Sergio.

"Then both of you will be given no food. If that doesn't convince you to play, then I have no compunction about torturing you."

Carmen looked at her brother but said nothing. She knew he could be stubborn to the point of petulance and tried to gauge his state of mind. He returned her gaze and indicated that he would resist compliance with Pedro's wishes. She knew where this was going and it didn't make her feel good. She believed Pedro when he indicated that torture was a valid option.

When he finished his cinematic session, he wheeled Sergio back to the room next door. Carmen heard him ask if they could return to the beds they had previously been in for sleeping and Pedro ignored her. The sharp sound of a heavy hand slapping a face in the room next door was unmistakable. Her brother's look of defiance hadn't gone unseen.

"I'm going to enjoy hurting you, boy" was all that Carmen heard before the ward doors were slammed shut for the night.

At Alicante Airport, Juan was in a quandary. Fernando Alvés hadn't called him back and he daren't leave in case his children were actually on a later flight. He considered calling him again but dismissed this. Fernando Alvés had said that he would call when he knew what was happening and would be angry at being bothered by his chauffeur. He wasn't a patient man and was best left to resolve the situation and inform Juan when he had decided what to do. Juan's dilemma was resolved in the arrivals hall a few moments later.

"Juan?"

He looked to see who had called his name and recognised an old comrade. Pepe had worked as a handyman with the Alvés family for some years before leaving after an awkward situation arose, allegedly with a housemaid, though there were other theories banded about.

"Pepe, what are you doing here?"

The question was totally unnecessary as Pepe was clearly wearing an airport security uniform.

"I've worked here for over two years now. Are you still with Fernando Alvés?"

"Yes. In fact, I've come to collect Sergio and Carmen. They were due in on a flight from Barcelona four hours ago but they haven't arrived."

"They have."

"What do you mean 'they have'? Have you seen them?"

"Yes. They arrived around four o'clock. Carmen waved at me and Sergio gave me the sneer that he always reserved for hired hands."

"Where did they go?"

"A chauffeur met them and led them to the car park."

"A chauffeur? What chauffeur?"

The hairs on Juan's neck were beginning to rise as the possibilities of something bad having happened ran through his head.

"Big guy. When I saw him I just assumed that you had moved on to something else and he was your replacement."

"I haven't been replaced, Pepe. I've come to collect them."

"I'll call the police," Pepe offered.

"Ok. I'll inform Mr Alvés straight away."

As Pepe dashed to the airport police office, Juan called his employer. In his lavish country home, Fernando looked at the caller ID and wondered what to do. In the excitement of the call from the kidnapper, he had completely forgotten about the chauffeur at the airport. His concern wasn't for his employee; it was more about what he might do now. The man who had taken Sergio and Carmen was quite adamant about no police involvement. He decided that he had to stop Juan before he got them involved.

"Fernando Alvés. Is that you Juan?"

"Yes sir. I have something odd to tell you. Sergio and Carmen were picked up by another chauffeur this afternoon. They arrived before I got here."

"Come straight back here, Juan. They have gone to some stupid party in Alicante and will be home before the nights out."

Juan, for the first time in all the years he had worked with Fernando Alvés, didn't believe him. There was something about his voice that betrayed his words. Fernando Alvés was hiding something. Juan considered his options and decided to obey the wishes of his boss but didn't stop Pepe from informing the police. Pepe returned with two policemen.

"Their father thinks that they may have been picked up and gone to a party in town."

Pepe read the face of his old comrade and knew that he was bothered by this explanation.

"You don't think they're at a party, do you?"

"It doesn't matter what I think, Pepe. I have been told to return to the house. There is no need for the police to be bothered by this. It's probably nothing."

With that, Juan turned on his heels and sped to the car park where his Limousine waited. The policemen looked at Pepe and asked if they should investigate or not. Pepe said that he would talk to the airline desks and find out when they arrived, if the police took the trouble to look at the CCTV in order to see exactly what happened when they met the chauffeur. One of the policemen said that they wouldn't be able to recognise the Alvés offspring and that Pepe would have to pick them out. They re-allocated their resources and set about getting to the bottom of what had actually happened in the arrivals lounge that afternoon.

Within twenty minutes, they had confirmed that Sergio and Carmen Alvés had arrived at three forty-five on Iberia flight 232 from Barcelona. They were clearly identifiable in the video footage being met by a chauffeur while their baggage was dragged laboriously by a porter.

"That's Geraldo," Pepe stated as he pointed to the man in airport coveralls. "He'll be off duty by now. Do we have another tape of the outside of the terminal?"

The policeman confirmed that all points were covered by their cameras and it took little time to pick up the chauffeur, two passengers, and the porter as they made their way to the large car that awaited them. The policeman who was operating the controls zoomed in on the number plates of the car, scratched the details on a notepad, and slid his chair across to another computer in order to check the ownership of the vehicle.

On the first screen, with his passengers in the rear of the car, the chauffeur watched as the porter struggled with the luggage. As Pepe and the other officer watched the replay from that afternoon, their comrade called to them.

"We have a problem. That registration plate belongs to a Renault 406, not a Limousine."

He returned to the others as they watched the tape with renewed interest. The driver had seen off the porter before entering and leaving the driver's position. He then opened the rear right hand door of the car and did something that the camera couldn't see while covering his nose and mouth with his left hand. He then seemed to lean into the car in a most un-chauffeur-like manner before taking a few deep breaths and driving away.

"Something's not right about this," one of the policemen said. "I'm going to call Alicante and get them to send an investigator down here."

All were in agreement that there was more to this than met the eye and watched the tape again as they waited for their colleague from the Commissary to shine some light on the matter.

In the Alicante Central Commissary, Investigator Sergeant Christiano Marcos had the dubious honour of being the duty senior detective. He had only recently been granted permission to fill this role and wondered if this was no more than an excuse for his boss, Inspector Carlos Rico, to enjoy a few more evenings at home. As the new man in the station, he accepted this as his lot. He had recently arrived from Valencia on promotion and knew that he had a lot to live up to. His predecessor had been killed in the line of duty, and he remembered all too clearly reading the horrific details of his death. At that time, he never considered that he would be taking his place and working with the legendary Carlos Rico, and so far had seen nothing remarkable about his modus operandi.

When the call came in about a suspicious occurrence at the airport, Christiano thought that there was little point in bothering his boss until he had checked exactly what was happening. He drove the short distance in fifteen minutes and sought out the airport police office.

When he knocked and entered the office, he was eyed with suspicion. People had often said that he didn't look like a policeman. He was of average height and build with thinning black hair. The hair he blamed on his father who was himself bald at thirty-three. His soft features belied a determined, sometimes belligerent nature, which had been misinterpreted by criminals to their detriment. The Chief Inspector had told him on arrival that he had been selected by Inspector Rico from a long list of candidates and should be honoured. Christiano decided to defer judgement on his appointment until he knew the lie of the land.

He flashed his warrant card.

"Investigator Sergeant Marcos, Alicante Central Commissary. What have we got?"

The airport officers and security guard Pepe ran the tape and told all. Christiano asked to see the salient points several times without saying a word.

"Who are the people who were picked up?"

Pepe gave him the details.

"You seem to know an awful lot about them, Pepe."

The airport police had also thought that this was a bit odd and perhaps he had something to do with whatever was happening.

"I worked for Mr Alvés for five years as a handyman."

"Did you leave on good terms?"

"I left because I was on too good terms with a member of the household. A handyman that was a bit too handy, perhaps."

The uniformed officers smiled but Christiano remained impassive.

"I need an address for Mr Alvés."

Pepe gave the investigator the details and actually felt a little relieved when he left. Christiano told them that he would keep them informed and left to talk to Fernando Alvés.

The impressive house stood in spacious, manicured grounds. Christiano knew that he was being observed as the camera on the large, ornate gatepost followed his approach to the intercom on the gate. A security guard answered.

"Yes" he said abruptly.

"Police. I'd like to talk to Mr Fernando Alvés."

"It's late. Can't it wait until the morning?"

"No."

Christiano could also be abrupt. A minute or so later there was a click and the whirr of an electric motor as the large metal gate began to move to one side. The security guard appeared on the other side and asked for ID. Christiano obliged, and was directed to follow the driveway up to the house.

The house was every bit as impressive as the grounds. He knew that when dealing with people who hired chauffeurs and security guards, he had to expect a degree of opulence in the house. A tall, powerful looking man waited at the front door. He was around

33

fifty with the lined face of a man who has worked very hard over many years. He walked to meet the detective and shook his hand firmly.

"Fernando Alvés. How can I help you, sergeant?"

"I've come to ask about the whereabouts of your son, Sergio, and daughter Carmen. Something odd happened at the airport today. Are they at home, sir?"

"No, sergeant. They were picked up at the airport and told me that they were going to a party somewhere in the city. You know what young people are like."

Christiano knew that he was lying but didn't know why. This was an assertive man but his words lacked sincerity.

"Do you have a number I can call them on, sir."

"There is no need to bother about them. They will have switched their phones off and drunk far too much champagne by now."

"For my peace of mind, I'd like their numbers anyway."

Fernando Alvés ran through what was happening in his head. The kidnapper would have taken their phones from them, so if the policeman called, there would be no answer. On the other hand, if the kidnapper were to answer, the interfering sergeant could be unwittingly signing their death warrants. To refuse would only fuel the flames of his suspicions. He pulled a smart phone from his pocket and dictated two numbers. The unfortunate deaths of Rene and Maria in a traffic accident two weeks ago meant that their numbers were unlikely to be answered and so could be passed to the investigator.

"If you would be so good as to call me when they return, I would appreciate it, sir."

Fernando Alvés agreed and waved off the snooping sergeant. Chauffeur Juan, watching from his quarters, knew that he was about to have an uncomfortable tête-a-tête with his employer.

*****

The night in the clinic passed peacefully as Sergio and Carmen, strapped to gurneys, were incapable of misbehaviour. Pedro knew that their inability to move would result in an uncomfortable night and leave them looking exhausted, and this was exactly what he wanted. He himself looked less sharp than normal but this was because he never shaved when he was on an operation. This always made him feel grubby for the first couple of days as he acclimatised to the stubble, but it was based on tactical considerations. He also wasn't prepared to waste the electricity produced by the small petrol generator he had bought on heating water. Unless it had been prepared to go into a coffee cup, there was no hot water in the building.

After the cold shower, he picked up his much-used Heckler & Koch USP pistol from his quarters as he dressed and inspected it as he did every morning. He looked out of the window at the almost lifeless landscape, his mind wandering back to his days as a Legionnaire. This could have been Algeria, Mali or any of a number of North African hellholes where he had served both Spain and France before going independent. He had learnt in the desert, but he earned in the jungle. The snapping of the magazine into the pistol grip brought him back to the present and he checked his appearance in the mirror before making his way down to the kitchen.

He prepared coffee and sandwiches, and placed them on trays that he put on a trolley. He felt a little demeaned by waiting on captives, but the balance of his savings account made his discomfort fade as quickly as it had come. He went to the girl first, knowing that she would present no physical threat.

The unlatching of the door caused her to strain her neck to see who had entered, although she doubted it could have been anyone but the man she knew as Pedro. He pushed the trolley into the room, walked over to where she lay and smiled at her.

"Good morning, Carmen" he said in an almost jovial manner.

He had obviously slept a whole lot better than she had and this was reflected in his general demeanour. She winced as he tugged at the straps holding her arms, dreading what was to come.

"Easy does it. I am releasing your straps. I don't want you to do anything silly. Your breakfast is on the tray and there is a toilet facility in the corner of the room. Complete your ablutions and eat your food. We have a busy day ahead of us."

She tried to sit upright and her frozen muscles refused to co-operate. Pedro held her under the armpits and eased her into the position she sought. Her instinct was to thank him but she managed to overcome a lifetime of good manners and said nothing.

"Take it slowly; your legs will also feel weak initially. I'll be back in an hour."

Her expression was as blank as her legs were useless. She wanted to shout, scream, and cry all at the same time but did none of them. Instead, she watched as Pedro left her room, her cell, with the promise of returning with the probable intention of inflicting pain or, at the very least, discomfort. The heavy door to her ward shut behind her tormentor and the clunk of the deadbolt removed any thoughts about trying to open it.

The sound was repeated a few seconds later as the ward next door was opened. Pedro knew Sergio had taken his abduction far worse than his sister, and therefore presented more of a threat. Pedro was a skilled and experienced fighter who weighed twenty kilograms of muscle more than the rich kid, so there was no real physical threat: it was the potential nuisance value of a minor injury inflicted by a lucky amateur that he wanted to avoid. In order to reduce the possibility of heroics, Pedro produced his pistol and waved it under Sergio's nose.

"There will be no nonsense when I release your bindings. Am I understood?"

Sergio used what little movement he had of his head to show he grasped the reality of his situation. One by one, the thick leather bands were removed and Sergio dared to use one hand to massage the blood flow back into the other and then repeated the process on his legs. He was given the same brief his sister ten minutes before and his almost overwhelming need to use a toilet meant that he would do nothing to question it.

With his breakfast duties complete, Pedro retired to the kitchen where he prepared something more substantial for himself. The smell of his fried chorizo and toasted bread merely added an olfactory element to the torment felt by his captives.

On completion of breakfast, he carried out a series of security checks on the building and surrounding grounds. He had devised a list of key points to be inspected in order to ensure the integrity of the area and fastidiously checked each. He knew from bitter experience what could happen when procedure wasn't followed to the letter. The trip flares and infrared light beam and sensor arrays were exactly as they should have been, with not even a fox leaving a footprint in his combed, sand pits. His next task was to contact the Fixer.

The phone rang six times before being answered. He knew that this was sufficient time to allow the Fixer to turn on his voice scrambler.

"Taker, I trust all is well?"

Pedro quite liked his new sobriquet. He'd never been called 'Taker' before.

"Everything is as I said it would be. They've had an uncomfortable night's sleep, just enough to make them start to take this seriously. How do you want me to proceed?"

"We have to consider all of the possible outcomes and arm ourselves against them. I want the father to be sufficiently worried such that he won't hesitate to pay the ransom immediately we demand it. We will not contact him for a couple of days. In that time, I want you to record video footage to cover every eventuality. This will require many hours of filming of your prisoners reading prepared statements."

"Where are the prepared statements?"

"They are in your post box."

Pedro cursed the Colonel for divulging the whereabouts of his personal post box to the Fixer who was merely a customer. Admittedly, the only post he ever received was from the Colonel and so he could argue that it was no more than a business

39

arrangement, but nonetheless he felt like he was being marginalised.

As it was, he had no further need to speak to the Colonel on this mission: he had done his job by arranging contact between the Fixer and Pedro.

"I will collect them this morning."

"I have been guaranteed that you have the requisite computing skills to edit the footage professionally?"

"You have nothing to worry about on that account. I have the knowledge and the best equipment available. How particular are you about collateral damage?"

The Fixer seemed surprised by this question. He hesitated for several seconds before responding.

"Is there any need for damage?"

"There will come a point where deprivation of food and water alone will not be sufficient to make them comply with my wishes. I know this from personal experience. A point will be reached where I will have to apply a little pressure."

Another silence indicated that the Fixer was considering his reply.

"As little as is necessary," he said in a measured manner. "This is a financial kidnapping, not a political one."

Pedro wasn't quite sure what he was being told.

"I have done my research on the father and he is a ruthless operator. He won't take the abduction of his brood without employing top-level operators to find them. For purposes of self-preservation, I need to frighten him and the most effective way to do that is through my 'prisoners' as you call them. Blood is thicker than water and this is especially true when it is your own blood."

"Do what you must but don't go too far. Call me when you have completed the videos."

Pedro thought about his call with the Fixer and reflected on how the balance of power had shifted towards him. In order to achieve their goal, someone would have to endure a little discomfort. Initially it would be Sergio and Carmen and this would be transmitted on to their father. When the pain became too much, he would pay and the situation would be resolved.

In the meantime, he had mail to collect and videos to make. He checked his inmates before leaving and felt vindicated in his hard-line approach when Sergio, sufficiently recovered from his overnight ordeal to be abusive, hurled a verbal barrage at him.

"I'm going to enjoy hurting you, boy" was all he said in reply but it left no doubt in the young man's mind that he sincerely meant it.

In Alicante Central Commissary, Sergeant Christiano Marcos related the events of the previous evening to Inspector Carlos Rico as the senior officer read his morning newspaper. He didn't appear to be listening to a word his sergeant was saying, seeming more interested in the croissant that was flaking over the front of his jacket. He licked his fingers as he deposited the final piece of the pastry into his mouth and dropped the newspaper slightly in order to speak to Christiano.

"So are they missing or aren't they?"

"The airport staff reported them being picked up by a strange driver and taken away in a car with false plates."

"Who was this strange driver?"

"No one knows. That's what makes him strange."

Carlos was assessing whether his new sergeant was trying to be smart or just stating the facts, as he knew them. Christiano continued.

"The family chauffeur arrived a bit later and missed them. They had already gone with the first chauffeur. Surely even Fernando Alvés isn't rich enough to have two chauffeurs."

Carlos slapped the newspaper onto his lap and sat up in his chair. Christiano had caught his interest.

"Fernando Alvés you say? Why didn't you tell me this before?"

"Does it make a difference, sir? Are we to treat this case differently because he is rich?"

Carlos let the remark pass without responding. His new sergeant knew nothing about the chequered history of Fernando Alvés, and now seemed a good time for him to start getting to know a bit more about the locals.

"Look at our files for Mr Alvés before you start chasing shadows. Tell me about the car."

"It was clearly a Limousine but the traffic department have it registered as a Peugeot 406."

"Find out who was the last registered owner of the Peugeot."

As Christiano stood to go, Carlos stopped him.

"You say you spoke to Fernando Alvés at his house?"

"Yes sir, a magnificent house with full-time security."

"What did he say about his missing offspring?"

"He said that they had arrived on a different flight and proceeded to a party in Alicante. I insisted that he gave me their mobile numbers."

Christiano proudly brandished the piece of paper with the phone numbers on it.

"Have you called the numbers today?"

"Not yet, it's only early, sir."

"Would you have called a working man at this time of day, sergeant, but not the Alvés?"

Christiano realised that he had fallen into Carlos' trap and held his hands up in the way of an apology for his earlier remark.

"Leave the numbers with me and check out the history of Fernando Alvés and the car. While you're at it, check the flights from Barcelona yesterday and see if they actually were on one of them."

The sergeant was pleased to see the newspaper flicked back up from the inspector's lap indicating that the awkward encounter had been terminated. As he made for the door of Carlos' office, a voice behind him called.

"Meet me in Avenida at twelve and we will discuss this further."

Totally unaware of what was meant by 'Avenida', he thought better of asking the inspector and decided that one of the constables would furnish him with this information. Behind his daily, Carlos smiled.

Smiling was definitely not on the agenda of the Alvés siblings. They called to each other from their respective wards in the hospital, but thick walls and an echo made most of what they were saying unintelligible. They ascertained that both were well and Pedro was absent. Windows and doors had been struck with a variety of objects to no avail. There was no obvious escape. Their last syllabised words were an agreement to wait for their father to pay.

They heard a vehicle draw up and both sat on the hospital beds in the wards in hope that they were allowed to use these, and not be returned to the gurneys.

Pedro had travelled a considerable distance that morning to do some basic shopping. He planned never to use the same town twice in hope that none would recognise his face were it to become known. He trusted no one, and included the Fixer in this category. This was a one-soldier mission. The material he received was substantial and would take many days to record and edit. If he were in a position to sub-contract part of this, he wouldn't have hesitated in doing so, but it was made clear from the start that this was not an option.

He had set up the green room very carefully. Previously, it had been a communal area and had one long unblemished wall that suited his purposes perfectly. He thought that it was perhaps used to screen movies or hang posters. However, it provided a long flat space where he could hang a batten framework.

He had procured twenty metres of two-metre wide cotton in a brilliant green colour from a market stall in Murcia, ironed out all of the creases and tacked it to the framework in such a manner as to appear seamless. The screen lighting was bought from a large, faceless electrical superstore on the edge of Alicante and levels adjusted against a calibrated meter. Diffusers were manufactured from batten and aluminium foil to set appropriate foreground illumination, spreading the light from four spots such as to leave no shadow, regardless of where he stepped across the individual contributions.

His chroma keying software was checked against the screen and foreground and adjusted to give the required result. The chosen background image was of a medieval dungeon. This gave the grim impression he wanted to portray. It was important that their father thought they were in a far worse situation than they really were.

Pedro had learnt the green screen technique while working as a film stunt man. He wasn't a particularly good stunt man but the director didn't discover this until it was too late to replace him. He had appeared in too many good takes to be replaced when he broke his wrist after landing clumsily, so was retained for facial shots.

During his idle time in the studio, he became acquainted with the special effects man who was all too keen to show off his newly acquired skills. Filming against a green background, another location is layered behind the original and the colour levels adjusted to remove the green. In this way, he could record the pleas and eventual abuse of the Alvés siblings in what appeared to be a horrific setting. The psychological effect was profound, with the additional benefit of disguising their actual location. Everything was set up and it merely required him to read through the prepared scripts and make adjustments as he thought fitting.

The editing of the collected material took him the remainder of the day, which left Sergio and Carmen with a lot of thinking time. Their very different natures dictated how they spent the day, with Carmen meditating while Sergio paced like a caged animal. It was seven in the evening when Pedro returned to check and feed them and they were almost pleased to see him. Carmen was the first to be visited.

He opened the door and ascertained her location before entering. He was taking nothing for granted; that would have been amateurish. She was sat on the bed where she had been when he left that morning, although she had clearly eaten everything he had brought earlier that day. Her look was expressionless and she said nothing as Pedro wheeled his trolley into the ward. He positioned it in the corner of the room furthest from her bed and took the tray of hot food to her. She looked at the plate of pasta and meatballs and was pleasantly surprised. Half a French stick had been cut and placed on a side plate and she had a full flask of coffee to wash it down. As he placed it on her bed, she thanked him.

"What has my father said?" she asked

"I haven't spoken to him. You are going to be my guests for a while."

"How long?"

"That depends on your father. If he pays, you will be released. If he doesn't, then you won't."

"Why wouldn't he pay?"

"He is a proud man who is used to being in control. Such pride can influence decisions."

"And if he refuses to pay?"

"We will have to convince him otherwise."

Carmen knew there was a threat thinly concealed in his words and this caused a shudder to run the length of her spine. The look on Pedro's face told her that he too was a man with great determination and that she and her brother were caught between two powerful wills. She looked away and toyed with her food until he collected the breakfast tray and left.

Next door, Sergio petulantly launched a verbal attack at Pedro as he entered. Pedro responded by taking the breakfast tray and smashing it across the young man's face. It made an impressive sound, although the physical damage was minimal.

"You must learn to respect your elders, young man," Pedro said with undisguised sarcasm.

Sergio wiped the blood that trickled from his split lip and inspected it. He considered charging Pedro but knew that the outcome was likely to be unfavourable. He had never been physical and this had bothered his father at times. However, he had always been rich and buying muscle had been an option he had used on many occasions. There was no muscle to be hired on this occasion and he felt frustrated that he was powerless.

"This will not end well for you, driver."

The 'driver' ignored the comment and picked up the distorted tray that had been his weapon of choice and placed it on the trolley. He picked up another tray containing the food he had prepared and looked at Sergio. He turned the tray over and deposited its contents onto the floor. The plate smashed, spreading the food over a large area. The flask of coffee cracked and the black liquid oozed through the food.

"Dinner hasn't ended too well for you, prisoner," Pedro smirked. "It's there if you get hungry enough but don't wait too long; it's bedtime soon. You have a long day tomorrow."

As he considered the implications of 'bedtime', he wished he had kept his mouth shut. Pangs of hunger rumbled through his stomach and he knew that if he wanted to eat, then it would be off the floor. His captor pushed his trolley out of the door without looking over his shoulder and closed it firmly behind him. The pasta was still steaming. Sergio looked at it and his hunger battled with his pride. In a ward all alone, there was little room for pride. He picked the pieces of broken crockery from the food and scraped the remnants of his dinner into one hand. As he ate, he felt embarrassed and demeaned, like a third world beggar scavenging scraps. He vowed that Pedro would suffer at his hands, though how this would come to pass wasn't too obvious at this time.

An hour later, Pedro returned and at gunpoint returned them to the gurneys they had occupied on the previous night. Both accepted that there was little point in resisting the vastly superior force of their captor, and he saw the absence of food on Sergio's floor. His will was beginning to break, as he knew it would. Isolation was the first step, followed by humiliation. This could be escalated to mental persecution before resorting to actual physical torture.

The Advanced Treatment Room was in the basement and Pedro didn't discover it until his second week of preparation in the building. He was washing a floor and noticed that the water appeared to be draining down a line between the tiles. There was what seemed to be a handgrip on one of the tiles and he pulled on it. A one-metre square hatch opened on creaking hinges to reveal a set of wooden steps leading into the darkness below. He fumbled and found a switch for the lone light bulb that hung above the steps. The steps led to a door, which was too tempting for Pedro not to open. When he did so, he found a four-metre square room crammed with implements the likes of which he hadn't seen since his time in Congo. The advanced treatment room was nothing short of a torture chamber. Shackles hung on the walls, a gurney with evil looking attachments sat in the middle of the floor, and worst of all was the chair that occupied the wall on the right-hand side. The chair was similar to one he had once been strapped into and electrodes attached to his testicles.

As a mercenary, you expected no mercy when captured by your enemies, and this was never truer than in the Congo. Outside of your own battalion, it was impossible to say who was friend and who was foe. These definitions changed with the political and military wind, with the only viable survival strategy being total distrust of all but your immediate brothers.

He shuddered as he recalled the three days he spent in the chair. He was told it was three days but it felt like three lifetimes. The same question was repeated endlessly; 'who are you working for?' He came across as a tough guy but the truth was much simpler; he didn't know. As their insistence increased, so did the wattage applied. When the flash bang announced his rescue, it was the sweetest sound he had ever heard, and continued to hear for several hours. He vowed that he would never apply such techniques to another human being, remembering what came to him in his frequent nightmares. These chambers were hell on earth. He left the Advanced Treatment Room and closed the hatch, hoping never to open it again. He knew 'never' was a dangerous word that could be adapted to suit the situation.

Christiano Marcos confirmed that the Alvés youngsters had flown in from Barcelona, this being confirmed by the airport security and police. Their father had lied to his chauffeur. Fernando Alvés' business success appeared to have been based on a series of lucky breaks, the sort that normally occurred when a powerful external influence is applied. Fraud Squad had investigated his dealings in several questionable transactions with seriously unsavoury criminals, and he always came out smelling of roses. The Peugeot 406 donor car had been written-off two years ago and the plates stolen from a scrap yard.

Inspector Carlos Rico contacted the phone company before calling the numbers. The numbers were registered to Rene and Maria López. When he tried one of the numbers, it was answered by someone with an unsure tone in her voice.

"Hello, this is Maria López's phone."

"Can I speak to Miss López, please?"

"Are you a friend?"

"No, I'm Inspector Rico of Alicante police."

There was a pause, as the person answering seemed to be bracing herself to speak.

"I'm sorry, my sister died in a car accident last week."

Carlos heard the snuffling and decided to end her torment.

"I'm very sorry to hear that. This was a minor matter that I needn't bother you with. Please accept my condolences."

He checked the traffic records and was not surprised to see that the other mobile number given by Fernando Alvés belonged to the passenger who also died in the crash. Fernando Alvés was playing games with them and Carlos wanted to know why.

Sergeant Marcos discovered that Avenida was a café bar much frequented by his boss. He thought it a nondescript establishment frequented by nondescript people. Carlos sat at the bar eating a plate of sardines.

As he approached him, the man sat next to him spoke.

"Are you his new bum boy?"

Christian took a few seconds to assess the situation before responding. The man with the attitude seemed to be in his seventies and this tempered his reply.

"You're not too old to get a slap. Watch your mouth, old timer."

Carlos introduced the two protagonists.

"This is Enrique. He is the most obnoxious man in Alicante. Enrique, this is Christiano Marcos, my new sergeant. You will be nice to him."

"He looks softer than the last one, and less intelligent."

Christiano knew the holy cow status enjoyed by the memory of Sergeant Salva Martinez and had decided when he took the post that he wouldn't ever challenge it. His predecessor had died in horrific circumstances at the hands of the serial killer known as the Alicante Assassin. Everyone said that he was a good copper. Enrique offered his hand to Christiano who reticently accepted. Carlos pointed to a stool and indicated that Christiano sat down.

"Do as your boss says and sit down."

"Tell me what you have found out."

Christiano related the fruits of his morning's labour, all of which Carlos had already surmised.

"Where do we go from here, boss?"

Carlos considered the question as he mopped the oil from his plate with his remaining bread.

"For now, we do nothing. I don't know what Fernando Alvés is playing at and am loathe to waste resources based on a long-standing dislike of the man. I will get the local patrols to keep an eye on the house."

"Should we let him know that we know he is lying to us? It might make him re consider."

"He will already know. He is buying time: but for what?"

Both investigators had enough live files on their desks to deal with, and agreed that Fernando Alvés, and whatever he was trying to hide, wasn't a priority. Nonetheless, Carlos ordered a twenty-four hour watch to be manned on his house. Something didn't smell good about Fernando Alvés' behaviour. Where were his son and daughter?

Pedro repeated the breakfast routine he had established the previous day, this time providing toast and jam for his guests at the earlier hour of six a.m. He enquired if Sergio wanted to behave himself or would he like his food deposited directly onto the floor again just to save time. Sergio saw no point in risking food poisoning for the sake of a cheap comment and agreed to keep a civil tongue, for now at least.

"We have a lot of work to do today, so I want you to be at your best."

"Work, what work?" Sergio asked.

"We are going to record a series of statements. I will then edit them and send a ransom demand to your father."

"My father is a man with a great deal if influence in Alicante. He will have men out looking for us, seriously bad men who will not hesitate to kill you."

"Bad men have tried to kill me many times in the past. The evidence shows that they failed. You do as you are told and no significant harm will come to you."

Sergio mulled over the use of the word 'significant' and decided that he really didn't want to know. Pedro said that he would return in half an hour to collect him and that he should forget about being found by his father's henchmen.

"If they are looking for you in Alicante, they will never find you."

Sergio thought on the journey from the airport and estimated that they had driven for approximately two hours, working on the times of news bulletins on the national radio station. That meant that they could be as far as two, maybe three hundred kilometres from the airport. The barren landscape he could see from the small, barred window favoured the country to the south, perhaps near Almeria but he couldn't rule out a remote inland valley. Unless he could devise a means of communicating with the outside world, their location was purely hypothetical.

The drive had been planned to give this impression to the blindfolded passengers of the Limousine, with the reality being that they were scarcely thirty kilometers from where they had been snatched. Pedro had put the extra miles on the clock in order to give the notion of distance, while ensuring the radio could be heard in order to allow a scratch calculation to be incorrectly carried out.

This made him think about the Limousine; it was due back to the garage In Malaga, but if it were suspected of being the vehicle involved in a kidnapping, forensics might find enough evidence to track him down. The owner would have insurance to cover his loss. Pedro found a tarpaulin in an attached garage building and threw it over the luxury car. A Limousine would certainly catch the eyes of a police helicopter, especially in this near desert environment. He knew that he couldn't trust Fernando Alvés to keep the situation secret from the police and had to assume that they already knew.

At the Alvés family home, Fernando was facing a dilemma of his own: to tell his wife or not. He had married Almudena Perez twenty-five years ago, and after the first five years, they settled into a routine partnership. Almu was a beauty and he was rich. She liked the good life he could afford to give her, but what she really wanted was his attention, his time. Fernando saw life differently and concentrated his efforts on his business, causing a distance to grow between them. This was partially filled by the arrival of Sergio and then Carmen, who gave Almu's life a new focus. She knew that they, Sergio in particular, had been spoilt by their father's affluence. He replaced love and attention with almost unlimited funds and this made her maternal bonds even stronger. Almu dismissed the nanny hired by her husband in order that she could enjoy motherhood, and her relationship with her children was closer than most.

If Fernando withheld what he knew about his absent offspring from his wife, she would most certainly divorce him when she found out, and he couldn't afford that. His business wasn't doing as well as he declared and he had other things occupying his mind. Three days had passed since they had last been in touch with their mother and she started to make phone calls to ascertain their whereabouts.

"Almu, sit down. There's something I have to tell you."

Despite her forty-five years, Almu was a striking woman. Her dark hair was now maintained in movie-star condition by frequent visits to her over-priced hairdresser, her clothes were from the best designer shops in the country and her figure would have been the envy of many a woman half her age. However, it was her eyes that everyone noticed. Large, brown, and shaped like almonds, they gave away every emotion that she ever experienced. Now they were displaying distress, bordering on panic. If Fernando didn't do something soon, she would mobilize every law enforcement officer in Spain to find her children. Her expression changed as she listened to Fernando. Tears began to appear when she heard the sober tone of his voice.

"What's happened? Tell me what's happened. Something has happened to the kids, hasn't it?"

Although Fernando knew this moment was coming, it didn't help him find an appropriate way of telling his wife. There was no point in trying to dress it up. He held her hands as he spoke, so she knew she wasn't going to like what he had to say.

"Sergio and Carmen have been kidnapped."

Almu could no longer hold back the tears. She took her hands from his and raised them to her face as the shock of what she had heard hit her.

"Oh my God. When?" she sobbed.

"Two days ago, they were taken from the airport."

"Two days ago and you're only telling me now? Why?"

"I thought that I could resolve the issue without worrying you."

"Resolve the issue? Someone kidnaps our children and you wanted to resolve the issue without as much as telling me? This isn't one of your questionable business deals we are talking about, they are our children."

The emotion being expressed in Almu's eyes now was close to rage.

"Why aren't the police involved?"

"The kidnapper said that they would come to harm if I involved the police."

"What does he want? How much? I assume it's about money?"

Fernando stood and paced to the far side of the large room.

"He said that he will send a ransom demand. I haven't heard from him since. I've got an acquaintance making enquiries about who the kidnapper might be."

The involvement of her husband's dubious friend did nothing to console Almu. She knew that he had dealt with people and organisations of unclear probate, but her children weren't involved on those occasions.

"What are we going to do?"

"The only thing we can do is wait."

Waiting, however, wasn't on the cards for the inmates at the former clinic. Sergio and Carmen were reunited for the first time in two days as Pedro led them at gunpoint from their individual wards to another room. They hugged tightly when Carmen walked through the doorway into the sterile corridor and cried in each other's arms. Pedro allowed this moment before encouraging them to walk towards another open door.

This was a bigger room that was badly decorated with posters relating to healthcare issues. One wall was completely covered with bright green material and carefully illuminated by a series of spot lamps and diffusers. In front of the screen sat two chairs with further lighting arranged around them, and it was obvious who was going to be sitting in them. The scene was completed by a video camera mounted on a tripod. Chalk marks on the floor indicated that the scene had been set very precisely.

Pedro gestured for the siblings to sit. They continued to hold hands until the last minute but Pedro had deliberately positioned the seats such that they would be physically isolated during the filming. He turned to a table sat behind the camera, lifted up two sheets of paper, and handed one to each planned participant. Their clothes still bore the dried blood smeared on them as they lay drugged in their cells, and Sergio's shirt had been torn to expose the knife mark inflicted during the incident in the car.

"This is the first of many scripts you will read. I want you to look directly at the camera and only speak what is written in front of you. If you get it wrong or try to improvise, we will carry on doing it until you get it right. Failure to co-operate is unadvisable. You will do exactly as I tell you or I will take measures to impose my will."

This undisguised threat prompted Sergio to look at Carmen, as if weighing up his options. She returned his look and shook her head, almost imperceptibly, in a negative manner indicating the futility of resistance.

"Why so many scripts? Surely you just say how much you want and wait for him to pay?" Sergio asked.

"My employer hasn't yet decided how this is going to end."

"So you're no more than a hired hand. I didn't think you would have the brains to pull off something like this on your own."

Pedro stopped making adjustments to the camera and glared angrily at Sergio. His concentration had been on the equipment and he instantly regretted his answer that gave away his employee status. He was also angry at presenting the younger man with the material required for a cheap shot. Yes, Sergio was going to make mistakes and he was looking forward to punishing him for doing so.

"Read the scripts," he snapped.

Pedro left them alone in the room stating his return was imminent. Carmen took the opportunity to talk to her brother.

"Are you ok? I heard you being struck last night."

Sergio rubbed the point of contact between the breakfast tray and his face.

"I'm all right. He hit me with a tray, no more. How are you? He hasn't, you know?"

"No. He only wants the money. I think we should do as he says and wait for daddy to pay."

Sergio didn't get the chance to reply as Pedro returned. He was carrying a flip chart, which he placed behind the camera.

"These say exactly the same as your scripts. I want you to look at the camera and read these. I'll turn them and point to who I want to speak. Do it right first time and we can all have an easy day."

He stepped behind the video camera and pressed the record button. With his left hand, he pointed to the first chart and then to Sergio, who took a few seconds before he started reading.

"Hello father. We are both being treated well and are in no danger."

Pedro flipped a preset position on the tripod and the camera now focussed on Carmen. A new chart and an unambiguous finger told her that it was her turn to speak.

"The person who has taken us means us no harm. He wants you to put together ten million Euros, ready for delivery at the time and place he decides."

Back to Sergio, who was amazed at the amount of money he had demanded.

"That's five million each. It is to be in unmarked and untraceable bills, and is not to include five hundred Euro notes."

"Under no circumstances are you to inform the police or send anyone to find us," Carmen read obediently.

"If the police get involved, we will be punished. Our taker will be in touch."

Sergio wondered about the use of the word 'taker' but thought no more of it when Pedro announced his satisfaction with their first recording.

"Good, well done. If we carry on like this, we can finish today and send the edited article to your father at the end of the week."

"Why not today? Why are you waiting until the end of the week?"

"As you took so much pleasure in pointing out, I am no more than an employee. I have orders, just like I give you orders. When people follow orders, things work. When they don't, they must be persuaded to comply for the better good."

"Fuck you and your orders. We're not your playthings."

Sergio would never realise how happy his words made Pedro feel. He hadn't yet actually refused to play along, but it seemed inevitable.

"Do you remember the rope with the clever knot I employed in the car?"

Both captives shuddered at the thought of the contraption that tightened around the neck of the other whenever either moved too much. How could he possibly arrange for that to happen in these circumstances? He anticipated their thoughts.

"I don't intend to use the rope again: that would show a complete lack of imagination. No, but I will be applying the principle. If Sergio is a bad boy, Carmen will be punished on his behalf and vice-versa."

The look held between Pedro and her brother chilled Carmen. She knew that he could be headstrong but had met his match in this man. He had the bearing of a soldier and many scars to prove that he was no stranger to close combat. She protested at his threat.

"You can't hold us here and hurt us whenever it pleases you. Make your demands for money but leave us alone."

Pedro responded with the speed of a snake. He covered the four metres to where Sergio sat and landed a heavy blow with his left hand to his midriff before he could raise his hands to protect himself. As his chair toppled backwards with the force of the blow, he landed another, equally heavy punch with his right. Sergio hit the floor hard, his knees jerking up to his chin instinctively to protect his stomach from further blows. The pain of his head striking the cold tiles seemed petty in comparison with what he felt in his abdomen. Carmen dashed to him and Pedro stepped back to allow this. Sergio was ashen. He had never experienced pain like this and wondered how much damage his internal organs might have suffered.

"You bastard", Carmen spat the words at Pedro.

He responded by picking up the chair and dragging Sergio onto it. Carmen raised her hand and slapped him as hard as she could. He drew his right fist back and bunched it for another blow.

"No, please. Don't hurt him anymore."

Pedro held his pose for a few seconds and looked deep into the eyes of the young woman. She was terrified, and that was sufficient to achieve his mission. He let her limp brother back fall into the chair. He remained doubled up for some time before trying to straighten. When he did so, his look was one of defiance. Pedro explained what was expected of them, his manner belying what had just happened.

"Take five minutes, drink some water and we will continue shooting."

Sergio could not bring himself to look at Carmen. He had always looked after her but knew that he was incapable of defending her against this man. He felt defeated and weak. She knew what he was feeling and laid a soft hand on his shoulder. He was crying and she pretended it wasn't happening.

"We will get away from him, Sergio. Just do as he says for now."

He gave the briefest of nods as he dried his face and tried to put on a brave smile.

"We'll do as he says." He repeated.

The remainder of the morning consisted of a series of ever more worrying messages being recorded. From the initial demand, they escalated to levels of increased threat and references to torture.

Both now knew that Pedro was capable of inflicting pain with little compunction and hoped that he would never be put in a position where he felt the need to do so. Thinly veiled threats of mutilation and increasing the amount demanded were also shot for what Pedro called 'contingencies'.

Scenes were then recorded individually and this was a further cause for worry. Was the intention to separate them at some point? The holding of a bright green placard seemed an act of futility until Pedro stated that a newspaper bearing any date or headline could be seamlessly superimposed to give the impression that they were still alive at a time in the future when perhaps they might not be.

With that chilling statement still ringing in their ears, he announced that he had had enough for the day. He escorted them back to their wards and closed the doors behind them. A supper was brought and this time accepted in silence. Pedro repeated the bedtime routine by strapping them to the gurneys.

The complete lack of resistance to his unnecessary punishment told Pedro that their wills were breaking. He remembered the Israeli mercenary, Aaron, he had worked with in Sudan. He was a master of what he called 'advanced interrogation techniques'.

"Break the will, and not the body. The body can mend, but a mind takes a lot longer."

Aaron broke strong Nubian men in no time. When they thought they had nothing else to tell him, he would start the physical torture. It had a remarkable effect on their memories, making them betray their own mothers in order to avoid further pain.

Sometimes just the threat of torture was enough to turn a brave warrior into a garrulous fool.

Pedro learned that every man had a threshold for both mental and physical pain, and like all thresholds, it was possible to return to the other side when circumstances allowed. He would monitor the situation very closely to ensure that he didn't take them too far, unless he had to. He didn't want either of these two young people dead but if it came to a choice, he wasn't afraid to make it. He had dealt in death for too many years to have any qualms about killing them.

The editing of the day's footage was a pleasant diversion for one so used to warfare. Initially, it amazed Pedro how easy it was to change what was perceived as the truth. The smell of blood and cordite were what he knew, but clever software in the right hands could produce much more effective results. By carefully marking the position of the chairs relevant to the camera and the lights, removing the green background was a simple task, even after the incident with the young man. The chosen background was a standard image available to anyone with the patience required to trawl through hundreds of pages on the internet.

The plethora of dungeons and torture chamber photographs available made Pedro think that his chosen lifestyle may not have been so different or extreme as he had once considered it. What did people do with this kind of imagery? He chose a background tagged as a French Medieval torture chamber and layered it beneath the footage he had shot that day. His preparation paid off as the green filter was adjusted to leave Sergio and Carmen, to all intents and purposes, sitting in a sixteenth century house of horror. Sound effects of dripping water seemed appropriate, and Sergio's face, blanched by the problems his kidneys were having after his beating, enhanced the final product.

He toyed with the newspaper he had bought that morning, and after several adjustments to the focus and angle, achieved a result that made him feel very proud. Tomorrow was going to be a little more difficult due to the very nature of what he had to do, so he set about making preparations. The discovery of the Advanced Treatment Room meant that he had to rearrange his lighting and calibrate distances from his camera to get the footage required, but at least he didn't have to worry about having a dungeon as a backdrop. Now, he had a real torture chamber at his disposal and Sergio's attitude caused him to have a change of heart about its use.

*****

With the now familiar breakfast routine complete, Sergio waited to be taken for further filming. He heard the footfalls as Pedro approached, followed by the sound of the key in the heavy metal door. He wondered why a door befitting a prison was necessary in what was obviously a hospital and concluded that it was designed to keep patients securely locked away. He thought that this must have been an institution for people with mental health issues, and this was confirmed a few minutes later.

Pedro indicated that he walked down the corridor in front of him and Sergio made his way towards the room with the green screen. As he reached the doorway, Pedro spoke for the first time.

"No, not there. Turn right."

Sergio looked along the corridor to his right and saw a gaping hole in the floor. A hatchway had been tied back and he could see wooden steps leading to an underground room. He had a bad feeling about this but the barrel of the pistol in the small of his back removed any question of non-compliance. The sign on the door indicated that this was the Advanced Treatment Room, but the furnishings belied this as being a location for anything other than torture.

The dominant feature was the gurney in the middle of the floor. It was bigger than the one he was strapped to for sleeping, with a number of clamps situated at each side. He froze when he saw this and was relieved when Pedro pushed him beyond the gurney towards a large chair. His feeling of relief was short-lived.

"It looks like the electric chairs they use for executions in America," he said.

His fear level began to rocket as he realised how close he was to the truth.

"They used to use these things for electro-shock therapy. Electrodes were applied to the side of the head and current passed through the targeted area of the patient's brain. I think this was a last resort before they went for the full-blown lobotomy. In places like this, they turned crazies into zombies. Society wanted them locked away but the staff were more certifiable than most of the inmates."

"Are you going to torture me?"

Despite the chill in the Advanced Treatment Room, he was sweating.

"Are you going to give me cause to?"

The question went unanswered. Pedro secured Sergio into the seat and walked to his camera.

"What do you want me to say?"

Pedro heard fear in Sergio's voice and this pleased him immensely.

"You have no more speaking parts. This footage is to convince your father that I mean business. I needed the light in the hall in order to use my special effects. Here, it isn't important. I want to capture the terror in your eyes. There will be no sound, a sort of film noire don't you think?"

Pedro attached electrodes to Sergio's temples, pushed the record button on his camera, and filmed the tethered, perspiring Sergio from all angles. No electricity was needed to convey the alarm he felt, but just for effect, Pedro stabbed him a few times with a skewer he found in the kitchen. The result looked the same as a jolt of electricity. If the truth were known, Pedro had no faith in the contraption and didn't plug it in for fear of electrocuting himself. The footage was very convincing.

In less than an hour, an exhausted Sergio was returned to the ward he never thought he would be happy to see. The door slammed closed and the heavy lock applied, indicating that for now his contribution was over. He listened as Carmen was taken and wept for the ordeal she was about to face. They had to get away from this sadist. It would have to be when they were out of the ward, as the doors were insurmountable objects. Pedro would have to be incapacitated, so an element of surprised was needed, as well as a means of doing so. Sergio had much to think about and he needed this to divert his thoughts from what he knew his sister was enduring in the Advanced Treatment Room.

Carmen displayed the fear desired by Pedro and his filming was completed in a shorter time than expected without harming a hair on her pretty head, though some may have prematurely greyed. Prodding with the skewer once again proved a sufficiently stimulating way of evoking a realistic response, and the capacity of the petrol-driven generator remaining unchallenged. Sergio heard her crying on her return and hoped that she was physically unharmed. Of course, she would be mentally traumatised and both would need counselling when this ordeal was over, but for now he hoped for a quick resolution to the whole affair and a return to his previous, privileged lifestyle.

Pedro contacted the Fixer and reported that everything was in place to make their demand.

"You were quicker than I expected. Is it good?"

"It's better than good. I found a room within the clinic where they applied old-fashioned therapy."

"What kind of therapy?" The Fixer sounded concerned. It was becoming obvious that he had little appetite for the physical aspects of coercion.

"Electro-shock therapy but don't worry, I didn't use it. The machine frightened me as much as it did them. The very thought of nineteenth century solutions to insanity was enough in itself. The simulation is very convincing."

The Fixer had chosen the Agost Clinic for Mental Health because of its remote location. He also chose it because he knew it well. He hadn't been inside the asylum for over seven years, when it was closed after a scandal relating to allegations of mistreatment of the 'guests'. He was unaware of the room Pedro referred to, but had always suspected there were aspects of the clinic they didn't speak about openly.

"We go ahead of schedule. Send the demand today. Remind him of the conditions and the consequences of not keeping to them. He will have people looking for you, and because of this, he will try to buy time. Convince him that this isn't an option."

The scrambled voice sounded assertive once more.

"How do you want it delivered?"

"Put the video on a DVD and lock the file. Arrange for delivery by courier. Buy a new SIM card, the pre-paid sort, and call him on the same number you used previously. Give him the password and let him watch the video. Remind him there is to be no police involvement. Tell him he has twenty-four hours to get the money, and then dispose of the SIM card. After twenty-four hours, call him again using a new SIM card and arrange the drop. Call me with the details. Have you got that?"

Pedro confirmed that he understood the instructions and drove to a supermarket twenty kilometres away in Petrer to buy the necessary materials. There were four mobile phone outlets, so he bought a SIM card from each before collecting the DVDs with his shopping. The schedule being brought forward suited him, as the longer he kept the hostages, the greater the chance of something going wrong. A quick payout would enable him to leave the country while the police chased shadows. And there would be no repeat of Barcelona.

On return to the clinic, he checked his prisoners. Carmen looked tired as the emotional rollercoaster was taking its toll on her. He said nothing as he observed her lying down on the bed in a foetal position, not bothering to plead or voice her resentment. Sergio seemed to have recovered from his visit to the Advanced Treatment Room but stopped short of speaking his mind for fear that Carmen would be punished.

Pedro knew the expression on his face; it said 'I know something you don't know', and Pedro wondered what it might be. He would have to be extra careful with this lad, as he was resourceful.

He went to his makeshift office cum production studio and put together the DVD with the ransom demand. He added a password to each video file and noted them for later use. He wore latex gloves throughout, only too aware of the fingerprint issue. Pedro had little doubt that the complicated and incompetent Spanish administrative system would have lost any record of his fingerprints many years ago, but couldn't afford to take any risks. He placed the DVD in a padded envelope and sealed it by peeling the adhesive strip and pressing the edges together. The label was produced using a computer programme, printed, peeled, and stuck on the front of the envelope.

He drove to the nearby coastal town of Santa Pola and looked for a courier office. The first one he found had an officious looking middle-aged woman behind the counter, and he decided that she was too observant to risk using. The next had a teenage boy who was busy playing a hand-held game. He was perfect, as he clearly displayed that he was bored and disinterested in his job. Envelope despatched with a cash transaction, Pedro stopped in a small café across the road from the courier's for a beer before his return journey to Agost.

He had always liked this small fishing town. It was a working town that flooded with Spanish tourists every summer and was probably reaching the end of this year's exodus. The golden sand was its main attraction, along with the deep blue Mediterranean Sea it bordered.

As he drank his cold beer in the shade, he realised that the cooking smell coming from the kitchen had him salivating. The Menú del Día was only ten Euros, so he decided to treat himself. As he moved on through the salad starter to the hake main course, he saw the motorcyclist arrive at the courier's office across the road. By the time he had finished his crème Catalan, the rider had left and was hopefully speeding towards the home of Fernando Alvés.

Fernando Alvés had briefed the security guard that any if packages or messages were delivered, he was to be informed immediately. When told of a courier delivery, he knew what it was before it was brought to the main house. Almu had been crying since being told of the kidnapping and knew by her husband's urgency that whatever had arrived was important. He returned with the envelope and went through the large living room to his office. He had been feeling the envelope and was relieved that he felt no fingers inside, as he had heard that this wasn't uncommon in kidnappings.

Almu followed and stood on his shoulder as he tore the top from the package. A DVD fell onto the leather-clad desk and both looked at it without daring to touch it. Almu unfroze first.

"For God's sake open it."

Fernando's hands shook as he took the DVD and slid it into his computer. The E-drive whirred into action and a few seconds later the screen showed it contained two files. Fernando clicked on the first.

"It wants a bloody password."

He sounded incredulous. Almu was only vaguely familiar with personal computing and responded inappropriately.

"Then give it a bloody password."

He looked at her and bit his tongue.

"It could be anything. This is part of his game."

"We have to tell the police. They will have experts who can open the files."

"He was most insistent that there was to be no police involvement."

Almu didn't have the opportunity to reply before the mobile on the desk rang. Fernando had been no more than one metre from his phone since the first call. He rationalised that if he missed a call from the kidnapper, bad things would happen to his children. Almu's eyes screamed 'answer it'. He did so nervously.

"Fernando Alvés."

"You will have received the package by now?"

Fernando peered out of the window, wondering if the kidnapper was watching him from somewhere nearby.

"Yes. I have it."

"Have you got it in your laptop?"

Fernando didn't think it was relevant or prudent to tell the caller it was actually a desktop and said that he had.

"It's password protected."

"The password for file number one is 'Brazzaville' with a capital B."

Fernando typed the password and a WMV file opened. Almu burst into tears when she saw Sergio and Carmen in what looked like a dungeon. As their mother, she could tell that they had both been crying. Sergio was in pain and it looked like his throat had been cut; the clothing of her son and daughter were covered in what looked like blood. She sobbed into her already wet handkerchief as she watched them plead for their lives on the small screen. It was obvious that they were reading from a prepared script, as the words weren't those they would have chosen. When the video finished, Pedro spoke.

"Remember the conditions I laid down in our first conversation; no police and no attempt is to be made to find me. Additionally, the ransom must be in non-sequential bills with no five hundred Euros notes included."

"It would take some time to put together ten million Euros, even if I had it, which I don't."

"You are a resourceful man, Mr Alvés. You will find a way of raising the money."

"It really isn't that easy, er ... What do I call you?"

"I am the Taker, apparently."

"Taker, I don't have that kind of money."

Almu interrupted.

"This is our children you are speaking about. You can't bargain with the lives of our children."

"Listen to your wife, Fernando."

Fernando Alvés' brain raced as he tried to find something to say that would save his children. He didn't have ten million Euros, even if he could sell his faltering business. However, he had to buy enough time to find a solution. Maybe his man could track them down and eliminate the Taker before they came to harm. Pedro, revelling in his role as the Taker, knew what Fernando was thinking.

"If you need further proof of my sincerity, open the second file."

Fernando had wondered about the function of the second file and tapped on the open tab. Once again, a password was required.

"Type in 'parenthood', all in lower case."

No one missed the irony of the password as Fernando hurriedly opened the file. This time there were no words. Firstly Sergio and then Carmen appeared, alone in a different dungeon and very frightened. Electrodes were attached to their heads and they appeared to be subjected to a series of electric shocks, which caused them to jump and strain against the heavy leather straps that held them in a monstrous wooden chair.

"No! No! No!" Almu screamed, unable to control herself at the sight of her petrified children.

"What kind of low life are you? There is no need to torture them. I'll get your blood money but I'll need some time."

"You have twenty-four hours."

The line went dead.

"What are we going to do?" Almu asked.

"I don't know. I really don't know."

"Do we have the money?"

"I could raise two million at a push but no more."

"Then we must inform the police."

"If the Taker finds out, he will kill them."

"If we don't pay him ten million Euros, he will kill them anyway. We must inform the police right away."

Fernando knew she was right.

When the call was received at Alicante Commissary, it was tagged to be forwarded to Investigator Sergeant Christiano Marcos. When he heard the uncertainty in the voice of the caller, he felt a sense of smug satisfaction.

"Hold the line for one minute please, sir" he said as he placed the receiver on his desk while he poured himself a cup of coffee. He didn't really want the coffee, just to make Fernando Alvés wait.

"You're not so arrogant now, Mr Fernando Alvés," he said to no one in particular as he walked slowly back to his desk.

"What seems to be the problem, Mr Alvés."

"My son and daughter are missing."

"Are you sure?"

Fernando Alvés was expecting this and ate the humble pie that was required to get the detective onside.

"Yes, there was a misunderstanding the last time we spoke."

Christiano enjoyed the lie and said that he would be with the Alvés family in thirty minutes. When he told Inspector Carlos Rico of the second reported disappearance of the Alvés siblings, his boss smiled.

"Well, well, well. I'll get my coat. I think I'm going to enjoy this interview."

On arrival, they were waved straight through by the security guard and parked outside the main door to the house. This time Christiano got further than the front door. As they entered, Fernando Alvés shook their hands.

"Inspector Rico?"

"Yes Mr Alvés. We met after that terrible incident with your ex-partner's factory. I assume the insurance company recompensed him?"

"The matter was resolved without issue."

Both men knew this was far from the truth but Carlos moved on.

"Five days ago the airport police reported Sergio and Carmen missing and you told my sergeant that this wasn't the case. Now you are telling me that they actually are missing. Can you tell me what's exactly going on?"

Carlos braced himself for a lie and Fernando Alvés obliged.

"They called me and said that they were going to Cannes for a weekend but after they didn't get in touch for nearly a week, I made some enquiries. They never went to Cannes at all. They were on the flight to Alicante and they arrived on time. They never came home and I have no idea of where they are. Can I report them as missing?"

Almu listened without speaking, but her expression made it quite clear that there was more to this than they had been told. Carlos noted that her eyes, incandescent with rage, were locked on her husband as she tried to hold something back. He decided to let the scenario play out.

"You gave Sergeant Marcos two phone numbers belonging to women who were recently killed in a road accident, telling him they were your son and daughter's numbers. Why did you do that?"

Fernando knew that the police had followed up on the false information he had given them and was beginning to feel foolish at being exposed as a poor liar.

"Did I really? That was a simple mistake. I'm not entirely comfortable with modern technology, inspector."

One of the region's most successful entrepreneurs was now trying to tell the police he was incapable of using a mobile phone. Carlos had had enough.

"Mr Alvés, I will give you one last chance to tell me what exactly is going on or I will ask my sergeant to book you for wasting police time. I know that you are normally a very competent liar; you would not be where you are in your line of business without being able to bullshit. But, you're not fooling me for one minute. Now stop playing games and tell me what has happened to Sergio and Carmen."

Fernando Alvés had never felt as helpless in his life. First the Taker, then Almu, and now the police; he was not in control. Every thought that came into his head had already been negated by one of the three. His decision was taken by Almu.

"Are you going to tell then or am I?"

Fernando Alvés raised his hands in a surrendering gesture and indicated that the investigators sat down. Christiano looked to Carlos who sat comfortably in a large sofa. He followed suit and their host propped himself on the arm of a nearby chair.

"My son and daughter have been kidnapped."

He waited for questions but none came. The detectives continued to look at him without saying a word. Unnerved by their lack of reaction, he wondered if he had done the right thing by telling them.

"I said my son and daughter have been kidnapped."

"When did this happen? Let me warn you before you answer that anything less than the whole truth will put their lives at risk."

Carlos was impressed by Christiano's ability to pick up on his own unfriendly questioning technique.

Fernando Alvés would have seen through any other strategy.

"They were taken from the terminal as reported by the airport police. Someone posed as a replacement chauffeur and took them away in a Limousine. Later that day, I received a call from a man telling me that he had taken them and that I would receive a ransom demand in due course."

"Why did you lie about the first report?"

"He said that they would be harmed if I told the police, and he sounded like he meant it."

"Has the ransom demand been made?"

"Today, for ten million Euros."

"Do you intend to pay?"

"I don't have ten million Euros. He sent a DVD. I'll show it to you."

Fernando Alvés beckoned the police officers into the adjoining office and booted up the computer. Christiano took the opportunity to ask some questions.

"How did the DVD arrive?"

"By courier. The security guard signed for the package and he will have the driver on CCTV."

Christiano noted this.

"At what time?"

"Three-thirty."

Carlos noted the request for a password to access the digital file.

"Was the password in the envelope?"

"No. The Taker called. He told me the password and I then watched the video."

"The Taker?"

"That's what he calls himself."

"What is the password?"

"Brazzaville, with a capital 'B'."

"Is that not the capital of the Congo?"

"The Republic of the Congo, sometimes called Congo-Brazzaville, as opposed to the Democratic Republic of the Congo, where the capital city is Kinshasa, sir."

The two other men frowned at Christiano and his geographical knowledge before returning their attention to the computer monitor.

They watched the video in silence

"I want you to try to remember exactly everything he said, Mr Alvés."

"He repeated no police and that the money was to be in bills less than five hundred Euros."

"What did you reply?"

"I told him that I didn't have that kind of money. That was when he told me to watch the second video. The password is 'parenthood'."

He typed the password into the box and once again, they watched the young Alvés' apparently being subjected to electro-shock treatment in what seemed to be a different dungeon from the one use in the initial demand.

"What are we going to do?"

"We have a lot of police work to do. I will post around the clock protection on the house. You and your wife are not to leave it. A communications team will be here shortly and set up monitoring equipment on your telephone. When he calls again, we will record the call to try to ascertain his location or perhaps identify any background noise than might give us an idea about where he is. We will take the

DVD for analysis and talk to the courier service. Do not hand over any money. Don't do anything without consulting with me. I will have an investigator from my team with you at all times until this is resolved. Do you understand?"

Fernando Alvés had no choice but to hand over control of the situation to the police, but for his own peace of mind, he would gather together as much money as he could for when they cocked it up.

"I understand, inspector."

Carlos left, giving Christiano instructions to find the courier and talk to his dispatcher while he returned to the Commissary with the DVD for dissection by forensics. He was certain that a check of phone records would lead to a dead end, but for completeness, it had to be carried out. Sometimes criminals made silly mistakes and he always lived in hope of an easy win. Before he reached the door, Fernando Alvés reminded him of the timescale.

"I don't have to remind you that we have less than twenty-four hours before this man starts to hurt my children, inspector?"

Carlos stopped dead and turned on Fernando Alvés.

"We have less than twenty-four hours, Mr Alvés, when we should have had five days more. Good day."

The lord of the manor looked to his wife for reassurance and it was not forthcoming.

"You should have told them as soon as you got the first call. You should have told me."

There was little point in covering this territory again. She would calm down after the kids had been returned, if they were returned unharmed. He had a lot to think about and a few calls to make on a line that wasn't monitored by the police. There were people who would lend him a lot of money, though he knew ten million was an unreasonable request. He could make guarantees, but first had to close as many loopholes as possible.

He would find the money.

*****

On return to the Commissary, Carlos called his team into the briefing room and told them about the kidnapping of Sergio and Carmen Alvés. He led them through the case, as told to him by Fernando Alvés, and showed them the videos while marking the salient points on the large incident board that dominated the room. He pinned up two recent photographs of Sergio and Carmen, which hadn't been hard to find as they appeared regularly in the celebrity magazines that followed the rich and famous. He was professional enough to ignore his personal feelings about their father: the lives of the two young people were at risk.

"Sergeant Marcos is pursuing the courier in hope of getting a lead on who sent the package to the Alvés household this afternoon. We have got very little time due to the reticence of their father to involve the police until the last minute, and he assures me he did so with the welfare of his children in mind. Be that as it may, we will tread carefully and not make our investigations too obvious in case the perpetrator gets wind of us. Complete discretion is required. I will be making enquiries with other forces to ask about any similar cases in recent years, as this may not be the kidnapper's first job. Velasquez."

"Yes sir?"

"Check the telephone company for all calls to the Alvés house and Fernando Alvés' mobile over the past week. I want to know about everyone who has spoken to him in this period. I also want you to get in touch with our communications monitoring people. We need a unit in place when the kidnapper next calls."

Velasquez indicated he understood and left.

"Mendez, I want you to take the DVD to forensics and sit with them until they have squeezed every possible bit of information from it. Tell them it is priority A and that no one goes home until this job is complete. I want to know where they are being held. Got it?"

Mendez confirmed and left with the DVD.

"Ferdinand. I need your computer skills and a bit more. I want to know all about Fernando Alvés. From the minute he was born, right up to what he had for breakfast today. Talk to the Fraud Squad, I know that he has been on their radar for some time. I think that he might have made an enemy who has decided to reap revenge by kidnapping, or at least arranging the kidnapping, of his son and daughter."

"Do you want me to look into the rest of the family, sir? I know that the son has a reputation for being rather controversial in public."

"Good idea based on bad reading habits, Ferdinand. Do it."

"Ferrera, I've saved the best for you. I need you to babysit the Alvés family. Nominally, you will be there to watch and wait for the kidnapper to get in touch. However, Mr Fernando Alvés likes to keep secrets from us. For a respectable businessman he has scant regard for the police and I don't trust that he would necessarily tell us if the Taker, as he likes to be known, were to contact him by other means. If you see him speaking to anyone, I want to know who it is; if it is a pigeon, assume it's a messenger, shoot it, and bring it to me."

Ferrera, somewhat confused by his boss's sarcasm, acknowledged his orders and thought that he had worse duties than waiting around in a luxury mansion. Carlos called to inform his long-suffering wife not to expect him home in the next twenty-four hours. Marta sighed as she had on many occasions in the past and agreed to have a change of clothes ready whenever he got the opportunity to collect them. After thirty years as a police officer's wife, she expected this call. He didn't say what had 'come up', and in such circumstances she knew better than to ask. If it wasn't on the local news channel, then it was for a good reason. There were very few aspects of an investigator's job that would make a civilian smile and she had long stopped asking him about his work, especially after Raúl Berbegal.

Their personal encounter with the serial killer had almost ended tragically, and as far as Marta was concerned, the further Carlos' work was from home, the better.

Carlos himself had only recently returned to work after that horrific incident and was relishing the involvement in real detective work again. He had only encountered kidnapping on a split family basis, where one parent abducted the child or children because of what they considered an unjust court order. No ransom was demanded in these cases, as there was no intention of relinquishing possession of the little darlings. Unless they left the country, these cases were usually resolved by Social Services with minimal police involvement.

Kidnappings, once common in the north of the country as the separatists tried to gain political leverage, were unheard of in Alicante. As he called around the forces in the major cities, only three ransom-based kidnappings had occurred in the past five years.

A banker in Madrid was taken on his way to work and held for three days before the police found him and his abductors, who, Carlos was guaranteed, were still firmly under lock and key. The second kidnapping for money happened in Bilbao and resulted in the hostage taker, the hostage and two officers being shot dead in an operation that bordered in the calamitous. The third was an amateurish attempt five years ago in Barcelona, which ended tragically with the victim hanging himself after being extensively tortured. Carlos thought of the second video on the Alvés DVD and requested the Catalan National Police, or Mossos d'Esquadra, as they are known, forward him the file in hope that there was a link that might help. The Barcelona incompetent seemed his only possible link.

Closer to home, Christiano's investigation into the courier delivery had initially proven fruitless.

"The package came from Santa Pola. The office was manned by something best described as half boy, half computer game. He noticed nothing and I sincerely believe him. I checked the CCTV in the office and it had been turned around to monitor the staff and not the customers. I found the manger in a local bar, drunk. He told me they had been having problems balancing the books and he suspected it was one of his part-timers, though I suspect the truth was a little more obvious.

"The sender paid in cash and gave a false name and address. This line of enquiry appeared to be going nowhere until I stopped for a coffee in a café across the road. On the off chance, I asked the owner about the courier service. He told me it was good for business as the delivery drivers always used his establishment. He even got the odd customer. At about the time the package was brought to the office, a tall athletic man of around fifty had a meal there. The owner saw him come out of the courier's. He had dark hair and the owner said he looked like one of ours."

"A policeman?"

"I assume so. He told me what he ate and that he paid and left without further conversation. I've asked the locals to get a sketch artist to the café as quick as possible."

"It looks like you're lucky. A detective needs luck."

Christiano would have preferred praise for good investigative work but accepted 'lucky'. It was more than he was expecting from one generally regarded as a tough taskmaster. As Carlos brought his new second-in-command up to date with what he had discovered, Constable Ferdinand knocked and entered the inspector's dingy office. He seemed excited.

"Ferdinand; if you were a dog, your tail would be wagging. Out with it, what have you found?"

Ferdinand blushed slightly. He had been with the investigation branch for just over a year, and knew that he was included for his IT skills. He was trained as a copper, like the rest, but was unlikely to be asked to single-handedly face any of the dregs of the city.

With data, he was very much in his comfort zone. He settled his lanky frame into the chair indicated by the inspector and read the printouts of his findings.

"Fernando Alvés has had a very chequered history. He started a dotcom business with Jorge Bocanegra in 1988. They were an overnight sensation, wiping out all local competition within three years. They became one of the top companies in their chosen field in Spain and made a lot of money, to the extent of refusing a buy out from one of the big players in Silicon Valley."

"Was everything legitimate?"

"Completely. They found an emerging market and exploited it. All was going well until 1994 when, for no documented reason, they had a massive falling out. I have made enquiries about the cause of this split, but no one seems to know. All of a sudden, they just hated each other."

"Did this coincide with a particular business event?"

"No, though it sounds like it was an acrimonious split. Both filed for the rights to their joint company with the outcome favouring Bocanegra. They formed competing companies and then Bocanegra began having accidents."

"What do you mean by 'accidents'?"

"Firstly, in 2001, his factory was burnt to the ground. Forensics said that an accelerant had been used to start the fire. Then in 2004, he had an almost fatal car accident. The insurance report said that the brake fluid had been drained from his car."

"Was it a leak?"

"Apparently not. It had been siphoned out. The brake failure was a deliberate act. He was lucky, if two broken legs and a cracked skull can be considered as fortune. In 2006, he wasn't to be as lucky. In yet another improbable car accident, he was left paralysed. The investigation into the crash was inconclusive but eye-witness accounts point to a failure of the steering mechanism, though the vehicle befell a series of thefts before a full examination could be carried out."

"Was Fernando Alvés implicated in any way?"

"His name was never mentioned in any official document."

"But?" Carlos knew there was a 'but'.

"These incidents coincided with major contractual conflicts between Alvés.com and BlackBull.com, as Bocanegra named his company."

"Where is he now?"

"Jorge Bocanegra is an invalid. He is wheelchair bound and totally incapable of walking."

"Is he capable of kidnapping or even promoting such a thing?"

"It seems unlikely, sir. His company was sold on and Alvés seems to have monopolised the dwindling market since. Jorge Bocanegra took his money and now lives in a retreat close to Denia. He requires constant care and the matron tells me that he spends most of his days studying chess; Kasparov mainly."

"I preferred Fisher myself. He was less predictable."

The interjection by Christiano was met with bemused looks from the others.

"Does the evidence indicate that Fernando Alvés was involved in Bocanegra's accidents?"

"Surprisingly, Fernando Alvés was always in a high-profile situation far removed from the mishaps of his former partner. Fraud Squad suspect a link between Fernando Alvés and the Russians but have no proof. The modus operandi of Jorge Bocanegra's accidents has Moscow written all over them in large letters."

"Could Jorge Bocanegra have commissioned the kidnapping of the Alvés pair?"

Antonio Ferdinand was taken aback. The famous Inspector Carlos Rico was asking his opinion. He almost felt unworthy but he bolstered himself to answer.

"Not in my opinion, sir. He requires full-time medical assistance. Unfortunately, it seems that he no longer has the capacity for deviousness. The matron said that he has no visitors and never uses a phone."

Carlos felt disappointed that an obvious perpetrator had been eliminated. He thanked Ferdinand and told him to dig deeper into the dealings of Fernando Alvés. There were many rich men in Alicante, why him?

Sergio Alvés was asking much the same question. He thought that this kidnapping was more than a financial venture. His father had powerful friends but he also had powerful enemies. Could this whole thing be an attempt to undermine him? Slowly, he was being bled into the ways of the family business with the eventual aim of taking over from his father, and this meant exposure to questionable practices. Had his father gone too far and was being reprimanded via his children? He knew Pedro was no more than hired muscle. He correctly classified him as an ex-soldier and built his escape plan around this. Pedro ran to a routine, routine was God.

Pedro thought that Sergio was a spoilt brat and, to an extent, he was correct in that assumption. However, this clouded his judgement of Sergio as a man. Sergio knew that his biggest obstacle, the steel door, was also his biggest strength. Strength is weakness and weakness is strength. He had learnt very little in his study of philosophy, but this phrase now rang true. He started timing Pedro on his methodical visits. Everything was done mechanically; Pedro knew no other way. He followed orders. Therefore, he could become a victim of his own routine. All Sergio had to do was to watch, record, and indentify the weak spot.

It took several days, but he found it. Every time Pedro came to feed him, he followed the same predictable sequence of actions. He opened the door and checked were Sergio was. He then wheeled in the trolley with the food tray on top. This was the gap that Sergio needed, between the check and the trolley. If he could use the weight of the door as a weapon, he had a chance. He wasn't sure he had it in him as the result of failure was unthinkable, but the alternative of being no more than a slave was intolerable. The door was the key. He had one shot at it, and failure was unthinkable.

He had to appear dormant and then move like lightning after Pedro checked his whereabouts. If he got it wrong, he had no doubt that Pedro would kill him, or even worse, his sister. He had made little pretence of liking Sergio and had taken every opportunity to hurt him, so he decided that today was as good as any other when it came to knocking out a psychopath; waiting for later would serve no purpose.

He had never done anything like this before, and his heart raced as the evening visit was anticipated. The past six days had given him time to reflect on his life and he wasn't sure he liked what he saw. He realised that he had been a shallow, arrogant egotist. His friends were mostly sycophants who liked him for his money and not his personality. Academically, he wasn't particularly gifted; he knew that in later life he would have to depend on whatever business acumen he had inherited from his father. Yes, his father, it always came back to his father.

He had managed to dominate their lives without ever being there. He provided for everything, but his personal contribution was negligible. There was even a period that Sergio thought was in his early teens, where his attitude towards him and his sister became quite offhand. By then they had been farmed out to full-time boarding schools in preparation for the pointless university degrees they would complete as a statement of the family status. When they came home for fiestas, more often than not his father was absent on business matters. Their mother had tried to cover for him but she wasn't a convincing liar. They accepted that he just wasn't paternal and left matters at that.

What would he do in this situation? Fernando Alvés was an aggressive man so Sergio guessed he would go for broke and try to take down his captor. Then, that was what he must do. At times like these, he wished he had inherited his father's heavy build rather than his selfish personality.

After release from the overnight gurney for breakfast, he had taken the opportunity to move the heavy bed a metre closer to the door. He wiped the marks that the wheels of the bed made on the linoleum floor with his towel and hoped he had left no evidence of the subtle change in the ward. He daren't push his luck by making the change too noticeable, and the early afternoon delivery of lunch without comment indicated he had been successful. The fraction of a second it would buy him just might be enough.

That evening, Pedro's routine was being played out like clockwork. Sergio heard the front left-hand wheel of the trolley squeak as it was pushed down the corridor. It stopped outside Carmen's ward and the large bunch of keys jangled as he searched for the right one. The positive click indicated success and the squeak returned. Pedro spoke but Sergio couldn't make out the words due to the sound of his own heart pounding in his eardrums. He felt like he was going to be sick as next door was secured and the squeak got closer. He had practised his lunge many times that day and adopted a position on the bed that he thought gave him the maximum chance of success.

He had observed that after the initial look to ascertain the lack of threat, Pedro returned to the trolley, leaving Sergio hidden by the door. Two squeaks of the trolley wheel would put his target in what he considered the optimum position to strike. Only after impact would he know if he had got it right. Pedro would either be hurt and hopefully unconscious in the doorway, or bruised and angry, fit to kill.

The heavy lock clunked as the key released the dead bolt, with the sound echoing around the ward. The top of Pedro's head appeared around the edge of the door and Sergio watched through half-closed eyes, as though just wakened by the noise. As Pedro's head disappeared, Sergio rolled off the bed and stood like a middle-distance runner awaiting the gun to start a race. The front of the trolley appeared from behind the door and the first squeak of the wheel told him it was time to move. By the second squeak, he was airborne, committed to this act of desperation.

He hit the inside of the door with the palms of both hands with his full weight behind them. His feet hit the ground at the exact spot he had hoped for and the additional thrust from his legs caused the door to move explosively. He felt contact with his target, accompanied with a heavy exhalation of breath and the crashing of the upturned trolley on the floor.

As Sergio dared to look around the door, he saw Pedro lying in the portal. Blood oozed from the side of his head and he wondered if he had killed him. The adrenalin coursing through his veins urged him to throw himself on top of his captor but when he landed on him, he wasn't sure why he had done it. He could see that Pedro was breathing shallowly and this scared him. He had to act now, before he came around.

He undid the buckle of the leather belt around Pedro's waist because he didn't have the time to attempt releasing the ring of keys with his trembling, almost uncontrollable hands. He would take the whole belt. When the keys fell from the belt onto the floor, he picked them up and turned to release Carmen. As he looked at Pedro, he knew that this man had been subjected to heavy abuse in the past and wouldn't be unconscious for long. He decided to drag his limp body into the ward and for the first time in his life realised what the phrase 'dead-weight' actually meant. Initially, he wouldn't budge and the feeling of nausea returned. When Pedro emitted a small groan, this supplied Sergio with the strength he needed. He dragged Pedro inside the doorway with one determined heave, pushed the trolley in beside him, and slammed the door shut. The sound was deafening and satisfying in equal proportions. He found the correct key on the third time of asking and locked the door. He leaned against the door and breathed deeply.

Carmen listened to the noises in the corridor and feared for her brother's welfare. Pedro's dislike of him was clear to see and Sergio could be very irritating. She cowered as her door opened for the second time in as many minutes and was surprised and relieved to see Sergio enter.

"Sergio. What's happened? How did you get away from him?"

"We don't have time for this now. We must get away. I've knocked him out, but I think he's coming round."

He hugged her as he said this, all the while guiding her out of the ward. They sped down the corridor, at first running blindly from the known danger towards who knows what. Sergio wondered if the man who employed Pedro to kidnap them was in the building, but his boldness had grown to the extent that he was prepared to face this lesser enemy. He pushed each of the doors as they reached them and soon found Pedro's quarters.

As expected, they were immaculate. He started emptying the contents of the drawers onto the bed, spreading them as he looked for something.

"What are you doing?" Carmen asked.

"Car keys, we need his car keys."

As he continued his frantic search, Carmen rifled through the pockets of the jackets that hung in the wardrobe. Her heart skipped a beat when she saw the chauffeur's jacket, expecting to find the keys to the Limousine. Both were disappointed, as there were no car keys to be found.

"He probably got them in his pocket. Is it safe to go back and check?"

Sergio considered this for a few seconds and concluded that the risk of releasing Pedro against walking to safety was too great.

"No. If he has even partially recovered, we would be in a lot of trouble. I should have taken his gun. He must have been lying on the holster. Damn it, I'm so stupid at times."

There was no time to debate his intellectual capacity. He grabbed Carmen's hand and they left the building by the same door they entered nearly a week before. They emerged into the weakening, evening sunlight and took a few seconds to breathe the warm air. Carmen walked directly to the Land Rover to check in case the keys were left in the ignition, and shook her head.

"I don't suppose you know how to hot-wire a car?" she asked.

It was Sergio's turn to shake his head.

"I only got as far as knocking out kidnappers at criminal school. Hot-wiring was the next lesson", he joked. "Let's get out of here."

They identified the shape of the Limousine under the tarpaulin as they passed it but neither wanted to waste any further time looking for a means of starting it. It was more important to get to safety. The dirt track was the only way in and out of the hospital, and they followed it as it wound up the hill. They stopped at the end of the track and surveyed the three-hundred and sixty degrees of surrounding countryside. They had seen a small sector of the terrain through the windows of their wards and it now looked even more barren to the naked eye.

Carmen looked at the layers of multi-coloured rock and thought that they reminded her of the liquorice sweets she had liked so much as a child. However, these were far from tempting or welcoming, and would become every bit as dangerous in the dark as the man who may soon be pursuing them. Time was moving on and they weren't.

"Sergio, this is a desert. We cannot go this way."

Her brother looked at the roughly carved rock formations separated by sand, clay, and rocks, and was forced to agree.

"We take the track. We will have to listen in case he escapes and follows us. If he does this, we will have to come off the road and wait for daylight. We can hope for another car and flag it down but I can see no reason for anyone to want to come down here unless they are associated with Pedro."

As much as it pained her to agree, Carmen followed him into the encroaching darkness. When they heard the gunshots from the clinic, they knew the chase was on.

*****

As his team of investigators reported to Carlos Rico, it became all too clear that he was facing a clever adversary. Velasquez, who was charged with all things telephonic, was the first to knock on his office door. His expression said it all but it was exactly what the inspector expected.

"So you're telling me kidnappers don't leave calling cards."

"I suppose that's what it amounts to, sir. Twenty-three calls to the Alvés household during the past seven days. Almost all were to his wife, relating to her search for the victims. One call was taken by Fernando Alvés from a public phone in a village near Murcia, almost one hundred kilometres to the south. This was the call informing him that Sergio and Carmen were at that point in time in the care of an undesirable. Local police are brushing it down for fingerprints. The last was from Alcoy, thirty kilometres to the north of here, using a mobile with a disposable SIM card. Surprisingly, there was no reply on that number. I expect the card is lying at the side of the motorway our caller appears to be driving up and down in an effort to keep us at arm's length."

"What about Fernando Alvés' mobile? What's been happening with that?"

"A constant string of business calls, all traceable."

"A remarkable feat for someone who wanted us to believe that he wasn't comfortable with cell phone technology while running an internet company, don't you think? Are the communications people in place?"

"Ferrera confirms that they arrived ten minutes ago and are setting up their equipment."

99

Christiano stated that this only proved that the kidnapper was nobody's fool, and Carlos felt obliged to agree with him. The inspector told Velasquez to find Mendez and return with him and Ferdinand to the incident room.

"We need to pool what we know and decide how we are going to proceed."

His new sergeant was surprised at Carlos Rico's openness to listen to his team. This behaviour flew in the face of all he heard about the gung-ho detective, but they were operating against the clock. They had six hours before the deadline was reached and seemed no closer to finding the victims. Mendez was their last hope of a breakthrough.

When the three constables arrived, Mendez pinned four large photographs on the display board at the front of the room. He looked particularly pleased with himself as he addressed his teammates.

"We have been fooled. It is a very elaborate special effect, but a trick nonetheless."

He pointed to the first photograph.

"Look here, on Sergio's right shoulder. It isn't clear to the naked eye but if we look very carefully with a magnifying glass, a green line can be seen."

Carlos accepted the instrument so loved by fictional detectives and peered at Sergio's right shoulder for several seconds. He gave Mendez a questioning look and returned to the photograph.

"So there is a green line. What does it mean?"

"It means that a process known as chroma-keying has been carried out. Sergio was filmed against a green background, the background was then removed, and the dungeon added."

"I thought these things were done with a blue background?" Carlos queried.

"The software has moved on and almost any colour can be used, the criterion being that it doesn't appear on the foreground subjects or their clothing. However, the director of this movie made a couple of small mistakes. With Sergio, he didn't get the lighting quite right, probably a light or the chair had been moved before filming."

He moved to the second photograph, this time of Carmen.

"Carmen was wearing a tiny lapel pin in protest at the treatment of prostitutes on Las Ramblas in Barcelona. She probably picked it up the night before, the pin I mean and not the prostitute."

"Keep your jokes for the bar, Mendez" Carlos reprimanded.

"Sorry, sir. If you now look on the collar of her blouse, you can see a flaw. This flaw lines up with the bricks on the wall of the dungeon."

Mendez produced a metre long rule and lined up the course of bricks to which he referred. Carlos approached it with the magnifying glass and slowly nodded in agreement.

"Either Carmen Alvés has a hole in her body or we have indeed been fooled into thinking she is being held in a dungeon."

Mendez pointed to the third photograph.

"This is the dungeon without Sergio or Carmen."

His teammates gasped as they compared the photographs. It was identical to the background with the siblings as hostages.

"How is this possible?" Christiano asked in amazement. "There were no shots in the video without them".

"This is the background shot that was added. I downloaded it from the internet while the boffins were doing the serious work."

Mendez was a solid team member who was seldom given the limelight, and was relishing his short-term celebrity. Carlos let him have his moment before returning the Mendez fan club to a police investigation.

"What is the relevance of the fourth picture?"

"It is a real dungeon. I say dungeon but the construction tells us otherwise. This was probably built in the middle of the last century. It could have been an interrogation room used by Franco's boys or even the basement of someone with an S and M fetish. This is the location we need to be looking for. This is where they are actually being held."

Mendez's finishing flourish was incorrect at the time of speaking. Sergio and Carmen Alvés were running for their lives up a dirt track in a barren valley. When they heard the shots, they knew that Pedro was shooting the lock from the door in Sergio's former ward. It would only be a short time before he came to find them, and he would be very angry. The temptation to run as fast as they could was almost overwhelming as the fear hit them, but Carmen said 'no'.

"We will get further if we maintain a steady jog. Run fast and we will burn out in no time. We need to be able to hear him coming. We must stay together."

Sergio breathlessly agreed. His sister had always been the athlete of the family. They set off at Carmen's pace, which was hampered by their stylish footwear and the uneven ground.

In the clinic, Pedro cursed his own ineptitude. He had let his guard down and been caught out by a complete amateur. Perhaps the Colonel was right after all and he really was getting too old for this type of work. At least Sergio Alvés had chosen to confirm his non-professional status by leaving him with the pistol. Without this, it would have been another embarrassing attempt at kidnapping. As it was, he knew he had concussion and his jaw was broken. The concussion would pass but the jaw had to be reset.

He used the trolley as a shield as he shot the lock out of the heavy door. An injury from a ricocheting bullet would have been the last straw. The door yielded behind a cloud of wood and steel, and the smell of the cordite acted like an aphrodisiac to the former mercenary. It took him back to bygone glories and bolstered his spirit.

He ran to his quarters and saw that his ex-prisoners had ransacked it. The medical box was under the bed but the hypodermic with the painkiller was intact. He injected his jaw in three places and waited a moment for it to take effect. It might as well have been a saline solution for all the difference it made, as the pain was blinding when he manoeuvred his jawbone into line. He wiped the tears from his eyes and thought that he would get it reset properly when this was over. However, this was far from being over.

The siblings had been making good progress when they heard the Land Rover engine gun into action outside the clinic, not nearly far enough away. They knew that he would be with them in no time.

"We have to get off the road," Sergio gasped.

Carmen agreed. They stumbled to a halt and scanned for cover from the road. A large rock on the left would shield them from the headlights of the Land Rover as it went up the dirt track. They took cover behind it and waited. When he passed them, they would progress up the track and continue in this manner until they reached safety. As they waited, they both prayed silently. It was a beautiful starlit night and, in other circumstances, they would be sipping Martinis. Now they were praying for their very survival.

The vehicle screamed up the road in an inappropriate gear. The driver wanted noise: he wanted them to know he was coming. He knew the effect noise had on the nerves of the uninitiated and he wanted them to be hurting as much as he was at that moment. This pass was purely to put the frighteners on them; the next was when he would pick them up.

The noise had the desired effect, making the blood in Sergio and Carmen's veins freeze. They cringed as they held each other in the now almost complete darkness and sensed that he was toying with them.

He knew they wouldn't go across country: that would have been suicidal and they weren't that stupid. He would have taken the road and hidden when he heard the vehicle approach, and they would too. It was three kilometres to the end of the dirt track and they would have covered one at best. If they strayed off the track, there was a strong possibility of breaking limbs in the impassable terrain. He drove to the end of the track and turned the Land Rover around.

He was looking for the signs that would give away those unfamiliar with tactical evasion. Sound was one of them, with shape, silhouette, smell, shadow, and movement also featuring high on the list. However, night vision glasses removed the necessity for too much effort.

It was downhill for most of the road to the clinic, so he could afford to turn off his engine and roll with gravity. With his headlights switched off, the slower speed suited the resolution of the glasses that gave him a tremendous advantage, and would also prevent him driving off the narrow track. They would glow like neon signs in the eerie black and green world he now saw.

They watched as he passed them on the uphill journey and started out again on the track when he was a hundred metres away. At places, the drop on one side or the other was precipitous, and this was something they had to be aware of. Listening for the sound of the engine to warn of his approach, they were caught flat-footed in the middle of the road in front of the silent vehicle. They were like rabbits in his headlights when he turned them on. Sergio looked to both sides and shouted,

"To the left."

Carmen blindly jumped into the verge and heard Sergio land nearby. He whispered that she should follow him as he crawled into the darkness but Pedro had them in his sights and wasn't going to lose them. What followed was punishment for daring to escape.

As they crawled across the ground littered with sharp rocks, he took aim. Carmen would have to be punished in order to teach Sergio a lesson, but it was he who took the majority of the pellets from the shotgun. When the shot rang out, they instantly stopped moving. The sound of the shot would have been heard for many kilometres and attributed to the frequent hunters in the area, so Pedro was in no hurry to pick his way down to where they lay.

When he did, he found Carmen unconscious and Sergio groaning a few metres away. He was face down and his shirt was crimson with fresh blood. He tried to crawl away but Pedro stood on his neck, pushing his face into the rough ground. There was no point in trying to get away and he knew it. Pedro felt the ache from his own broken jaw as the painkiller started to wear off and was tempted to viciously kick Sergio, but in a moment of professionalism, imposed the self-restraint he had been taught. He had the satisfaction of having found his prey and recaptured his prisoners, mission accomplished. There were other, more important issues to consider.

As the twenty-four hour deadline approached, he had to inform the Fixer of the details of the drop, though he would keep these deliberately vague to prevent a double-cross where he might not receive the rest of his fee. He had mulled over taking the lot and fleeing but didn't want to spend the rest of his subsequent short life looking over his shoulder, waiting for one of his own, better qualified and equipped for the job, to take him out.

Experience had shown him that he was a good soldier: thinking was best left to others. He had to confirm that Fernando Alvés had the money. It was a huge amount of money and would not have been easy to put together, especially in lower denomination notes. This would have to be an extraordinary order that would draw a lot of attention. Police involvement was guaranteed, so the drop had to be special.

A gasp from the girl lying nearby brought his thoughts back to the present. She was obviously in shock and trying to get up, though kneeling was as far as she got. Pedro ignored the brother who was going nowhere and took the two paces required to stop Carmen falling back onto her face.

"Steady young lady. I think I should get you out of here and back to somewhere you will do yourself less harm."

Carmen recognised the voice and instantly knew that their game was up. She peered into the darkness to find Sergio, but was pulled upright and faced towards the lights of the waiting Land Rover by Pedro's strong hands before her eyes could focus.

"Can you walk?" he asked.

She remained defiantly silent and moved slowly towards the source of the light. Both knew that Pedro was bearing most of her weight but it served the purposes of neither to emphasise this. He had to carry her up the embankment that separated the dirt track from the ditch they had thrown themselves into, and the indignity of this made her weep silent, bitter tears. On reaching the vehicle, he sat her on the waiting tailgate and walked to the front seat. He returned seconds later with cable ties, which he used to bind her wrists and ankles.

"Get inside and make yourself as comfortable as possible for the trip home."

"My father has paid?"

The word 'home' gave her hope beyond her wildest dreams and her heart lifted.

"I haven't spoken to him yet. When I said 'home', I meant the ward that you will call home until he does pay."

His meaning now obvious, her anticipation of a hot bath, fresh clothes, and a comfortable bed disappeared in an instant, leaving her lower than she had ever felt. She was bleeding from several places and felt the shotgun pellets in her flesh.

"I'll be back in a minute. I'm going to collect your brother."

She had nothing to say to this and it would have mattered little if she did, as he had already left her sitting alone and injured in the dark.

On return to the ditch, he was surprised to see that Sergio had been foolish enough to make another attempt to escape. With his flashlight, he followed the blood streaked, snake-like trail he had left in the barren soil. After only five metres, it reached what seemed like a sheer drop of twenty metres to the next strata of the rock formation. Pedro painted the surrounding area with light in order to identify any dangers before peering over the drop. He scanned the ground below and all he saw were rocks: no blood and no body. He was beginning to admire the ability of the younger man to make good an escape in such circumstances when he heard the grunt. He had heard such grunts before and they always indicated that someone had just thrown something that required all of their strength.

Partly by instinct and partly by training, he threw himself to the ground with his hands over his head. As he did so, a large rock missed him by a few centimetres and clattered amongst its relatives below. In a routine recovery position, Pedro thrust to one side as he turned. This was the only thing that stopped him going over the edge with Sergio, who had launched himself at the bigger man in desperation.

In the half-light that the torch on the ground provided, He saw Sergio drop from view and heard the sickening sound as his bones broke on the unforgiving rocks below. He crawled to the edge and once again shone his light below. This time there was both blood and body.

"Shit" was his initial thought.

He couldn't leave him there, but he didn't have what was needed to rescue him. He could put something together at the clinic, but was it worth it? A trained paratrooper couldn't have landed without a chute in that type of terrain in the daytime without sustaining serious injuries, let alone an injured kid, headfirst in the dark.

Something had to be done but it wasn't going to happen until dawn. If Sergio died, that would be a tragedy of sorts. If Pedro himself were to die in an ill-considered rescue attempt, that would also be a death sentence for Carmen. For the greater good, Sergio would have to wait until daylight allowed a possible rescue. Pedro cursed Sergio and his attempted heroics, while admiring his spirit.

Before leaving, he shone the torch one last time at the prone figure below. He looked for any sign that he was alive and there was none. His efforts might result in no more than recovering the body, but he had to do it. He had been forced to leave good men's bodies in bad situations before, and those were the thoughts that still haunted him at night. Not the killing of enemies, nor the collateral damage that the women and children too often became, but the comrades who fell, their bodies far from home and liable to be mutilated. He would recover Sergio Alvés, dead or alive.

When he arrived at the Land Rover, the girl awoke as he slammed the door shut.

"Where is he? Where's Sergio?"

"He's had an accident. He did something stupid and fell quite a distance and ..."

"Is he all right?"

"I don't know. I'm going to take you back to the clinic and then bring the equipment I need to get him."

He heard her cry the short distance back to the clinic and wondered if he needed her help. That would be a last resort. If he were alive, he would be in poor condition. If he were dead, then he wouldn't ask her to help carry his body. He would have to be buried where he lay.

As they pulled up outside the Agost Clinic for Mental Health, he felt the heat and hoped that this would at least stop the onset of hypothermia. Carmen was escorted back to her ward. She was told to take her clothes off and put on an operating robe he had found.

She looked at him and was horrified on two counts. Firstly, she thought that he was going to rape her. Secondly, his face was badly swollen. Whatever Sergio hit him with was extremely heavy. He saw the look on her face.

"I need to take the shotgun pellets out before they cause complications."

Her rollercoaster of emotions hit another spiral but she was tired beyond resistance. Pedro returned with a bowl of steaming hot water and a medicine box. For the next twenty minutes, he applied a surface painkiller to the area where each pellet had entered, bathed the area in a hot water and iodine solution before extracting the small metal balls using tweezers. He then wiped off the area with the iodine once again before applying a small dressing. After removing twelve pellets from her back, buttocks, and thighs, he declared that there were no more.

She hurt all over but was numb, physically and emotionally. 'Where was Sergio?' was her only thought before the sedative knocked her out. He left her to sleep on the hospital bed he had used as an operating table.

Pedro also felt terrible. This was like Barcelona with bells on. The kidnapping had gone so well and then this. If he hadn't shot them, it might not have happened. If he had taken the boy, the most dangerous, first to the Land Rover, it would not have happened. If he had even just secured him in place, it could not have happened; but he didn't. His head hurt, his jaw ached, and he wondered if his actions had been impulsive. He knew that this wasn't so, or he wouldn't have taken the shotgun. His intentions were that someone was going to get hurt for wounding his pride. He badly needed sleep and decided that whatever mess he had made could wait for the sun.

He drank half a bottle of brandy in less than ten minutes and this helped him drop off.

His dreams were of the worst kind. He relived his bad days and nights in the desert towns of North Africa and the jungles in the west and central belt of the same continent. He saw faces from the past, friends and foes, and they were all dead. Some at his hand, others not, but dead nonetheless. Eyes flashing in the dark of night as someone or something stalked, not daring to shoot through fear of giving away position, waiting and fearing the end. These dreams were brought on by memories of malaria, yellow fever, and above all else, fear. Fear of dying, but also fear of living.

He woke with a start and found his bed soaked with sweat. His head hurt and his distended jaw made its presence known. He regretted the brandy but needed the sleep. He washed his face carefully in a basin of cold water and made strong black coffee as he devised a plan of action.

He hadn't contacted Fernando Alvés on his deadline and this sent out the wrong signal. It said that he was haphazard, disorganised, and vulnerable. He could address that later.

Sergio was his immediate problem and would be taken care of right after breakfast. The sedative he had administered to Carmen would mean that she was unlikely to awaken much before noon, so he left her to rest. He tested the flexibility of his own face and decided that squashed fruit and milk were all he was capable of taking in without pain. He needed the energy for whatever faced him.

He gathered a stretcher, as many bindings and ropes as he could find, and his rapidly emptying medical kit into the back of the Land Rover and drove up the dirt track to the pile of rocks he had left to mark the spot. He was dreading looking over the edge where Sergio had fallen the night before, just in case his body wasn't there. He had no idea where this thought came from, but this lad had got under his skin. When he reached the edge, he checked all around. This time, he was alone. He looked down and saw that Sergio hadn't moved from when he last saw him. He looked dead.

"Sergio" he shouted.

He repeated his name, this time a little louder. The figure below made the slightest movement of his head.

"Sergio, I am coming down to take you back to the clinic."

There seemed to be another slight movement, which Pedro took as acknowledgement. He looked around for a safe route down to where Sergio lay and identified that the rock formation he was standing on tapered to the left and joined the level of the lower strata fifty metres away. He returned to his vehicle and retrieved as much of his equipment as he thought he needed. He knew that the stretcher would be much harder to negotiate back up from the lower level but he would be dealing with fractures that would exclude the possibility of carrying him without causing further damage.

He slipped on the scree twice on the way down, losing the skin on his own left arm and lower back. Coming back up with Sergio on a stretcher would be even more treacherous.

When he eventually reached Sergio, he saw that he was breathing shallowly.

"Sergio, I'm here. I'm going to take you up the hill to the Land Rover and then back to the clinic where I can clean you up."

While he doubted the veracity of his own words, he knew this was what he was meant to say in such situations. The response to his morale booster was muted, with Sergio merely mouthing 'Get on with it'.

Pedro ran his hands along Sergio's limbs in order to ascertain the damage incurred in the fall. He wasn't too bothered by the shotgun pellets as Carmen's wounds indicated that they had penetrated less than two centimetres due to the distance between the gun and the targets. The blood on his clothes had dried and this told Pedro that he was no longer bleeding. The wincing as his leg was gently pressed pointed to his right thigh and shin bones being broken to some extent, His left forearm was clearly shattered as the protruding bone confirmed, and the bruising on the right side of his face was a sure sign that his skull had sustained serious damage.

His first act was to administer a large dose of morphine: what he had to do would be extremely painful. Next, he turned him as gently as he could and poured water into his mouth. At first, he choked and the coughing made him scream in agony, but the need for liquid forced him to persevere.

Pedro moved the stretcher into position behind Sergio and placed a series of splints and bandages on either side. The sun was barely up and he was already covered in sweat. He had to get this done before the temperature rose, but allowed ten minutes for the morphine to take effect. He put himself on the other side of the stretcher from Sergio and told him that he was going to move him onto it.

"I know it will hurt but you must try not to move."

As he slowly rolled Sergio onto the stretcher, his scream would have been heard for many kilometres. Pedro struggled to hold him on the stretcher as the possibility of both tumbling further down the dried riverbed began to look likely. Before their situation became any more precarious, Pedro fastened the heavy straps across the waist and chest of Sergio, preventing him moving his body. His next step was to bind his shins and thighs together against the splints to minimise movement. As he did so, he aligned the bones as much as he could under the circumstances, and the limited effectiveness of the morphine became apparent.

His final act of battlefield first aid was to fit an improvised head and neck brace. This was actually some kind of restraint formerly used to prevent patients biting staff, but was fit for purpose. This done, he placed a cloth over his face and explained that it was for protection from the sun and dust, though it was more to do with the precipitous climb they faced. Sergio was as ready as he could make him for the move; however, he himself needed a few moments before he had the energy to attempt raising him.

Pedro's head pounded and his jaw throbbed. He ignored his new scratches as just that, and drank a litre of water before bracing himself for the physically challenging task ahead. He took a few deep breaths and grasped the end of the stretcher nearest to Sergio's head. As he started off, he used a one stint at a time technique and focussed on his immediate target, a long straight section with a gentle incline. This was achieved with relative ease and he stopped for a water break as he assessed the next leg. He walked on ahead and removed some large rocks that would have proven problematic, though others weren't for the moving.

This time the going was much tougher and his lungs burned with the effort he was exerting. When he reached his second waypoint, he collapsed on the ground beside the stretcher. Sergio hadn't moved since they had started off from his overnight location and Pedro feared the worst. When he checked him, he was relieved to find that he was breathing and apparently unconscious.

Pedro knew that he was fast running out of energy and would soon have to abort the rescue. He had one shot at getting them back to the ridge Sergio had fallen from and decided to give it his all. The sun was getting hotter and the flies had found the sweat that poured from him, making it all the more important that he didn't stop. He had carried out many physically exhausting tasks in his lifetime, but this was the most trying. As he dragged the heavy stretcher and its load the last few metres, he was on the point of collapse. He went all the way to the Land

Rover before lowering his end of the stretcher and falling across the front seat.

He stretched for a water bottle and drank greedily while heavily panting heavily. He didn't move for ten minutes, and when he did, his legs felt like jelly. He knew that there was no one to help him, so found the strength from somewhere to lift first one end of the stretcher, and then the other onto the tailgate and into the back of the Land Rover. He almost had to support his weight by grasping the side of the vehicle when he returned to the driver's seat, and on sitting, he took a few moments before attempting to drive.

"Be a shame to drive back over the bloody side", he said to himself and laughed.

Almudena Alvés was beside herself with worry about her beloved children. She had sat with her husband, three policemen, and a communications expert for hours on end, looking at the phone she had come to hate.

"Why hasn't he called? The twenty-four hours was up nearly ten hours ago."

Carlos had been asking himself the same question. The modus operandi for kidnappers was normally to reduce the timescale, increasing the pressure and the subsequent likelihood of being paid. No one gained by stretching the period of confinement of the victims: not unless money was not the real reason for the kidnapping. However, the massive amount demanded told him that this was very much about money.

Thomas, the communications man, was getting threadbare with being asked if the phone was working or if there could be a problem with his equipment. When Fernando Alvés looked at him, he knew what he was going to say and replied without waiting for the question. His bedside manner was one befitting a techno-geek.

"No, there isn't a problem with my set-up, and yes, the telephone is functioning as it should. No one has called; it's as simple as that."

This wasn't strictly true, as two well-meaning friends had contacted Almu to enquire about Sergio and Carmen. She had been directed by Carlos to say that all was well and they were staying with friends. She didn't sound particularly convincing but

Christiano told her to finish the calls in case the one they were waiting for was trying to get through.

Almu stared, Fernando Alvés paced, and the three investigators went through the mental processes that prolonged periods of waiting, so often part of their job, required. Thomas twiddled with various knobs and listened to classical music in his earphones: this was just another assignment to him.

"Why aren't you doing something?" Fernando Alvés asked Carlos.

"What do you suggest we do, Mr. Alvés? Until you speak to the Taker, we have nothing more to work with. There are three officers at the Commissary looking for the dungeon. They have identified some of the equipment in the room and are making enquiries. Manufacturers, distributors and end users are being questioned, but the items are very old and may have been sold on many times."

"How many dungeons can there be in Alicante?"

Fernando Alvés' question was soaked in sarcasm and Carlos was in no mood for it.

"In my job, Mr. Alvés, I have days when I think there are too few."

The tension in the room was tangible, with two people very worried and four extremely bored. Carlos decided that he would give it another thirty minutes and then head back to the Commissary. He would brief Christiano on what to do, if and when the call came in.

The Fixer was also feeling this frustration. He knew the schedule and was at a loss as to why the Taker hadn't been in touch, as briefed. He took it upon himself to contact Pedro and when he did so, he could tell by his voice that something was wrong.

"What's happening? Why haven't you called me with the details of the drop?"

"There has been a complication but I've sorted it."

He had considered saying nothing about the attempted escape but realised that it would come out when he released them and do his credibility no good. He tried to speak normally but the restricted movement he had in his jaw made him sound drunk.

"What kind of complication?"

"They escaped. Don't worry; I recaptured them and they won't be trying that again. They are under lock and key and will remain so until I hand them over."

The Fixer sounded angry without uttering a word. Pedro sensed his discomfort and tried to patch over the damage he had done.

"I'm going to call Fernando Alvés now and make sure that he has the money. When I have done that, I'll call you back."

"Make sure you do."

Pedro was pleased to hear the line go dead. He had other matters to consider.

Sergio Alvés was in a bad way, and it was going to take more than the contents of his First Aid box to make him better. The broken legs needed resetting properly, the shattered forearm was beyond his capabilities to realign, and he had no idea about the potential internal injuries he might have suffered. He could scarcely take him to the hospital at Elda or Alicante, but professional medical attention was required or he would die.

He unscrambled an address in his computer and dialled the number. He didn't know if either the recipient or the number were still valid, but took the chance, as he had little choice.

A woman answered the phone and he asked for Alex. He could tell by the change in her tone that he had hit a nerve.

"Who is calling?"

There was no point in lying to her, and it might make the difference between the man he wanted to speak to accepting the call or not.

"Tell him it's Pedro."

It took a moment for Alejandro Basseta to come to the phone, and when he did so, he sounded guarded.

"Pedro? Fusilier Pedro?"

Pedro hadn't been called that for many years now and it made him feel good.

"Yes, Fusilier Pedro. How are you? Are you still active?"

"I haven't been active for over eight years. After our narrow escape from Mogadishu, I called it a day. I spend my time doing the more mundane things in life. No one calls me Alex any more. My wife knows that you're from the past. What do you want, Pedro?"

"I'm in a fix. I have a young man who fell onto some rocks. He's is in a bad way. I need medical assistance."

"I don't practice any more. Take him to a hospital."

Alex knew there must be a reason why this wasn't an option and wanted Pedro to come clean.

"I can't do that. I can explain to you. There's a fee involved."

121

"How much?"

Pedro considered how much of his pot he was prepared to part with and arrived at a figure.

"Two grand, cash."

"Make it five, and I don't want any explanations. The less I know the better."

This sounded totally unreasonable but Pedro knew that he was asking, and therefore not in a strong bargaining position.

"Can I collect you now?"

"You know where I live. I'll be at the Bar Argentina in an hour. What's the extent of the damage?"

"Broken limbs and possible internals."

"Meet me in one hour. For five grand, you get my services today, after that I don't want to hear from you ever again. Agreed?"

"Agreed."

Pedro checked Sergio before making his next call. The morphine had worn off and he was in a state of shock. He looked a small, pathetic figure and there was no way he was going to let Carmen see her brother in this condition. He hoped that Doc Alex could mend him. He had been the very best field medic in his day, performing apparent miracles on a regular basis in the worst of conditions. If anyone could save Sergio, it was Alex. For now, there was nothing more he could do for him. He had to call his father, and tell him that his son and daughter were fit and well.

When the phone rang, everyone in the Alvés' lounge jumped. It was as though they had come to believe that it would never happen. Fernando Alvés' arm shot out to pick up the receiver and he was restrained by Christiano. Thomas threw a switch and nodded that he was ready. Christiano released Fernando Alvés' arm and Almu moved next to her husband.

"Fernando Alvés."

"Have you got the money?"

"I have two million Euros. I can't get any more."

"That wasn't what I asked for. I want ten million Euros."

"I don't have that kind of money."

"You're not listening, Mr. Alvés. Ten million Euros will buy the release of your son and daughter, not two."

"Are they OK? Has any harm come to them?"

"Until now, no", he lied. "However, I think that you need convincing that I mean business. This is most unfortunate."

"No, please don't harm them. We'll find the money", Almu screamed.

"Do that. I'll be in touch."

Almu burst into tears and ran from the room crying "Oh my God. He's going to kill them."

Fernando Alvés looked around as if seeking guidance and Carlos obliged.

"Go after her."

He dashed from the room to comfort his wife.

"Well?" Carlos asked Thomas the communications man surrounded with equipment.

Thomas responded by holding a finger in the air while he tapped on the keyboard of his laptop. After a few moments, he beckoned the detectives to look at the screen.

"The call came from a service station just outside Albacete. A prepaid SIM card that I would bet you will find in or near the location. The background noise is what you would expect from a service station; cars starting and stopping with fast road sounds in the background."

"Ferrera, get the locals to search the service station with a fine-toothed comb. Look for the SIM card. There may be prints. Get them to check for CCTV footage. We need to start having some luck if we are going to break this case."

"Where do we go from here, sir?" Christiano asked Carlos.

"We go back to the Commissary and hope that our team have found the dungeon. I'll get Ferrera to come back and hold the fort here, but our perpetrator isn't going to make it easy for us. Old-fashioned police work is the only way we are going to catch him. Old-fashioned police work and the hope that he makes a mistake. He may get over-confident and give himself away."

At that moment, this seemed unlikely, though Pedro didn't share their confidence in his abilities. He called the Fixer who didn't answer, and he thought this rather strange for a man who insisted on knowing what was going on. He considered leaving a voice message but due to the nature of their business, that seemed less than prudent. Bad news could always wait. He had to attend to medical matters.

As he approached Bar Argentina on the outskirts of Albacete, Alex walked through the doorway with a canvas grip in his hand. He didn't acknowledge

Pedro. When the car stopped, he opened the passenger door and got in without comment.

"You're not pleased to see me then?" Pedro enquired.

"You were part of who I was. I'm not that man any more. Someone needs medical attention and I seem to be his only chance. I don't want reminiscences or even to know what you are doing. The less I know, the better it will be for me if it all goes wrong. I'm going to close my eyes now and sleep. I don't want you to waken me until we are at our final destination."

The frosty reception almost hurt Pedro but he understood why Alex had to act in this manner. They weren't in Africa now. Alex was as good as his word and didn't open his eyes until Pedro applied the handbrake indicating they had reached their destination.

Alex got out and stretched. He looked at the bleak clinic in the barren landscape without comment. Pedro thought Alex had aged by more than eight years since their last meeting, and Alex read his face perfectly.

"It takes a lot to slow down. Inactivity has pressures of its own. Like you, I enjoyed the buzz at the time. The money helped, but it was never important to me. All I really wanted was to be involved."

Pedro forced a smile. He had never wanted to analyse his reasons for doing what he had. Perhaps he didn't want to find what he knew was lurking inside. He knew Alex would bring back memories.

"Where's the patient?"

"This way."

As they walked through the reception area of the Agost Clinic for Mental Health, Alex shuddered as he remembered how barbaric institutions like this had been.

"If you weren't mentally ill on admission, it wouldn't take long."

"He's in here. He fell about twenty metres onto rocks. I put the splints on to evacuate him."

"Did he fall onto a shotgun too?"

Alex spoke distractedly as he examined Sergio. Pedro didn't answer. Sergio winced as he was moved and Alex apologised.

"I'm a doctor and I'm going to patch you up. The first thing I'm going to do is knock you out."

Sergio nodded in hope that he would lose the pain when he lost consciousness. Alex opened his canvas bag and produced a white coat and two surgical masks, one of which he handed to Pedro.

"I'm no medic," he protested.

"And I'm no juggler. I would prefer a pretty nurse but they seem to be in short supply. Scrub up. This boy's in a mess."

They worked for four hours without rest before Alex pulled off his latex gloves. Both of Sergio's legs were set from waist to ankle, the broken arm was put as straight as the swelling would permit and the plethora of shotgun pellets were removed.

"How does he look, Alex?"

"Bloody awful. His legs will heal but he may lose the arm. As for the internal injuries, I don't know. There is blood in his urine and this indicates damage to his kidneys or liver. He has head injuries that require a scan to determine the extent of the damage. Blood poisoning is a strong possibility because the shot was in him for so long. I'm tempted to ask you what happened to him but in this case, ignorance is most definitely bliss. Pay me and take me home."

Pedro was hoping for something more positive.

"Will he be OK on his own for a couple of hours?"

"I've put him under again to allow him to recover from the extensive work I've done on him. Give him these pills, two every four hours. He will be like a zombie but the alternative is a world of pain for the next two or three days, if he lives at all."

When Pedro removed the surgical mask, Alex noticed his swollen jaw.

"Walk into a door?"

Pedro rubbed his aching face and confirmed that was almost exactly what had happened. Alex ordered him to sit on a chair while he examined his jaw by running his fingers along the extremely tender flesh.

"You did a decent job of resetting it, though it'll never be quite straight again. I'll leave you some pills for the pain, but you'll live."

Pedro considered the irony of a wimpy youth succeeding where many seasoned professionals had failed, and once again thanked Alex.

"You've come through for me again, Alex. Thanks. I've got to feed the girl before I take you back. She hasn't eaten today."

"Girl? Good God Pedro, what the hell are you doing?"

As he said this, he covered his ears indicating that he didn't want an answer.

"Feed her. I'll wait."

Carmen was frantic with worry over her brother and sprang to her feet when Pedro opened her ward door.

"Is Sergio OK?

"He's resting."

"That's not what I asked."

"He had a fall and a doctor has put him together again."

Alex was no more than a paramedic and Sergio was far from fighting fit, but knowing this wouldn't help Carmen's state of mind.

"Can I see him?"

"Not now. I have things to do."

He had almost forgotten his failure to secure the full ransom sum in his efforts to save Sergio, and knew that he now needed a plan B. He had two hours of silent driving in which to contemplate the way ahead and no easy answer presented itself.

When he arrived at the Bar Argentina, Alex awoke and rubbed his eyes.

"I need a cognac. I won't invite you in. You're driving and I don't want to be party to anything illegal."

He leaned across the car and shook Pedro's hand.

"Have a nice life, Fusilier Pedro, and remember; I don't want to see or hear from you ever again."

Pedro watched him walk into the bar without looking back. This was how men like them had to live their lives, no reunions, no emotions. On the road back to the clinic, he considered what he had to do to get Fernando Alvés to pay the full amount.

He had prepared hours of footage for this very possibility, but after what had happened they seemed tame. Sergio was the obvious star of any further video but he didn't really want to display the extent of his injuries. It gave the impression that paying the full amount wouldn't stop his bones from being broken. Facially, he looked like he had been hit by a truck. No, he couldn't use Sergio. That left Carmen.

He wanted the maximum effect for the minimum damage. She was a beautiful young woman and he a war-weary soldier, but he didn't torture innocents unless he wanted them to confess their guilt. How do you use a young woman to convince her father that he must do something he professes impossible? He didn't feel pleased with his solution but it was guaranteed to work.

On arrival at the clinic, he checked Sergio. He looked terrible: his face was ashen and his breathing shallow. He looked at the bottle of pills Alex had brought and decided that he would be better left to his dreams. Regardless of how frightening they were, his present situation was much worse.

His next visit was to the Advanced Treatment Room below the corridor floor. Despite the late evening heat, this room felt cold. The combination of white tiled walls, heavy wooden furniture, and thick leather straps exuded evil menace. How many poor souls had been subjected to unthinkable horrors in this confined space? Pedro tried to block these thoughts, but his immediate environment oozed misery and suffering. He reflected on the fear he had felt when strapped into a chair just like this while being punched, stabbed, and subjected to the raw power of electricity, and decided that this was not how he was going to proceed. This girl wasn't an enemy; she was merely a means to an end. No, the chair was out of the question.

He could possibly use the iron shackles that hung from the wall, but the techniques involved would mean exposing too much of himself to the camera. When this ends, every policeman in Spain would be looking for him and there seemed little point in gifting a full portfolio of photographs. It had to be the table. He checked the integrity of the straps before he collected his lights and camera. It took a few practice runs to get the angles right such that he appeared only in profile and there were no facial shots. Lights were adjusted to illuminate what he considered would be the areas of maximum impact and the scene was set. All it needed was Carmen.

He had seen the look in her eyes when he removed the shotgun pellets, and that was what he wanted to record. What this intelligent young woman feared more than anything else in the world was to be defiled, especially by someone like him. No permanent physical damage would be incurred; however, the impact was disproportionately powerful. Daddy would find the money and mummy would make sure of this.

"Are you taking me to Sergio?" was her first question.

"No. There has been a setback. Your father appears to have a cash-flow problem and we're going to help him solve it."

"Where are we going?"

She now had fear in her voice, and as they glided past the room with the green screen, she knew the answer to her own question.

"No, not there please".

The tone of her voice intimated that she knew what was going to happen. She tried to resist being moved down the corridor but Pedro was too strong. She started to cry and this seemed to irritate him.

"Don't make this any more difficult than it already is. It's not personal."

Carmen felt both rage and fear.

"How can rape be impersonal? There is nothing more personal than what you intend to do to me. Don't do it."

She could tell that he was uncomfortable with what he intended and carried on pleading as she was roughly guided down the stairs into the torture chamber. His face remained expressionless as he strapped her onto the heavy table, completely preventing movement with the unyielding belts of leather. She thrashed out at him with her legs but he caught them one at a time and strapped them to the table. She was utterly helpless to prevent what followed.

Pedro pressed the camera to record and removed his trousers and underpants. Then, for the benefit of the camera, he ripped her panties off and threw them across the room. He made sure that his erection was in clear view before he knelt between her legs. The screams that followed were more of repulsion than terror or pain. He positioned himself inside her and completed the act without once looking at her face. True to his word, for him this was impersonal. Even the grunt he gave as he climaxed was for the benefit of the recording.

He dismounted as theatrically as he had started, clearly displaying there were no smoke and mirror tactics involved for the sake of the camera. To anyone watching the video, it was obvious that Carmen had been raped.

She sobbed uncontrollably for what seemed hours. Pedro left her to do this for the camera until it was time for him to move on. As he loosened her bindings, he expected a violent outburst but it never came. It was at this point he realised that he had completely broken her will; there was nothing left. She offered no resistance as he took her back to her ward, only silent compliance. When she entered the ward that was now her home, she stopped where he left her.

He suggested that she went to bed and got no response. When he touched behind her elbow to steer her to the bed, she winced on contact then obeyed without a word. All the while, she stared at something unseen in the distance. He had seen these symptoms before, usually in soldiers with shell shock or civilians after their families, villages, and complete lives had been obliterated. It was the brain's way of dealing with a severely traumatic event, a closing down of all thought processes, a kind of silent mental breakdown.

While this was never his intention, it also wasn't his highest priority. The recording had to be edited and delivered. He spent an hour cutting and sticking what had occurred in the Advanced Treatment Room before he was happy with the end product. The DVD and its box were wiped clean with surgical spirits to remove any prints and placed into an A4 envelope.

He checked Sergio and was pleased to see him awake. He complained about the pain he felt in his legs and that he felt nothing in his broken arm. Alex said that there may be nerve damage that was beyond his limited means, and Pedro considered this as probably a blessing for the young man. He was reticent to take the pills when offered but Pedro convinced him that he hadn't paid a lot of money for a doctor so that he could then kill him with a pill. Sergio accepted the argument, took the pills, and was soon unconscious again.

Carmen lay on top of the bed where Pedro had left her. She didn't look towards the door as it opened nor did she respond when he asked how she was. She looked blankly into space.

Pedro rationalised that there was little he could now do for either of the Alvés offspring other than arrange to return them to their family as soon as possible. He gathered the envelope and locked the clinic before getting into the Land Rover.

He ached from head to toe and was more tired than he could ever remember being at any time in his troubled life. Only this morning he was dragging Sergio from the gully into which he had launched himself. It seemed a lifetime ago. He had talked to Fernando Alvés and the Fixer, commissioned, collected and returned Doc Alex, and raped a young woman. He thought of the pressure of doing nothing expounded by Alex and knew this was something he would try in the very near future. This was his last job.

He drove to an area of Alicante where he knew the drugs trade was very active and scanned the streets for what he wanted. It didn't take long to single out the middle-aged man with a sad tale he wanted to tell anyone who would listen: anyone who would listen while paying for his next hit.

"Get in" Pedro barked unequivocally. The man obeyed without question.

"Are you interested in scoring?" the man asked with hope in his voice.

"I need a favour. There's fifty in it for you. Interested?"

The question was rhetorical but the muddled mind of Pedro's new passenger was beyond nuance. He reached for Pedro's crotch.

"Take your hands off me or I will break them."

"What do you want then? Is it head?"

"I want you to deliver a parcel. But first, I want you to score."

Pedro handed him a twenty Euro note and the man noticed the discrepancy.

"You said fifty."

"Twenty now, and the rest when you deliver the parcel."

The man looked at Pedro suspiciously but focussed his attention on the twenty Euro note that would make his night so much better. He snatched the note and indicated that Pedro pull over into a side street. The men who stood in the doorways were no more than cheap muscle, who at least had the sense to stay away from Pedro. They could tell that he was in a different league. After five minutes, the man returned and seemed a completely different person.

He had energy and confidence, so obviously missing before, and was keen to earn the rest of his money.

He was taken to the end of the street where the Alvés mansion stood and told to take the envelope to the security post. With thirty Euros and the envelope in hand, he strolled up towards the bright lights, unaware that he was in for a long police interrogation. In his drug-induced stupor, he would remember nothing of the man who sent him. Pedro waited and watched until the man called the attention of the guard in the security shack.

Fernando Alvés was about to get a message he would never forget.

*****

Ángel Fuster had many bad experiences in his drug-fuelled life, but nothing had prepared him for this. The security guard appeared completely casual as he called the main house and said that a gentleman had arrived with a package for Fernando Alvés. Michael Ferrera could scarcely believe being called into action; it had never seemed likely. No one knew where this case was going but none expected it to turn up in their laps. He quickly informed Carlos Rico that there had been a development before rushing to the gate. When he got there, the security guard guided him with his eyes towards the dishevelled figure holding the envelope.

"Are you Fernando Alvés?"

"No. I am Constable Ferrera of Alicante police. Who are you, sir?"

No one had called Ángel 'sir' for a very long time. Before his rapid demise, it had been the norm, but those days were very much in the past. Ángel responded by swelling out his chest, ignoring the question and presenting the envelope to Ferrera.

"Please see that Fernando Alvés gets this, if you don't mind."

The security guard and Ferrera swapped a bemused look.

"I would appreciate it if you accompanied me to the main house, sir." Ferrera was polite to the last.

"I've got things to do, constable."

"This isn't a request. I think you can help us with our enquiries."

Ángel had been no stranger to the police in recent years. His habit required appeasement, and how it

136

happened was on an opportunist basis. It was beginning to seem like tonight's opportunity might have been ill chosen. Ángel, head still buzzing from the heroin hit, complied without resistance and Ferrera led him to a room in the main house allocated to the police. It was obvious that this man wasn't in a fit state to give responsible answers, but what little he knew of the here and now might be lost if he didn't start the questioning process.

"What's your name, sir?"

"Ángel, Ángel Fuster."

Ferrera weighed up the usefulness of asking for an address and came down on the side of it being unimportant.

"Where did you get the envelope?"

"The man gave it to me. He asked me to deliver it to this address. He paid me."

Inspector Carlos Rico and Sergeant Christiano Marcos had joined them at this point and the inspector took the reins.

"Who was this man?"

Ángel recognised the voice of authority and addressed Carlos.

"I don't know. He stopped me in the street and said that he would pay me thirty Euros to deliver the envelope."

Carlos looked to Ferrera, who responded by showing him an envelope. He indicated that Christiano took it directly to Fernando Alvés.

"You didn't walk here. We're too far out of town. What kind of car did he have?"

"I don't know. A high one. I had to climb into it."

The glazed look on Ángel's face supported his lack of knowledge about cars. There seemed little point in wasting time interrogating him. He was in a state of advanced confusion and anything said would be inadmissible in court.

"See if you can get anything else out of him, Ferrera, and then arrange for him to be taken to the drunk tank."

As Ferrera raised Ángel by the arm, Carlos pressed thirty Euros into his hand.

"Take the thirty Euros from his pocket and replace it with this. He will only have thirty Euros, and there is a possibility that our Taker has left his prints. Get the notes dusted."

Ferrera said he would sort it right away and Carlos believed him. He was ambitious and eager to make a mark. By the time he joined the others upstairs, Fernando Alvés was on the point of pressing the play button to reveal the contents of the DVD. When he did, it took only a few seconds before they knew what they were watching. Almu collapsed onto the thick rug before anyone could stop her, as Fernando Alvés looked aghast at the screen.

"Take your wife to her bedroom, Mr. Alvés. We will take this from here."

Carlos made it clear that this wasn't a request and Fernando Alvés was glad of an excuse not to watch his daughter being raped. Christiano and his boss watched the complete tape without uttering a single word. It was frozen on the last scene with a voiceover that said this act would be repeated every day until the ransom was paid in full.

"Same dungeon" Christiano offered.

"And very carefully set to avoid showing much more than the kidnapper's genitalia. Where was Sergio?"

Christiano thought that the question was inappropriate having just witnessed the rape of his sister.

"I don't see the relevance, sir?"

"The kidnapper is a meticulous man. If he carefully choreographs the sexual assault of Carmen Alvés, as he did, why didn't he include Sergio in some way? Perhaps tie him down and make him watch."

Christiano was beginning to doubt the morals of his inspector and it showed.

"Put yourself in the kidnapper's place, Christiano. Would this video have had more impact with or without Sergio? He would have been horrified and humiliated and this would have been additional leverage against the parents. Something is missing."

Christiano agreed superficially, though he would have to consider this theory more deeply before committing himself either way. Carlos Rico's mind worked in different ways to most others.

"I will talk to the Alvés'. I want you to take the DVD and the envelope down to the overworked forensics lab and ask them to work even harder. Get traffic to look for any CCTV they may have of this area for the past two hours. We are looking for a high vehicle, maybe a people carrier. Don't forget to check the money from the junkie for prints. It's only a question of time before the Taker becomes a mistaker."

Carlos gave Fernando and Almu Alvés the degree of detail about the contents of the tape that they required, and no more. Carlos considered using the phrase 'not overly violent' in his description of the rape of their daughter, but thought better of it.

"He says that he will repeat this act every day until he receives the ransom in full."

"Then I must get the ransom."

Almu hung tightly to his arm as he spoke.

"You clearly said that you don't have that kind of money, Mr. Alvés."

Carlos didn't know where this was going.

"I don't, but I know people who do. They are my children and I will do anything to save them."

"Very well, it is not illegal in this country to pay a ransom and I cannot stop you doing so. In the meantime, we have new evidence that I hope will mean that you don't have to pay and we can find Sergio and Carmen. An officer will be here soon to replace Constable Ferrera. Let me know if you hear anything else from the kidnapper."

At the Commissary, the team had been busy. They had found that the chair in the second video had been manufactured by a company called Valls of Córdoba, as Ferdinand explained.

"That particular model of chair was made for three years in the nineteen fifties and only twenty were actually sold. The police in Madrid bought ten of them and they have long since disappeared, along with any record of their use. Four went to prisons and their probate is similar to that of the police. The other six were procured by mental health institutions. A 'medical supplier' bought them and we are currently trying to find any records that might tell us who they were sold to. The supplier stopped trading twenty years ago but the family who owned it now operate under a different name after being declared bankrupt. They now import tea."

"What about the table? It is very distinctive."

"All the evidence points to the table being locally manufactured, adapted for their particular needs. The original table, not too surprisingly, was a butcher's bench, designed for cutting up carcasses."

"And the shackles?"

"Available from any blacksmith or modern sex shop."

"And they say romance is dead."

Christiano's comment was ignored.

"Ferrera, tell me about the money."

"There were dozens of prints on the notes. Forensics are going through their database but have said that you shouldn't hope to base your case on them finding anything."

"Traffic?"

"Tall vehicles aplenty, but none appearing to have two male occupants in the front seats."

Carlos scowled at the lack of fruitful progress.

"Keep on looking. I want that chair traced. Christiano, we are going to have a word with Jorge Bocanegra. He has an axe to grind with Fernando Alvés. He may not be responsible for the kidnapping but this doesn't mean he knows nothing about it."

Before the trip up the coast to Denia, Carlos took the opportunity to go home and collect a change of clothes. His wife Marta was pleased to see him and also to have the opportunity to meet the new sergeant.

141

She had treated his predecessor as a son and, with no disrespect to his replacement, didn't want that degree of closeness again to Carlos' job. She kissed her husband and ushered the younger man into the living room.

"Sergeant Christiano Marcos, my wife Marta."

"I'm very pleased to meet you Mrs. Rico", he responded.

"I'm a civilian and my name is Marta. Please sit down. I'll so glad to meet you. I've heard a lot about you."

This surprised Christiano and he hoped that whatever his boss had said about him was at least not too damning. Carlos said that he was going for a shower and Christiano accepted Marta's offer of coffee.

He was left alone to absorb the inner sanctum of his inspector and, to his surprise, it looked like any other living room; there was no indication that the occupant was a senior police officer who had been decorated on many occasions, no photographs of him posing with the high and mighty, not even any indication of family.

Marta returned a few minutes later with a tray of coffee and biscuits. He thanked her and she joined him on the sofa.

"You mustn't let him bully you, you know."

"I don't know what you mean, Mrs. Rico. Sorry, Marta" he corrected.

"His sergeants all start off scared of him and that's how he likes it. He has some odd ways but he isn't a tyrant."

Carlos reappeared, knotting his tie.

"I hope you're not giving away my secrets, darling? If she says that I'm not a tyrant, believe her at your peril, sergeant."

Marta winked and Christiano smiled his compliance. Carlos said his goodbyes. He indicated that the case they were working on was ongoing and not to cook dinner for him. Marta kissed her husband and pecked Christiano on the cheek as he followed him out of the door.

"Our secret" she said.

The sergeant smiled and disappeared into the lift of the apartment building feeling bolstered by having found an ally in life.

The retreat where Jorge Bocanegra now resided was an old bodega converted for the purpose of housing disabled patients. It stood in the foothills of the mountains that fringed the Mediterranean Sea, at the end of a long green glade. It was built of red brick and had three floors, all of which were served by an elevator suitable for wheelchairs. The immediate grounds were well maintained and it gave the impression of being beyond the financial means of many.

A tall middle-aged man with receding, reddish hair and casual clothes walked into the car park to meet them. He introduced himself as David Campo.

"You must be the detectives from Alicante who have come to visit Jorge?"

"That is correct Mr. Campo. Is there anything we should know?"

"He has rested today, so you should have no problems. Sometimes he gets irritable, and if he does, please cut your interview short. Otherwise he will be in a black mood for days."

"Does he have any problems with his memory?"

"Not that I know of, though I think he chooses not to speak about his accident."

"What about visitors? Does he have any?"

"His brother used to come once a month but that stopped about a year ago after an argument. He has no other visitors."

Carlos and Christiano were led into a large room with windows running almost the complete length of the building, facing the field. A solitary figure sat in a wheelchair with a crocheted blanket over his legs, staring silently into the open countryside on the other side of the glass. He was thin with black hair and a shaggy beard, and didn't hear them approach until Carlos spoke.

"Mr. Bocanegra?"

He turned and took a few seconds to remember who his guests were.

"Inspector Rico. Please sit down."

They sat and a young woman in a lilac uniform brought them a tray of coffee. She smiled and left.

"I believe that you want to speak about Fernando Alvés. He's not my favourite topic of conversation."

"This hasn't always been the case. In the late 1980s, you were the hottest team in town. Your company was an overnight success and remained top of the pile for over six years. What happened between you?"

Jorge had been expecting the question and had prepared what he considered a suitable answer.

"We had diverging opinions on the direction the business was going. He wanted to branch out to the United States and I wanted to conquer Europe first, so we split."

Ferdinand's research had found nothing to collaborate this and Jorge Bocanegra didn't make a convincing liar. Christiano decided to push this point.

"It appears that you won the battle and the company, but never made a move to 'conquer Europe' as you said."

Jorge knew they would have done their homework. He also knew that they were policemen and knew little about business.

"By the time Fernando and I had finished our bickering, the window of opportunity had closed. You see, business depends much on good will, and we weren't exactly exuding that quality for a couple of years. Our network of contacts, like our assets, was split. Third parties didn't want to get caught in the middle and chose to work with a competitor."

"What about the fire? The fire brigade investigator said that it was started with an accelerant. Did you suspect Fernando Alvés had a hand in this?"

Jorge frowned at Carlos as though he had said something very stupid.

"I suspected Fernando Alvés of everything in those days. We lived in each other's pockets for eighteen hours a day during the early years. You don't do that without noticing things that annoy you. After the split, these were the things that became important. We hated each other and I would be the first to say that my thinking was far from objective for quite some time."

"So you do think that Fernando Alvés had something to do with it?"

Carlos was pushing for a reaction and could see it was close. Jorge hadn't played mind games for a long time and was enjoying the verbal sparring with someone who didn't back down just because he was disabled.

"Fernando Alvés was capable and would have had the opportunity. If he was guilty, it was never proven."

"What about the accidents?"

"Why are you asking these questions? Has something happened to Fernando Alvés? If it has, I'm not guilty and I don't give a damn."

"Someone drained the brake fluid from your car. Was it Fernando Alvés?"

"Definitely not. He knew nothing about cars. He understood computers but he didn't know how to change the bag in a vacuum cleaner. He had no technical knowledge this side of the cyber world."

"You had a second accident, the one that resulted in you being here. Do you think that had anything to do with your BlackBull.com versus his Alvés.com rival bids for the European Union contract?"

Jorge wasn't enjoying the thrill of the chase any more. This was the accident that put him in a wheelchair for life. His demeanour changed, now distinctly darker.

"As I said, Alvés didn't have the ability to sabotage my car, but he was moving with people who did."

The change of reference from Fernando to Alvés prompted Carlos and Christiano to exchange a glance acknowledging they had hit a nerve. Carlos went in for the kill.

"Who were these people, Jorge?"

"The Russians. He started dealing with companies in the newly emerging Russian markets and they had contacts in Alicante."

"Are we talking the Russian mafia?"

"If you choose to glamorise these thugs with a Hollywood name, that is your business, inspector. Those bastards put me in this chair and Fernando Alvés was behind it."

"Do you know this as a fact?"

Jorge now knew that something had happened to Fernando Alvés and his family.

"Is it Almudena? Is it the kids?"

There was a sense of urgency in his voice that Carlos knew he was incapable of faking. Whoever was behind the kidnapping of Sergio and Carmen Alvés, it certainly wasn't Jorge Bocanegra.

"For God's sake tell me."

"There is no need to worry yourself, Mr. Bocanegra. Thank you very much for your time. You have been very helpful."

"You need to tell me what's going on."

As Carlos left the residential care home, he warned David Campo to expect dark moods for several days.

The prognosis in the Agost Clinic for Mental Health was also dark. Overnight, Sergio had taken a turn for the worse. His temperature had risen and he had a fever. Pedro mopped the young man's brow as he sweated through the night and forced the pills left by Alex down his throat in hope that they would

147

promote a change in his condition. He had no way of telling if the change in his condition was due to internal injuries or blood poisoning and had no one to turn to for help. He knew Sergio was a fighter and hoped that he had enough will to live to fight his own way out of his current condition. Pedro was no more than a bystander.

Carmen remained in a catatonic state. She no longer ate or drank, and even conversation seemed unlikely until he raised her in order to pour water into her mouth.

"Do what you want with me."

Pedro was surprised at the first thing she had uttered since the rape.

"What did you say, Carmen?"

"Do what you want with me. I won't fight you; I don't care anymore. You have already taken everything I had: my liberty, my dignity, and my pride. You have won, so you can do what you want. You win."

Her face remained expressionless as she spoke and her eyes were focussed on something in a distance that she couldn't possibly see from her hospital bed in the desolate ward. Pedro felt no pride in what he had done to this innocent girl and knew that he couldn't go through with his threat to rape her again if payment weren't made. If her father didn't find a way to get the money, Pedro would devise another way to convince him.

The money was also foremost in the mind of Fernando Alvés. Jorge Bocanegra had been correct in his identification of the Russian mafia as bedfellows of his former partner, and Fernando Alvés had a big favour to ask of them. He made a phone call from his office and asked for a meeting. The man he was meeting with was a well-known local entrepreneur with fingers in many questionable pies.

Oleg Petrov was a long established pillar of the local Chamber of Commerce. He arrived on the Costa Blanca in the late eighties and had a string of fortuitous business ventures, where his competition fell by the wayside one after the other. Where others had problems raising finances, or with the unions, Oleg remained moneyed and untouched. When he branched out into construction, he never found the need to resort to court action in order to purchase a prime piece of land for his projects. Residents seemed all too willing to sell their family homes for well under the market value. Indeed, Oleg had lived a charmed life on the Costa, with the local and national police unable to find witnesses to speak against him whenever they tried to put a case together. Because he was such a respected businessman, it was only natural that he would mix with the likes of Fernando Alvés.

"Fernando, what can I do for you?" he asked as he shook his hand.

Fernando Alvés looked at the henchman who had escorted him in and now blocked the exit, wondering how many men had suffered at his enormous hands, the same hands that had professionally frisked him before entering.

"Don't worry about Danny. He doesn't speak any Spanish, he's just for decoration."

"I'm in a bit of a fix and need help. Someone has kidnapped Sergio and Carmen and is demanding ten million Euros for their release. I can only put together two million. I need to borrow eight million Euros."

Both men knew that the figure mentioned was both ridiculous and unlikely to be lent, but Fernando needed an ally. Oleg observed at him carefully, looking for a telltale sign that this was some kind of joke, but there was no such sign.

"Who has got them?"

Oleg was genuinely interested in the answer. If anything of this magnitude happened in Alicante, he was usually behind it. He needed to know if someone was using Fernando Alvés to get to him.

"I don't know, Oleg. They were snatched from the airport last Saturday and I got the demand for the ransom on Thursday. Whoever it is, he has been torturing them."

"How has he contacted you?"

"First of all, by telephone, then he sent DVDs. The bastard raped Carmen. He has threatened to repeat this every day until I pay. You are their only hope."

Oleg didn't like the way Fernando Alvés had passed the responsibility onto him and deflected it back.

"You have a problem. Are the police involved?"

"Yes."

"And you have brought this to my door. Why? Our dealings have always been on a 'private' basis."

"Almu found out and insisted. I didn't know that they were going to ask for so much money."

"You said 'they', is there more than one person involved?"

"I don't know. I'm desperate, please help me."

Oleg continued to look intently at Fernando Alvés in hope of ascertaining if there was more to this than met the eye. He knew his company was going through a rough spell and wondered if this was anything more than an elaborate attempt to raise collateral for a lucrative deal in the offing. There was very little chance of him releasing eight million Euros to anyone and both knew that to be a fact.

"What you really want is for me to find out who is holding your son and daughter and where they are? Am I correct?"

"Of course, that would be fantastic. Would you do that for me?"

Oleg Petrov didn't skip a heartbeat as he answered.

"No, but I will do it for the two million Euros you have raised."

This was not where Fernando Alvés had wanted this conversation to go. He wanted a loan and now he was being put in a position where he had to buy a service. Oleg made it quite clear that refusal wasn't an option.

"The police have the money. I can't give it to you."

"But you can give it to the kidnapper in exchange for your children. I will supply the rest of the money, for show purposes only, and you will deliver it to the kidnapper. My men will kill the kidnapper and release Sergio and Carmen. In the eyes of the police, the kidnapper will have disappeared with the money and you get your children back unharmed. Except for a little rape damage that occurred before you brought this proposition to me."

Fernando Alvés felt like he had just been hit several times by the silent Danny on the door. How the hell had this thing been twisted so badly? He felt trapped and helpless. He agreed. He had no option. Oleg was to deliver eight million Euros in 500 Euro notes to the Alvés house under police escort. Oleg had insisted that the larger denomination notes be used, contrary to the wishes of the kidnapper.

"You wouldn't be able to carry that much money in small notes, Fernando", he said as he indicated he needed time to organise the release of the money.

"Go and tell the police the nature of our business arrangement, and let me know the instant the kidnapper gets in touch for the delivery of the money. My best men will be on it."

When Carlos heard that the man dubbed 'the Godfather of Alicante' was to supply the money, he smelled a rat.

"I don't know if this sneaky, evil, Russian bastard is behind this, but I do know that he isn't lending that amount of money as a gesture of friendship."

Christiano agreed and enquired how they were going to proceed.

"With great care, sergeant. We have a kidnapper who appears also to be a rapist, a father with a questionable past and a volatile ex-partner, and now Ivan the Terrible throws his hat into the mix. There is much more to this case than meets the eye. Everyone involved in this case is lying to us. We will only be able to solve this case if we find out who is behind it, and that's exactly what I intend to do."

The frustration felt by Carlos was shared by the Fixer. Pedro knew before he answered the phone that it would be him and bolstered himself.

"Pedro, I need to know what's happening now."

"In two hours, I will call the father and he will tell me he has the money."

"How do you know this?"

"Trust me, Fixer, he will definitely have the money. I made sure of that. When I arrange the drop, I'll tell you. I will take my share and arrange for you to collect the rest."

"What's to stop you running with the lot?"

"The Colonel would have me terminated. His organisation operates on the basis of trust, and he wouldn't let a foot soldier like me tarnish his reputation. You will get your money, Fixer."

On the other end of the phone, the Fixer had a grin of satisfaction. This was working out better he had than planned.

The joy felt by the Fixer at the imminent payment of ten million Euros by Fernando Alvés was in stark contrast to how Pedro now felt. On return to the ward, he found Sergio dead. He checked for a pulse and any signs of respiration but knew from experience that Sergio Alvés was no longer with him. The dead always had a colour that no living person shared. He looked at peace, but was nonetheless dead. He now had decisions to make about who he told; Fernando Alvés and his wife, definitely not; Carmen had enough on her plate without adding grief to her current feeling of worthlessness, and the Fixer could wait. When he had his money, he wouldn't care less about the victims.

He looked at Sergio's face and had to admit to himself that the boy had earned his respect for his pluckiness. He thought him a spoilt little rich boy but conceded that he had shown considerable backbone over the past week in the face of insurmountable odds.

"Goodbye soldier" he said as he covered his face with the sheet.

When the sun dropped behind the mountain, he would dig a trench and lay him to rest. In the meantime, he had to call Fernando Alvés. He'd been put off for too long; Pedro wanted this sad series of events to come to an end. There had been a tragedy and he wanted to avert a disaster. He prepared his telephone with yet another prepaid SIM card, checked the semi-comatose Carmen and locked up the clinic before heading for Alicante Airport, where he parked in a long-stay parking facility.

He knew there was no CCTV on this site and the irony of finishing the kidnapping in the very place it started, appealed to him. The phone rang three times before being answered. In his head, he visualised the police communications man engaging the tracker before allowing Fernando Alvés to lift the hand piece.

"Fernando Alvés."

Not surprisingly, his voice sounded different to the last time they had spoken. The rape of Carmen had instilled a hatred that wasn't previously there. This change heartened Pedro; he now had their undivided attention, he was being taken seriously.

"Do you have it?"

"Not yet but it is coming. I need another five or six hours."

"Do you need another reminder of what happens when my demands aren't met?"

Almu screamed in the background.

"You touch her again and I will track you down and kill you with my bare hands."

"That's a very unreasonable attitude, Fernando. Just for the record, you and your police friends are incapable of tracking me down. I am too many steps ahead of you. On the second matter, you are not sufficiently familiar with the art of unarmed combat to stand a chance of killing me."

Fernando Alvés began to feel panicky. The Taker knew that the police were involved and he was worried that his children may suffer further punishment.

"I didn't tell the police. They found out ..."

"Don't make the job of your friend with the tracking equipment too easy by keeping me talking.

Because of the amount of money involved, I will give you another three hours. I will call you then and if you don't have all of the money, I'll send you a final reminder."

The click of the call being ended generated a flurry of activity in the Alvés living room. Carlos Rico and Constable Ferrera hovered over Thomas as he tapped and cross-referenced his signals. Fernando Alvés dashed to his office to call Oleg to find out when he would deliver the money and Almu ran after him in tears.

"What does he mean 'a final reminder'?"

Fernando Alvés told her it was no more than a threat to hasten things along but he didn't sound convincing. The police constable filling the role of Family Liaison Officer needed all of her strength to sit the heavily sedated Almu down. Her words were wasted on Almu as she careered towards a full nervous breakdown and the officer saw the warning signs. She called the family doctor and asked him to come immediately.

Thomas correctly identified the airport parking facility and Carlos despatched two of his men to check the area, all the while expecting nothing in return.

"He's military or ex-military," Carlos said to Ferrera.

"The unarmed combat references, sir?"

"Exactly, Ferrera. This doesn't really help, as there are tens of thousands of serving and veteran soldiers in Spain. I have an idea."

He called Christiano at the commissary and told him about the call.

"I want you to look at the Barcelona case again. This time target anything appertaining to the military. The Taker knows about unarmed combat. I'm going to keep an eye on Mr. Alvés and his dealings with Oleg Petrov. Keep me informed."

The sergeant agreed to keep Carlos up to date with any developments and retrieved the Barcelona files from his office. There were aspects of the scene where the dead victim was found that pointed to a military connection. The equipment recovered was army surplus and this pointed to familiarity; there was far better civilian equipment available that would have been the choice of a non-military man. The language used in the faltering negotiations was distinctly military, and there was an economy of effort in the field craft that only came after years of practice. However, the perpetrator then, as now, wasn't volunteering his name, rank and service number. Christiano decided to visit the local army barracks and run the evidence past their experts in hope of finding a lead.

Oleg Petrov didn't appreciate being reminded of the timescales he had set. He deliberately delayed the delivery of the money in order to make it clear to all involved, Fernando Alvés, the police, and even the kidnapper that he was now in charge of proceedings. This had the appearance of being a legitimate humanitarian act and his two million Euros reward was strictly between him and the fraught father. It also sent a message around the region that he was stronger than he had ever been.

In recent years, a rival Russian organisation had been trying to make inroads by redrawing previously agreed demarcation lines. This was not acceptable and a high profile scam would do his credibility no harm whatsoever.

"He said three hours or something bad would happen."

"Your money will take four hours to put together. For ten million Euros, he will wait, I assure you."

"I don't care about the money. I'm worried that he will rape my daughter again."

"When you deliver the money, he will never rape anyone again."

This didn't reassure Fernando Alvés but he could do no more than wait. This was now between the Taker and the Russian. He doubted the ability of the police to intervene between the two and make a significant contribution, their involvement being nothing more than a gesture of appeasement for Almu. He sat next to her on the elaborate sofa and took her hand. There was no point in telling her the details of his conversation with Oleg; if she heard and understood, she would only become even more upset. He felt the distance that had built up between them over the years but looked into her large, sad eyes and regretted that things had come to this. She deserved better and he hoped that in the future things might be different, but he still had secrets that he would never reveal to her.

The disclosure three hours later that the money would take one more hour to put together angered Pedro. Once again, he had performed the ritual of changing SIM cards, driving to an unlikely location, and calling Fernando Alvés only to be told that the ransom wasn't ready.

"I warned you that there would be a penalty for failing to meet my deadline. You will be receiving a package and I will send another every hour until you tell me you have the money."

There was no opportunity to protest or negotiate with the Taker as he cut the call. Thomas failed to locate the source of the signal from such a short call and Carlos could do no more than shrug. The only consolation Fernando Alvés could take was that Almu wasn't in the room to hear the call that announced her daughter was in all probability just about to be raped for the second time.

Carlos put a call out to all forces in the region to monitor courier offices for a tall man with a military bearing. He was hoping for a stroke of luck but knew it was a long shot. Christiano confirmed the military connection with the local camp training corps.

"The language isn't just army but very clearly infantry. The terms used are specific to one particular regiment. Unfortunately, this is the biggest regiment in the Spanish army."

"Well done, sergeant. Check army records for men who were serving in the north at the time of the Barcelona kidnapping and in the Alicante region now. If anyone fits the bill, find out where they have been for the past week. If this produces nothing, we will have to assume that our man has left the army. Get a list of everyone who has served in this regiment over the past thirty years. Our kidnapper will be on this very long list, I can guarantee you that."

With the sergeant chasing soldiers past and present, the investigators at the commissary looking for chairs built as instruments of torture, and several policemen in the region looking for tall men lurking around courier offices, Carlos couldn't have been accused of not doing anything, though he himself doubted that any of it would pay dividends.

He had asked Thomas to monitor the calls between Fernando Alvés and the Russian. Thomas was far from keen to collaborate as this exceeded his terms of reference, but a reminder of how few jobs there were on the market for communications experts whose employment had been terminated for 'technical reasons' soon changed his mind. Carlos knew the game Oleg was playing and was equally determined that he wouldn't succeed. This was a game of cat and mouse, though the roles were yet to be ascertained. The important thing for the police was the safe release of the Alvés siblings.

Pedro was at the end of his tether and his response was unambiguous. On return to the clinic, he took the opportunity of venting his frustration by digging Sergio's last resting place. The ground was baked hard and it took a considerable effort to make a hole large enough for a body. When he had caught his breath, he wheeled his dead victim out on the gurney that had once been his bed. He took the sheet that covered him and placed it in the hole. Sergio's broken body was then laid gently on top of it and covered by a second sheet. He thought about inviting Carmen to give her the opportunity to say goodbye, but the hysteria it would provoke was a complication he didn't want. She was better left in ignorance of what was happening only twenty or so metres from where she lay.

Pedro stood in silence over the white clad figure and reflected on their short and tumultuous time together. He had never been a religious man and there was no chance of that changing now. He had killed too many people over the years to ask for repentance. The hypocrisy of religion had paid his wages for many years when he sold his gun to the highest bidder. Sergio was no more than collateral damage, once again.

His mind returned to Fernando Alvés and his final reminder. He could not bring himself to harm the girl again, and Sergio would have volunteered an ear to save the honour of his sister. He cut the right ear from the side of his head, apologised, and replaced the sheet.

"You have no further use for this, soldier."

He covered him with some of the earth he had dug out and moved the rest to another location so as not to leave an obvious burial mound. The sun and wind would do the rest. Before he moved away from Sergio's last resting place, he saluted and bade him farewell.

A tray of coffee and sandwiches was wheeled into Carmen's ward in hope that she might eat them. She hadn't eaten since the rape and Pedro was hoping to hand her back before this became a major issue.

"I'm going out and I hope to be able to tell you that I am releasing you when I get back."

She showed no sign of having heard what he had said. He left her and wrapped the ear in a plastic bag, which he placed in an envelope. He drove to within a kilometre of the Alvés house and left the envelope behind a water meter cupboard.

161

"Go out of your gate. Take the third turning on the right and you will find a small brick construction containing a water meter. There is an envelope behind it. I will call you back in fifteen minutes."

Thomas drew yet another blank as Carlos clicked his fingers at Ferrera.

"Get it and come straight back here."

Fernando Alvés protested that he should do this and Carlos silenced him.

"It is more important that you are here on the end of the phone. Ferrera is well trained. He wouldn't dare open someone else's mail."

Fernando Alvés wasn't sure how sarcastic Carlos was being but understood that he wasn't being given a choice.

When Ferrera returned with the envelope, he didn't find anyone dashing to open it. He had squeezed it in order to get an idea of what was in it and had correctly guessed at the contents. He placed the unopened package on the table in front of Fernando Alvés and Carlos, and neither seemed keen to open it. Carlos took the initiative and resisted the temptation to have a pre-emptive feel. It obviously wasn't another DVD and this indicated that perhaps Carmen hadn't endured a repeat episode of her earlier defilement.

He carefully ran his penknife along the end of the envelope and emptied the contents onto the table. The plastic bag clearly contained an ear and Fernando Alvés jumped back from the table in shock.

"My God" he gasped, unable to take his eyes off the plastic bag.

The same question was being silently asked by all three of them, with Thomas, the communications expert, vacating his seat on seeing the ear. Fernando Alvés supplied the answer.

"It's Sergio's. Carmen has small, pixy-like ears."

As they stood transfixed, Almu came into the room. Before she could see the object that held their attention, Carlos pushed it back into the envelope and passed it to Ferrera.

"To forensics. Now."

Ferrera was all but pushed out of the room by the inspector. Almu knew something had happened that was being hidden from her.

"What is it? What aren't you telling me?"

"It's just a note from the kidnapper" Carlos lied.

He looked directly at Fernando Alvés as he spoke, demanding complicity. It would do Almu no good to know that her son had been brutalised. He expected nothing from forensics and merely wanted to protect Almu from the horrific truth. The awkward silence was broken by the telephone ringing.

Carlos shouted for Thomas to return and indicated that Fernando Alvés hold back until he was in his seat. Thomas scanned the table to make sure that the ear had gone before he resumed his station.

"Answer it" Almu demanded.

Pedro had no intention of beating about the bush. He didn't wait for Fernando Alvés to speak.

"Do you have it, or will I return your children one piece at a time?"

"What does he mean?" Almu asked.

Fernando Alvés held his wife but made no attempt at answering her question. He knew that the money was going to be available soon and told the Taker that he had it with him.

"I don't want anything else to happen to Sergio and Carmen. I have the money and I want to give it to you now."

"There is to be no police involvement. If I see that you are being followed, I'll walk away and you can guess at what I might do then."

"There will be no police."

Both knew that this was unlikely and the look on Carlos' face confirmed this.

"I want you to put the money in a holdall. It should only be as big as is necessary to contain the money. You will be directed to a number of locations and you will be given instructions at each of them, directing you to the next. I will be watching you every step of the way. If there is any funny business, our deal will be terminated, as will your children. Do you understand?"

"I understand. Let's get on with it."

The impatience displayed by Fernando Alvés told Pedro that he was now in complete control. In a matter of hours, he would have the ten million Euros and he would return Carmen to her family. He would then be fifty thousand Euros better off and on a flight to Brazil until the heat died down. Perhaps he wasn't too old for action after all.

"Go to Santa Pola. There is a churros stall on the beach. Next to it is a public telephone. Be there in one hour and you will be given your instructions. Remember, no police. I will be watching you and if I get the slightest indication that you are being followed, you know what will happen."

164

Fernando Alvés agreed the Taker's terms. He hoped that Oleg had the money available and that Carlos would appreciate the necessity of no police involvement. He knew that Oleg had no intention losing sight of his eight million Euros for an instant and hoped that his men would be more subtle than the police.

While Fernando Alvés finished his call with the kidnapper, Carlos scowled at his mobile before answering it. He saw it was Ferrera and couldn't think of what was so urgent that he would call when he knew the kidnapper was talking to Fernando Alvés.

"It's the ear, sir."

"What about it?"

"Forensics say the previous owner was dead at the time it was cut off. They said that they can't be one hundred per cent, but Sergio Alvés had been dead for at least four hours before the ear was cut off."

"Shit."

Carlos didn't relish telling the Alvés parents of this development. Fernando Alvés was barely holding himself together and Almu was quite clearly in the throes of a breakdown. Sergio's death was an irreversible fact and could only have a derogatory effect on how the rest of this scenario played out. Carlos became aware of the questioning gaze of the Alvés parents and ended the call telling Ferrera to gather all of the investigators together for briefing on the money drop.

"You heard what he said, quite clearly no police involvement. I don't want you anywhere near the handover."

"That is not your call to make, Mr. Alvés. A crime has been committed and I am duty bound to investigate. My officers will be unobtrusive. We will stay at a respectable distance from the happenings and only move at the last minute to apprehend the kidnapper. You would do better to keep your Russian friends away from the proceedings."

Fernando Alvés had worried about this too. Subtlety was never part of Oleg Petrov's modus operandi, preferring a more blatant show of force that left no one in any doubt about who was in charge. He excused himself and went to his study to call Oleg.

"Yes, the money is ready. Do you realise how bad eight million Euros smells?"

Fernando Alvés wasn't in the mood for discussing the aesthetics of currency and confirmed that he had his own two million Euros waiting to combine with Oleg's generous loan. This two million Euros was all he had in the world after a lifetime of graft, and the Russian made no apologies for his intention to take it from him in exchange for the lives of his children. He would have to address this later, because now was all about the handover.

He went to his bedroom and found a holdall he used when he went hunting. He took the two million Euros from his safe and found that it filled more than half of the bag. Oleg was right in his estimation of the volume of money and his insistence on five hundred Euro notes was accurate. Ten minutes later, two large Russian messengers arrived with the money that had offended Oleg's olfactory senses. Under the scrutiny of the Russians, Fernando Alvés packed the money into his holdall.

Carlos had left to brief his team and promised Fernando Alvés that they would be in Santa Pola when he got there. Fernando initially refused to wear a wire but Carlos made it quite clear that this was not a request.

"You want your son and daughter returned and we need to ensure that this man doesn't think that he can do this every time he feels like it. You will wear a wire and our friend Thomas will be listening to every word exchanged between you and the Taker."

Fernando Alvés agreed on the condition that it was invisible.

Meanwhile, Pedro was preparing for the end game. He had walked through the sequence of events that Fernando Alvés was about to enact, and was confident that it would go without fault. Perhaps it was over elaborate, but the more layers of protection he gave himself, the better. He checked Carmen before he left and was pleased to see that she had eaten the sandwiches left the previous evening. She seemed more depressed than traumatised, and he wasn't sure that this was an improvement. In a matter of hours, she would be returned to her family and receive professional attention. He had to make one more call before he left.

"Fixer, it's Pedro. Alvés has the money. I'm going to collect it."

"Where?"

The voice distortion made the Fixer sound evil. Pedro was feeling the effects of the past week's events and didn't need the Fixer's negativity.

"In Alicante. You don't need to know any more than that."

"What about the police? Are they involved?"

"Almost certainly. They won't be an issue."

"How can you be so sure?

"I have taken precautions. By tonight, we will have ten million Euros. How do you want it delivered?"

"When you have it, I will give you instructions on how I want it to be handed over."

Pedro thought that this was an odd response. Was this really about the money or was it a personal issue between the Fixer and Fernando Alvés? As far as Pedro was concerned, it made little difference. The death of Sergio was something the Alvés family would have to deal with and had little importance to the Fixer.

With everything now going to plan, Pedro visited Carmen and told her that her father had agreed to pay for her release.

"You said 'my release'. Does that mean that you don't intend to release Sergio at the same time?"

"Sergio has already been released."

Pedro was pleased at the profundity of his statement and turned on his heels before Carmen could interrogate him further. He had work to do and couldn't guarantee being able to keep Sergio's death from his sister for much longer. He gathered the items he thought necessary for the drop and headed to Santa Pola. This was going to be the most complicated few hours of his life and he would need all of his wits about him if he was to succeed.

*****

Fernando Alvés hadn't been to Santa Pola since he was a child and it made him feel that his adult life had passed so quickly. As he looked around, he thought that it hadn't changed significantly over the intervening half a century and it could have been any one of a dozen other Costa Blanca towns. It was a nice working town that was blessed by being on the Mediterranean Sea. However, he wasn't in Santa Pola to write a travel guide review, he wanted to bring his son and daughter home to his now almost broken wife. He parked his car as close to the beach as he could and looked around for the churros bar.

He disliked the doughnut-like delicacy so loved by his fellow countrymen, with the dunking in chocolate compounding his abhorrence of this breakfast treat for so many. He looked around and found the public telephone. The police presence that he knew was inevitable was at least subtle.

This couldn't be said for the Russians. Doorman Danny looked exactly like a Russian hood trailing a bag full of money. His partner appeared to have more muscles and fewer brains, making them stand out like two very large foreigners in a small Spanish town. Fernando Alvés hoped that he could explain their presence to the Taker before he made any assumptions about what was happening.

Pedro sat in his car at a discreet distance from the public telephone and clearly saw the Russians hovering fifty metres from Fernando. He instinctively knew they were Russian; they looked Russian. He had worked with them often enough to know that he was right. He mulled over their interest and quickly arrived at the correct conclusion that they had supplied the additional funds. This was turning out to be more interesting than he had anticipated. He had worked with them in Africa and never liked them. They had callousness in their dealings with others that went beyond soldiering. They took pleasure in inflicting pain and this made them useful in situations where others might have asked questions. To make fools of these goons would make the drop all the sweeter for Pedro.

He looked for the police and couldn't make up his mind about two or three men who appeared to have little purpose about their presence. He decided to avoid them. After all, he didn't need to pay any attention to them. He was just another citizen going about his daily business.

Fernando Alvés hovered around the phone, his knuckles white with tension on the holdall. When the phone rang, he snatched the handset from the cradle.

"I have the money."

"I can see that."

Fernando Alvés scanned through three hundred and sixty degrees in vague hope of identifying the Taker. He later thought that he didn't know why he did this, as there was no plan of action to support a possible discovery. Pedro knew that many pairs of eyes would be doing the same thing, though they would have very clear instructions on what to do if they identified a possible kidnapper. He had taken the precaution of investing in a hands free installation that would fool those looking for a man with a mobile.

"I told you no police. Who are the guys with the lumps in their jackets?"

Fernando Alvés didn't know how to respond to this. Were the Russians so obvious?

"I had to borrow the money from someone that I wouldn't normally do business with. He is a very careful man."

"He will want to kill me and keep the money, I assume."

"I want no part in his business. I want to pay you the money and for you to release my son and daughter. If I could shake them, I would."

"Go to Arenales. There is a café in Victoria Square. Order a coffee and ask for Pepe. He has a package for you."

"Where is Arenales?"

"It's about five kilometres up the coast. I will be watching you. If I see a policeman, Carmen dies."

This was the first time that the Taker had directly threatened his victims with death, and the significance wasn't lost on the police team monitoring proceedings.

"Those bloody Russians have got him spooked" Carlos said to Christiano.

"What are we going to do about it?"

Carlos had been considering this very question and was in two minds. Take the Russians and let the Taker know that they were in attendance, or leave their raw menace to keep the kidnapper on his toes? His prejudices came to the fore and made his decision for him.

"The Taker will be expecting us to be nearby but he specifically mentioned them. Take the Russians off the street."

"On what charge?"

"In my experience, being Russian is enough. I don't have to justify myself to criminals who are most probably illegal anyway. Get them out of this scenario. They will give you some reason when you stop them. Take Ferdinand in the second car and intercept them before they reach Arenales. Call uniform for back up. These guys don't always play nice, especially with ten million at stake."

Christiano was far from comfortable with his instructions but Carlos had made his mind up. This was the unconventional side to his inspector's character that he had been warned about but still wanted to experience for himself. Carlos didn't want the Russians littering his crime scene and that was the end of it.

Somewhere between Santa Pola and Arenales, a roadblock stopped a luxury car and arrested the two occupants. Their permitted phone call was to Oleg Petrov, who despatched more resources to find Fernando Alvés and the money. The chase was on.

Fernando Alvés stopped in a news kiosk in Arenales, bought a magazine he didn't want, and asked for Victoria Square. He easily found the café in the peaceful square and ordered a coffee. Once again, he looked around for the Taker. A derelict hotel occupied a complete block on the opposite side of the road, preventing a direct view of the sea. In other circumstances, he would be considering this beachfront property as a business opportunity.

Around him in the adjoining cafés, he found a group of Brits noisily comparing their shopping from the souvenir shop, an elderly man feeding his dog with the remains of his sandwich, and a jogger wearing a pair of ridiculously tight shorts. None of these looked like a kidnapper. The Russians were conspicuous by their absence and if Carlos Rico's men were in attendance, they were suitably subtle.

He checked the holdall as he had done every ten seconds, as the pretty young waitress brought his coffee and a small tapa. Ten million Euros has that kind of effect on people. He didn't want the coffee or the scrap of ham on bread, but needed to fulfil the role of casual customer. When he saw the all too familiar Constable Ferrera taking a seat at the next table, he thought it was time to act. He summoned the waitress and asked about Pepe.

"I'll get him for you" she said and returned to the counter where she spoke to the middle-aged man. He looked over her shoulder at Fernando and wiped his hands on his apron before nodding acknowledgement. As he approached the table, Fernando Alvés' blood ran cold when he saw the envelope in the man's hand.

"You are Fernando?"

"Yes. Is this for me?"

"The man said you would collect this."

He laid the envelope on the table and returned to his kitchen with a remarkable lack of interest about the envelope or its contents. Fernando Alvés saw it was flat and heaved a sigh of relief. He carefully opened it and was all too aware of Ferrera's unguarded interest. He half turned to shield the contents from the detective and was surprised to find a railway timetable. The schedule for the Alicante to Valencia service had the two-thirty departure underlined. It seemed like the Taker intended him to catch this train. Was the handover going to happen during the journey?

He left a five Euro note to pay for his coffee, waved the timetable at Ferrera, and returned to his car with the holdall and its precious cargo. Carlos waited and watched. He wasn't concentrating on Fernando Alvés; he was looking for the man he thought would be cajoling the bag with ten million Euros safely into his custody. So far, he was making a good job of being unobtrusive.

This was largely due to him being five kilometres away, in Alicante. Pedro had no intention of meeting Fernando Alvés in person. To put himself within striking distance of a man in such an emotionally charged state would have been foolish. He was too close to successfully pulling this off to risk being caught. He knew that Pepe in the café would be interviewed by the police, and had taken the precaution of asking the bread deliveryman to pass him the envelope. Pepe had volunteered his name to the tall stranger after being complimented on his tapas three days previously.

"Can you pass this to Pepe please mate? Tell him it's for Fernando. I'm so late and my boss will have my arse if I'm not in Elche in ten minutes."

Pedro didn't wait for a reply. The van driver shrugged and threw the envelope carelessly on top of the day's bread delivery. Pepe also shrugged and tossed it onto the far end of the counter. The postal system meant that it wasn't an uncommon occurrence for mail to be left in a local café bar or shop, and if it was still there at the end of the day, he would throw it out with the leftovers.

The next stage of the handover at the railway station would be tricky, but he was confident that his partner was up to the job. Once again, he had observed what happened on an everyday basis and knew that the man jealously guarding the bench outside of the station would be available for simple short-term employment.

"How would you like to earn twenty Euros? I want you to give someone an envelope and a message."

"Is it drugs?"

"It's not drugs."

Pedro pulled the crisp twenty Euro note from his own top pocket and inserted it into that of the street dweller.

"Is it legal?"

"Yes, it's legal. It's a map. His name is Fernando Alvés. Tell him to find the archer and I will call him. Now repeat it back to me."

Pedro's new partner looked at him suspiciously, as he repeated the instructions.

"Who do I give it to?"

Although he didn't smoke, he had come prepared with cigarettes and a lighter just for such an occasion. He passed them to his new friend and indicated that they were a gift. The man looked guarded; he wasn't used to unsolicited gifts. Pedro suggested that they might have to wait for a short time before the man arrived and he wanted him to be relaxed when he delivered the envelope. The man lit a cigarette and pushed the rest of the packet into his pocket without offering his new employer one.

As the man savoured the tobacco, made all the sweeter by knowing he had nineteen more in his coat, Pedro turned to peer into the car park that the bench overlooked. He saw Fernando Alvés' car approach and turned away. He didn't want there to be any chance that he might be recognised as having been in Santa Pola earlier that day. He also saw the cars containing men who were unmistakably policemen, though the Russians that were so prominent on the coast were now conspicuous by their absence.

When the entourage had passed, Pedro told his friend that the man he had to make the delivery to had just arrived.

"I will point him out as he enters the station. I will be watching to make sure you do as you have been told but I won't be here when you return. It is important that you forget what I look like. Do you understand?"

"Do I look like someone who remembers a face?"

The tramp laughed at himself and Pedro joined in, albeit only to keep him focussed.

"That is the man, just walking up the steps, wearing a blue jacket."

"I see him. I won't let you down. Remember, any time you need a ..."

"Go. Go now before you lose sight of him."

The tramp was propelled by Pedro towards the stairs. As he strode into the station, Pedro observed at least five men close behind Fernando Alvés, watching everyone in the vicinity. He avoided making eye contact with them and left as his messenger neared Fernando.

Fernando Alvés had parked his car and made his way into the station, well aware of the police presence. He wasn't sure if he was meant to buy a ticket for the two-thirty to Valencia, or not. He looked around for anything that might suggest the course of action expected of him and saw plain-clothed policemen aplenty. If the Taker was watching, he would have no problem in identifying the investigators from the Alicante Commissary.

As Fernando Alvés looked again at the timetable he had been given in the café, a tall, unkempt figure approached him. Could this be the kidnapper? He looked like a genuine homeless person; he was wearing too many clothes though a cold winter's night might question this, shaving hadn't been a priority in his daily routine, and the odour of too many days since he had troubled a shower was all too obvious.

All of this could easily be faked and Fernando Alvés looked around, this time to ensure that the policemen were watching. The tramp knew who he was; this meant that if he wasn't the Taker, he was nearby; watching and waiting.

"Fernando Alvés?"

"Yes, I am Fernando Alvés. Are you to collect something from me?"

The tramp looked confused at this suggestion.

"No. I am to give you this."

He handed the envelope to Fernando Alvés, who gingerly accepted it.

"Who told you to give this to me?"

"A tall man. He pointed to you and said I was to give you the envelope. He paid me twenty Euros."

"Where is he?"

The messenger looked around and shrugged his shoulders.

"He said that he will call you. You are to find the archer."

"What are you talking about? What archer?"

"That's all he said."

Fernando Alvés could see that the police were closing in on them, and wanting to put some distance between him and them, made his way to the car park. When his phone rang, he expected the kidnapper but was disappointed to hear a very angry Oleg.

"Where the fuck are you? The police lifted my men."

"I had nothing to do with that."

He considered lying but knew Oleg would make him pay dearly if he did.

"I'm at the railway station."

"Stay there until my men are with you. Have you made the drop?"

"Not yet. The police are busy harassing a down and out. He gave me an envelope."

He placed the holdall on the ground at his feet and opened his instructions.

"It's a map of the castle."

Castillo de Santa Bárbara dominated the Alicante skyline as it had for over a thousand years. Fernando Alvés had visited it as a child but had taken it for granted most of his adult life. History certainly wasn't high on Oleg's list of priorities.

"What is he playing at? A trip to the seaside, a visit to the castle; next he'll have you buying an ice-cream."

"I just want Sergio and Carmen released. I will do whatever he wants to make sure that happens. Your two million payoff is in the bag."

The hissed conversation on the other end of the phone confirmed that Oleg's replacement foot soldiers had found Fernando Alvés. As he looked around the car park, he saw the four by four with the darkened windows and knew that he once again had a full entourage of minders. As he pulled away, the car containing Inspector Carlos Rico blocked his path.

"Where are you going?"

There seemed little point in trying to lose them, but he worried about the wellbeing of Sergio and Carmen and attempted to buy himself a little time.

"The marina."

Fernando Alvés drove around the police car and headed out of the car park.

"He's lying, sir" Velasquez reported from the back seat.

"What do you mean 'lying'?"

"I saw what he had on the passenger seat. It was a tourist handout for Castillo de Santa Bárbara."

"Well spotted, Velasquez. I don't know what his game is but we will find out later."

Carlos called the Commissary and demanded that the castle be sealed when Fernando Alvés was safely inside.

"I want every available officer in that castle. There is only one entrance. There is no way he can escape if he picks up the bag."

Being relatively new to Alicante, Sergeant Christiano Marcos welcomed the opportunity to get to know its oldest structure. He utilised the openings his siren and blue lights allowed to cut through the busy afternoon traffic and parked close to the beach, where they were met by a dozen uniformed and plain-clothed officers. Carlos wanted everyone in place before Fernando Alvés arrived.

"No one is allowed to leave the castle after Fernando Alvés enters. Keep your eyes open for anyone carrying a bag. Treat this man as armed and dangerous. Spread out and try not to look too conspicuous."

Access to the castle was via a long, metal-clad tunnel that ran the three hundred metres from the busy street to the elevator that carried the visitors to the second floor entrance to the historic fortification. The crunch of heavy police boots reverberated in the confined space and the surprise on the face of the young attendant at the large number of policemen was all too clear.

She called the reception desk at the head of the elevator to warn them that an invasion, the first for over one hundred years, was under way. Soon afterwards, Fernando Alvés purchased the €2.70 ticket required for the lift and was followed by the Russians. They had to wait for the elevator as it took two trips to ferry the police contingent to the top.

The police officers arranged themselves in all of the best vantage points, looking inwards at the castle. The whole city of Alicante could be seen from the castle, from the surrounding mountains to the horizon on the deep blue sea. However, it was pointed out in unmistakable terms by the inspector that now wasn't the time to admire the breathtaking views offered from the ramparts; a considerable sum of money was about to change hands and a kidnapper was to be apprehended.

Fernando Alvés saw the lack of alternative exits available and wondered how the Taker intended to make good his escape. The sheer cliffs that had made the castle almost unassailable for centuries formed a formidable escape route. The Taker's getaway was a puzzle for him and a problem for the boys in blue; he was looking for an archer.

As he looked at the map given to him by the tramp in order to find a bowman, it seemed that every pair of eyes in the castle was firmly focussed on him and this didn't help placate his jangling nerves. He knew that the Russians and the police were armed and a shoot out wasn't beyond the realms of possibility, so kept a wary eye on the cover the heavy fortifications would offer. This was something that Carlos was also aware of and he didn't intend to let matters develop in this direction.

"Mendez, take four uniforms and round up the Russians. They will be armed, so do not let them put their hands inside their jackets. I want them cuffed and removed without disturbing the public. Call me when they are in the car."

The constable found the Russians easily. They were the guys who were bigger than the policemen. He took the recommended four uniformed officers and approached them from behind. They were concentrating on Fernando Alvés and this made their arrest relatively straightforward. Their removal was based on carrying an unlicensed firearm and they looked far from pleased.

Mendez reported that they were being placed in the back of a police van and Carlos told him to take them for a drive.

"I don't want them calling Oleg Petrov until our business here is concluded. He will only send more of them and the large influx of Russians will upset the custody sergeant."

Fernando Alvés noticed them being escorted from the castle forecourt and knew that his financial sponsor would be livid, but that was something that could be addressed later. He considered asking a member of staff about the archer but decided against this. He wanted to find the Taker before the police did.

He was amazed at the restoration that had been done on the castle and how large it actually was. There seemed to be so many layers, each with a story to tell. He had a picture in his head of what the kidnapper looked like and scanned the faces of his fellow visitors for telltale signs of someone with something to hide. The investigators were playing the same game and knowledge of the Taker's nether regions didn't help.

"Is the castle completely sealed?"

Confirmation that no one was going to leave the castle was forthcoming.

"I'd like to see how he intends to get out of here," Christiano said to no one in particular.

It was at this point that Fernando Alvés saw the archer. He was made of iron and stood proudly in the ramparts above his head. He looked at his map and followed the pathway that led to the sculpture of the soldier. When he reached him, he was impressed with the larger than life construction. The archer stood two metres high, wore full armour, and pointed a crossbow in the direction of the castle approaches on the Mediterranean side.

Fernando Alvés looked around and saw no obvious kidnapper. Three elderly couples posed for photographs and two of Carlos' team tried and failed to look like tourists. "Where was the Taker?" he asked himself.

The police were asking the same question and the increase in tension was palpable. When Fernando Alvés' phone rang, everyone looked around in hope of identifying the caller. Several people appeared to be using the built-in camera every phone now had, but no one seemed to be paying any attention to Fernando Alvés.

"Taker, I'm with the archer."

"I know. I can see you."

Fernando Alvés again looked around and saw no one suspicious. Carlos listened on the wire worn by Fernando Alvés and indicated to his officers that the drop was about to happen.

"Where is he?" Christiano was feeling the same frustration as the others.

Pedro gave his very precise instructions to the man with the bag containing ten million Euros.

"Walk away from the archer towards the battlements on the other side."

Fernando Alvés walked across the courtyard to the fortifications from where the castle would have been defended against an enemy attacking from the city.

He leaned on the crenel space from where real life archers would have fired, and looked between the protective, upright merlons.

"Do you see the bullring?"

Fernando Alvés scanned the cityscape below.

"Yes. I can see it."

"There is a plant growing in a crack in the crenel."

Fernando wondered at the relevance of a weed that had miraculously placed its roots in such an unlikely location, but confirmed that he saw it in front of him.

"Is the bag tightly closed?"

"Yes, the bag is very tightly closed."

"Run your hand through the plant on the crenel. You will find a piece of thin rope tied around the stalk."

As Fernando Alvés followed his instructions, Carlos started to feel very stupid as he realised what was happening.

"He's not in the bloody castle."

"What do you mean, sir?" Christiano said in disbelief.

"He is not in the castle. He is somewhere below us. He's drawn us into the castle and he's outside."

"Tie the rope around the handles of the bag and raise your hands when you have done it," Pedro ordered.

Fernando Alvés did as he was told, and raised his hands to signal compliance.

"Don't let go of the bag," Carlos shouted to him, but it was too late.

The bag disappeared from the crenel as Pedro tugged on the rope. Carlos and Christiano joined the astonished Fernando Alvés as they watched the bag containing ten million Euros freefall from the castle. It hit the rocky facade twice before landing near the dirt track fifty metres below. The tall figure waited until it had come to rest before picking it up and strapping it onto the rack of a trail bike.

He waved at the faces peering from between the merlons above before kicking the bike into life and speeding down the track leading to the coach park.

Once he had reached the tarmac, Carlos knew they had no chance of catching him. He gave them another cheery wave, as a man with ten million Euros would, and disappeared into the winding streets of Alicante old town.

"He has led us a merry dance," Christiano said.

None could disagree. The three men stood without uttering another word for several minutes. When the uniformed sergeant approached and asked what had happened, Christiano repeated his previous statement.

"Where is the money, sir?"

"The money has gone, sergeant."

Fernando Alvés didn't know how he should be feeling. He had made the drop and the Taker had his money. He hoped that he would keep his end of the bargain and release his son and daughter. Carlos, having deployed half of the Alicante police force, had failed to catch the kidnapper and felt no satisfaction.

"Get someone down there and collect the rope he used."

"Do you think forensics will find anything on it, sir?" Christiano asked.

"No sergeant. I think the chief inspector will use it to string me up."

Chief Inspector Roberto Martinez had been a colleague and friend of Carlos Rico for thirty years but he had a duty to perform. It was made more difficult because on this occasion, unlike many others, Carlos hadn't actually done anything wrong. He just didn't get anything right. They both knew this had to be done; after all, that was how the police operated, but it didn't make it any easier for either of them. When Carlos entered his office, he sat as invited, and awaited the judgment of his superior officer.

Roberto was in his last few months as a serving officer and had hoped to cruise towards retirement without further drama, but that was improbable when working with Carlos Rico.

"We are lucky that this isn't in the public domain. A clown on a motorbike manages to steal ten million Euros from right under the noses of the Alicante police and half of the Russian mafia. What went wrong Carlos?"

Carlos had re-run the scenario in his head many times in order to find the answer to this very question, and every time arrived at the same conclusion.

"He outthought us, pure and simple. I don't know if he anticipated the Russian involvement and lined us up to remove them, or he planned the whole elaborate wild goose chase as a piece of theatre for reasons known only to himself. Either way, it worked. He has ten million Euros and we have a piece of rope, two expectant parents, and a very angry Russian gangster."

"The Russians are a problem. Their Consulate has been in touch and wants to know why you have been shepherding a number of their citizens into cells."

"Do you want me to justify that?"

"No, and don't be a smart arse with me. I'm on your side. Leave the bloody Russians alone for a few days. They're obviously more sensitive than you think."

Carlos raised his hands in the way of an apology.

"They were a complication that I didn't need. Petrov is a malignant entity in Alicante and I wasn't going to let him dictate what happened on my crime scene. As it worked out, his goons would have been left looking every bit as stupid as me. I did them a favour."

"Be that as it may, it looked like you were arresting tourists. I managed to stifle the issue by stating that all four were carrying automatic pistols. There were mutterings of the weapons being planted by our officers but none other than Oleg Petrov intervened and the consulate backed down. Petrov is as embarrassed as he is angry. He will send people to find his money, and we could do worse than tail them."

Carlos confirmed that this was already happening.

"We now know what the kidnapper looks like. The CCTV from the castle caught him entering and leaving twenty minutes before we arrived. He fits the description, and only stayed fifteen minutes; just enough time to drop his rope from the fortifications and leave before we arrived."

"Does the rope tell us anything?"

"Nothing. Bought from a supermarket."

"And the ear in the envelope? Why haven't you told the parents?"

"We can't be sure that it's his. Forensics asked for something they could cross-match for DNA but I took the decision that it wouldn't help our enquiries if the Alvés' were grieving, perhaps for no reason. I hope we are wrong and the ear was procured from another source. The kidnapper, or kidnappers, has been very careful, and I don't think murder would be a path of choice."

"Where are we at this time?"

"The lab people are sharpening up the images we got from the CCTV at the castle and we can then look for a match on our criminal database. We will also be checking through the records of military identity card photographs from the infantry. This might tell us who we are looking for but it won't tell us where to find him, or the Alvés offspring."

Roberto knew that there was little else he could have expected from Carlos and his team, but the pressure was on him to produce nothing less than miracles. He was in a difficult situation because any criticism of Carlos would be unacceptable to the press, and therefore the general public, as he held celebrity status following his very public contribution to the death of serial killer Raúl Berbegal. Carlos almost lost his life but, with the assistance of a notorious bull, slayed the 'Alicante Assassin' in front of a viewing audience of millions. He was a hero who, for the credibility of the department, couldn't be made to look a fool.

"I don't see what else we can do until the kidnapper contacts the Alvés family. Keep chasing all of your leads, Carlos. I want a report every hour on our progress."

Carlos knew that he was being cut more slack than he deserved. He agreed to keep Roberto up to speed and stated his intention of pushing his team of investigators even harder.

"The kidnapper may have been clever but he will make a mistake, and I will find him when he does."

Roberto knew from experience, if the perpetrator made the smallest mistake, Carlos would find him.

"After all, he is only human."

At this moment, Pedro felt superhuman. He initially thought that his plan was over-elaborate; was he making his own life difficult by introducing too many twists into the drop? He wanted to stand back and see who the players were before he put himself into a potentially compromising situation. He knew that there would be police involvement but was unsure of their approach. Would they be heavy-handed and protective or more subtle and unobtrusive in hope of catching him red-handed?

Santa Pola gave him the opportunity to observe from a distance. Men in suits weren't the norm on a sunny seafront and looking disinterested was a questionable omission from police college training. He now knew who to avoid. The Russian involvement came as no great surprise as Fernando Alvés had to get the money from somewhere, and very few organisations could raise that amount in cash in such a short time. Their absence at the station surprised him, as he didn't believe for a moment that Fernando Alvés was capable of shaking them. This had to be down to the police.

The café in Arenales was no more than a way of buying time. His meeting with the bread deliveryman in his early morning visit to drop off the train timetable was fortuitous. It added one more layer of obscurity between himself and the police. He trusted the café owner's sense of duty to deliver the envelope, but knew that he could call Fernando Alvés and simply tell him to come to the station if all else failed.

He had noticed the street dweller the previous week as he planned the drop and thought of the confusion he would bring to proceedings. If he took up police time or resources, then this could only be a good thing. He dropped a few coins in the hat that lay beside the man as he slept and took the opportunity to sniff the surrounding air. He smelt damp clothes and body odour, but no alcohol. He didn't work with drunks, as they were too unpredictable. He felt vindicated when the detectives pounced on the tramp, giving him plenty of time to get into the castle, place the rope, and exit before Fernando Alvés arrived.

It turned out to be much closer than anticipated, as he and Fernando Alvés passed each other in the long access tunnel. The castle had proven to be the ideal location for the drop, and the literal application of the word allowed him to be far away from the clutches of the many policemen who would be in and around the fortifications. He wore the rope around his body and his motorbike leathers kept it out of sight as he entered the castle. To anyone looking, he was just another sightseer enjoying the dramatic views out over the city.

He had to ensure that he had enough rope to reach all the way to the dirt track below, and sufficient weight to take it there. On his first attempt, he cursed as it landed on a ledge halfway down. The sweat that ran down his back as he pull the rope back up had nothing to do with the physical effort and everything to do with being caught. His second attempt was successful, and he secured the end of the rope around the inappropriately growing weed. After a scan of the castle to ensure that he wasn't being watched, he beat a hasty retreat back to his trail bike that was parked close to the entrance. He was ignored by Fernando Alvés, whose focus was intently set on whatever awaited him.

From the coach park, he clearly saw Fernando Alvés as he stood by the iron archer with the crossbow. He saw him look around as he was being given his instructions, but his gaze was directed inwards. Everyone expected him to be in the castle. As he walked across the courtyard to the defensive positions on the other side, as directed, Pedro sped his bike up the dirt track to where the end of the rope lay. He was waiting on the end of the rope as the bag containing ten million Euros was attached to the other, and with a committed tug, he launched the grip down to earth. After securing it to the bike, he couldn't resist giving the faces peering at him from above a wave.

He had cleared the dirt track in five seconds and knew that now he was on a tarmac road, there was no way he was going to be caught. The bike was abandoned only a few streets into the town, the money transferred into another bag and clothes

191

changed before catching the tram that took him to the railway station. The money was then placed in the front seat of his waiting Land Rover, one doesn't throw that amount of money into the boot, and the short drive back to the countryside around the remote town of Agost was completed with a lightness of heart not often experienced by a mercenary.

Pedro had all but completed his mission and would soon be fifty thousand Euros better off and on his way out of the country. He had a few things to do before he left, but as far as he could see, the hard work was over.

On return to the former Agost Clinic for Mental Health, he realised that he hadn't tended to Carmen for over eighteen hours. When he opened the door to her ward, she almost looked pleased to see him. She had evidently been crying and he wasn't going to give her the opportunity to tell him why; she had far too many.

"I thought you had left me to die."

She had a desperation in her voice that was previously absent.

"I have been collecting something from town," he said cagily.

"I told you that my father doesn't have the kind of money you were asking for."

"Perhaps he doesn't, but he knows someone who does. Or, to be more accurate, did."

"He's paid?"

The smile on Pedro's face meant he didn't have to answer her question.

"Does that mean you will let me go now?"

He was still uncomfortable about telling her of Sergio's death and saw no reason to spoil her brightening disposition.

"I need to talk to someone first, but I don't think it will be long before you're home."

He left, telling her that he was going to prepare some food. As he reached the door, she called to him.

"Sergio's dead, isn't he?"

She couldn't possibly know this but now there was certainty in her voice.

"What makes you think that?"

"So you're not denying it then?"

Pedro felt trapped. He was a murderer, kidnapper, and rapist, and he could appease his conscience with the necessity of these acts, but lying? She could see he was struggling to find a suitable reply.

"I haven't heard his voice since the escape. Did you kill him?"

"No. I didn't lay a finger on him. Ok, I shot him but that was never going to kill him from that distance."

"Did you torture him?"

"No, I did everything I could to save him. I brought a doctor for him. He had a fall during your attempt to escape."

Pedro wasn't sure how much detail was appropriate in such circumstances. It was easy with soldiers, but Carmen was a sweet and delicate young woman. He had already defiled her and had toyed with apologising for this, but somehow 'sorry I raped you' had a hollow ring to it. He had done everything within his power to save her brother and doubted that the finest surgeons in the best hospital could have put him together again after his twilight encounter with the force of gravity and Spanish sandstone.

"You killed him, you bastard," she screamed as she launched herself at him.

He could have warded off the blows she pounded him with, but let her vent her fury at the expense of his discomfort. She wasn't capable of hurting him. The tears weren't far behind, as she fell exhausted to the floor.

"You bastard" she repeated time after time.

There was nothing Pedro could do for her and he didn't think that her thoughts were on food. It was better for all involved if he could bring this evolution to an end as soon as possible. The joy of the drop had gone; it was time to move on.

He dialled the number for the Fixer and waited for the scrambled voice to answer.

"Taker, have you got it?"

"I have it. It went like clockwork. The police were running around in circles."

"I said there was to be no police involvement. I made this quite clear from the start."

"The amount of money that you asked for meant that they were always going to get involved. It's ok, they have no idea who or where we are."

The Fixer went silent as though he were assessing Pedro's words. Ten seconds passed before Pedro spoke.

"I will take my fifty and we can arrange for you to collect the rest."

"I will be collecting nothing. You will take the money to the place I tell you at the time I tell you. Do you understand?"

Pedro would have accepted this tone from a senior officer or even a respected NCO, but baulked at putting up with it from a civilian. This had been the cause of several bars and not an insignificant number of bones being broken over the years.

"For a man who stands to lose nearly ten million Euros, your attitude stinks, 'Mister' Fixer."

There was another silence, this time because Pedro's words rang true. The Fixer was aware of Pedro's fear of the Colonel and his organisation, but he didn't hold the same authority and thought that he may have overstepped the mark.

"I could have put that a little better. Forgive me. I'm new to kidnapping. When you return Sergio and Carmen Alvés, we will arrange the delivery of the money and you can be off to do whatever you like."

Sergio seemed to be haunting him from beyond his grave in the arid earth. The Fixer was unaware of his death and this didn't feel like the best time to tell him. He tried to deflect the conversation away from the young man.

"In my experience, it would be better to hand over the money, in any way you like, before taking them back."

"This wasn't what I agreed with the Colonel."

Even the scrambler couldn't hide the impatience in his voice.

"They are to be taken back today."

There was no hiding place for Pedro anymore.

"The boy is dead."

The words seemed to echo down the line.

"What do you mean 'dead'?"

"He had an accident. He fell during the escape attempt, twenty metres onto rocks. I brought a doctor to attend to his wounds but there was nothing he could do. He died the following day. I've buried him in the grounds."

The Fixer had a lot to take in. What had started out as a kidnapping for money was now a murder. His first reaction was to distance himself from Pedro and his homicidal ways. If he were to be discovered, he would never see the light of day again. However, he had instigated this whole affair for money and the money was there for the taking. When he next spoke, it was falteringly.

"You damned fool. You brought a doctor. Did you also put an advertisement in the local newspaper?"

"It's ok; the doctor was one of ours. He cost a lot but he won't say a word."

"What about the girl? Please don't tell me that you have killed her too?"

"The girl is unharmed" Pedro lied. "You can always return half of the money with the girl if that helps to appease your conscience. Sometimes these things don't work out exactly as planned."

"Get the girl returned to her family right away," he said, with undisguised anger.

Pedro had little reason to take the moral high ground and agreed that it would happen that evening. The brilliance of his collection of the money had been completely overshadowed by Sergio's death. The Fixer knew nothing about the rape. If this were ever to become public knowledge, which he doubted, then it would be long after they had gone their own ways.

There was no bonhomie to be had from this exchange so it was better cut short.

"She will be returned tonight."

"When she is back with the Alvés family, I want you to return to the safe house. Then, we must assess just how much the police know before I give you instructions for handing over the money. In the meantime, you must make sure that Sergio's grave is well hidden."

The click indicated the call was finished.

Pedro had considered his options for taking the girl back and concluded that an uncomplicated deposit at a safe location close to her home was all that was needed. He couldn't take any risks at this point, and felt suitably guilty about Sergio not to leave Carmen in any danger.

Inspector Carlos Rico was also thinking about the return of Carmen Alvés. He gathered his team together to brainstorm the situation.

"We have no reason to believe that he won't return one, or both, of the Alvés offspring. If we are to catch the man known as the Taker, we have to outthink him. We need to predict when and where. Ideas?"

Mendez stated that they now had a reasonably clear image of the face of the man they thought set up the bag recovery rope at the castle.

"We could issue this to all patrols. The return will be in some kind of vehicle. The secret nature of the kidnapping doesn't need to be revealed; just that he is of interest to an enquiry and is to be detained if seen."

"Good, Mendez. Arrange for this to happen."

"I don't think he'll want to wait too long before making himself scarce, sir. If I were him, I'd return as many Alvés' as I had as soon as possible."

Christiano had a point. It was important that whatever they chose to do, they set it in place with immediate effect. Carlos agreed.

"So we will assume it will happen within the next twenty-four hours. Where will it happen? We can rule out a busy, public location. My worry is that he has proven his ability to tie together an elaborate trail, and this might tempt him to present us with another paper chase."

"We know that Sergio is probably dead but he doesn't know that we know this. I think he will want to bring the girl home unharmed and will choose somewhere close to her family home."

Carlos silently considered the words of his sergeant before answering.

"I think you may just have something Christiano. Let's look at the map of the area surrounding the Alvés house and distribute our resources in that area. I doubt that he will call before depositing her somewhere."

Carlos identified the places that he would bring Carmen to if he were a kidnapper returning her to her family, and positioned his team accordingly. He gave them a final warning before they deployed.

"Remember that he is cunning. He is also probably armed so I want no heroics. Salva's death is all too recent. Ears and eyes open, brains and radios switched on and we'll get this bastard tonight."

In the Agost Clinic for Mental Health, Pedro had made his preparations to escort Carmen back into the family fold and only waited for the cover of darkness to execute his plan. He would use a local sawmill as his return location; it was near the Alvés home and it was closed for the weekend. The only occupant at the weekend was a large German Shepherd dog that would make a lot of noise and draw the police to where he would leave the girl. This would guarantee that she would be picked up soon after he left her.

Carmen was limp, showing no sign of resistance or resentment, as he applied a blindfold and the inevitable cable ties around her wrists. He had no words that would make her feel any better and so decided to say nothing. She was carefully led to the Land Rover and secured by another cable tie to the tubular seat frame. He looked at her in the decaying sunlight and felt sorry for her. Sympathy had seldom been an option in his career, but he hadn't been dealing with innocent, young Spanish girls. She seemed to sense that she was being observed and half turned away towards the front of the vehicle.

"Let's get on with this," he said, desperately wanting an end to this whole sorry affair. He didn't expect, nor did he get a response from Carmen.

He drove carefully up the dirt track, all too aware of the delicate state of his passenger. When he reached the main road, he guided the Land Rover slowly over the bumps and gently round the bends in an attempt to make Carmen's last journey with him as comfortable as possible. He felt guilty about Sergio and knew he had to shake it before it affected his performance. When he hit the dual carriageway, he changed down the gearbox and accelerated aggressively to re-assert control of the situation, at least to himself. The rag doll in the rear of the vehicle was tossed backwards, with only the cable-ties tethering her wrists stopping her hitting the tailgate. She didn't care; she was going home.

Around the Alvés mansion, Carlos Rico's men sat in the dark and waited, each hoping that they would get lucky. If Pedro could have chosen which detective was to be the fortunate one, he would have elected for Ferdinand. As the Land Rover approached, the rookie detective peered at the headlights and made the expected call on his police radio.

"Ferdinand at location Delta. Vehicle approaching."

"Keep me informed, Ferdinand" Carlos ordered from his control position in the house.

Pedro recognised the sawmill looming in his main beam and slowed over the last fifty metres in order to scan the area. He didn't expect anyone but didn't want to be surprised by a courting couple, or a group of hunters stopping for a drink. He stopped in front of the sawmill gate, killed the engine, and got out. He stood still for ten seconds and listened. He heard nothing.

This was because Ferdinand was almost too excited to breathe. He saw the man get out of the Land Rover and recognised him as the man in the photograph he held in his trembling left hand. The man had left the headlights on for some reason and was clearly listening for the presence of others. Whatever he was up to, it wasn't good. He waited until the man started to walk towards the back of the vehicle, his feet crunching in the gravel, before he called in.

"Ferdinand in location Delta. A vehicle has stopped in front of sawmill. The man who has just got out is the man in our photo. How do you want me to proceed, sir?"

"Do nothing until reinforcements arrive. Maintain visual contact. Do not approach him on your own."

Carlos called all officers to move directly to location Delta. It seemed like their luck was changing at last.

"We've got him," he said to Christiano as they ran to their car.

The click of the police radio would have gone unnoticed by most, but Pedro had heard field radios too often to confuse it with anything else. He assessed his situation and decided to go ahead with his plan and vacate the location as quickly as possible. If the police had the resources in his immediate area, they would have had him in cuffs by now. He snapped the tailgate open, removed her blindfold, and produced a large knife that caused Carmen's eyes to assume saucer-like proportions.

He didn't wait to explain, and cut the cable tie that secured the girl to the seat. He launched her onto his shoulder and carried her to the sawmill gate, where he unceremoniously dumped her on her backside in the gravel. The air that was involuntarily expelled from her lungs when she made contact with the ground didn't disguise the sound of a police-issue pistol being cocked. On hearing this all too familiar sound, Pedro turned with his own gun in his hand.

Ferdinand had observed what was unfolding in front of him and knew that he couldn't wait for his colleagues to arrive; he had to act. He broke from his cover behind a low wall and closed the distance between them as Pedro carried the girl. He had never used his pistol outside of a firing range and didn't feel comfortable handling an implement of death. Pedro saw the fear and knew that he was in control as they faced each other, guns in hands. Pedro turned his gun onto Carmen.

"We both know that you are not going to shoot me, but I am all too willing to kill her. I have nothing to lose."

Ferdinand looked between Pedro, his gun, and the prone girl. Inside his head, he was screaming for someone to come and make this en passé go away, but he heard nothing other than the beating of his own pounding heart. Pedro cocked his weapon.

"Throw your gun and your car keys into the field. You have one chance or I will kill both of you."

The man's eyes, illuminated by the headlights, showed that he meant what he said. Ferdinand slowly pointed his pistol to the side. He grasped the barrel with his left hand and threw the pistol into the darkness. They heard it land in the field on the other side of the wall that had been his stakeout position.

"Keys" Pedro ordered.

Ferdinand carefully extracted his car keys from his pocket and co-located them in the field near to his service issue pistol. The other man flicked the barrel of his pistol in a horizontal action that clearly indicated he wanted him to move aside, and Ferdinand obeyed.

Pedro kept his weapon pointing at the nervous young policeman as he got into the driver's seat of the Land Rover. He placed the gun into the door pocket and noisily drove off with his right foot hard to the floor. When he reached the junction, he saw headlights approaching from his right, and this determined his escape route. He switched his own lights off, pulled hard to the left and sped off in the direction of the city. He would drive to where he had dumped the trail bike when he collected the money and change his mode of transport. The police would be looking for the Land Rover, and as far as Pedro was concerned, they could have it. It had served its purpose.

His priorities now lay elsewhere.

*****

The detectives from the three other locations arrived at the sawmill and spread out. With pistols in hand, they waited for Carlos before moving in. He arrived less than a minute later and saw that their prey had flown. Ferdinand knelt beside the pathetic figure of Carmen Alvés, with neither brother, Sergio, nor the kidnapper to be seen. The distressed look on the face of the young detective told him all he needed to know about what had occurred at the sawmill gate.

"Is she all right, Ferdinand?"

"I don't know, sir. She hasn't spoken a word. She is just staring into the distance. I think she is in shock."

Christiano Marcos was already on the phone for an ambulance as his fellow officers scanned the area near to the gate for any possible evidence.

"Mendez, take over from Ferdinand. Come and tell the sergeant and me exactly what happened. Don't worry; I know you did the right thing."

Ferdinand didn't seem convinced but had little alternative but to tell it as it happened.

"He took the girl from the back of the Land Rover, I've remembered the registration number. He then carried her to the gate. I saw that no one was coming and that he would have got clean away if I didn't challenge him, so I did. He pulled his gun and threatened to kill the girl and me if I didn't throw my gun into the field, and my car keys."

His head dropped as he continued.

"I did as he told me. I would like to say that I did it solely for the girl but I would be lying. I was afraid."

"Be that as it may, Ferdinand. My interpretation is that you were very clearly obeying my orders, and I thank you for doing so. I don't want to be thinking about how I would tell your fiancé or parents that you died a brave man. Graveyards are full of brave men. Get the Land Rover number to traffic and find your gun. You did the right thing in backing down. Remember, this is only a job."

All three knew that Carlos meant everything except the last statement. If any of his team were ever to take this attitude, they would find themselves writing parking tickets the next day. Ferdinand appreciated the support of his boss and visibly straightened. Christiano patted him on the shoulder and suggested that he looked lively before the inspector changed his mind.

"Where do we go from here, sir?"

Carlos looked at the girl and knew that he wouldn't be allowed to pursue the obvious line of enquiry until she had been medically cleared for interview. He had to make the best of what was left, and that meant trying to clear up the loose ends they hadn't had the opportunity to chase.

"We should break the good news to the Alvés family. We will also have to break the bad news about Sergio, although this will remain supposition until we find a body or the Taker confirms that he is dead. We also have the matter of why Fernando Alvés lied to us about the final location of the drop. Did he strike some kind of a deal with Oleg Petrov that would have allowed his men the opening to catch the kidnapper before we arrived and therefore potentially recover the children and the money? I think that Fernando Alvés has some explaining to do."

The only sound that could be heard over Carmen's sobbing was the siren of the approaching ambulance. Mendez wrapped a blanket around the girl and was all too conscious that she would be wary of a man getting too close after her rape ordeal. He kept at what he considered a sensible distance and attempted to console her. It appeared to have little effect. She continued to cry and mutter incoherently causing Mendez to look around to his seniors for guidance on what to do. Carlos indicated that he did nothing and awaited medical assistance. Christiano had told ambulance control that the victim had been raped and they said a female crew would attend. They were with them a few moments later.

The paramedics pointed at Mendez and signalled that he should move away from Carmen. The first attendant spoke softly to Carmen in order to reassure her that it was all over, and was met with another barrage of tears, this time they were tears of relief that it really was all over. The second brought a stretcher and they gently placed Carmen on it and covered her with more blankets before carrying her to the ambulance.

Carlos looked at Ferdinand as he emerged from the darkness with his pistol in his hand. He had a grin on his face and was obviously pleased that he had found his weapon. The inspector removed this in an instant.

"Have you found your car keys, Ferdinand?"
"No, sir."

"In that case you aren't going anywhere. Tape off the scene and wait for forensics. It's only six hours until dawn. You will have more chance of finding your keys in the daylight. Give me a full report of their findings when you return to the station."

As the ambulance departed, four other cars followed leaving Ferdinand to wait alone in the dark for the men in white overalls. The other three constables were sent home to get some well-earned rest as they hadn't slept for thirty-six hours and would be of no use to Carlos the following day in this condition. Christiano correctly suspected that his lot wasn't going to be quite so comfortable.

"We will go directly to the Alvés house and tell them what we know."

"What about Sergio?"

"We can't hide the forensics report on the ear any longer. I must tell them that the evidence points to him being dead. We have kept it from them for too long."

The reaction of Almu Alvés predictably was one of hysteria. The expectant look on her face was wiped away as Carlos spoke. She stared at him in hope that she may have misunderstood his words, but his lack of facial expression told her that he had got to the point very succinctly.

"Carmen has been taken to hospital. This is a routine precaution taken in such circumstances and we have no reason to suspect that she has been subjected to any further physical harm. Sergio was not returned. Forensics think that the ear sent two days ago was removed post mortem."

"What do you mean 'post mortem'?"

207

Almu was in denial heading towards shock. The past week had been a nightmare for her and it had just got worse. Carlos didn't consider an explanation of the differences in blood behaviour before and after death would have helped, and went for the direct approach.

"We think that Sergio was dead when his ear was cut off. We will confirm this with a DNA sample. In the meantime, we have to concentrate our efforts on Carmen."

Almu threw herself into her husband's arms as he stoically tried to maintain his dignity for both of their sakes, but couldn't hide the tears that ran down his face. He indicated to the housemaid that she escort Almu to her bedroom.

"Give her a sedative and try to calm her down. I'll call the doctor. Inspector, I must see my daughter."

"I will save you the trouble of pacing the hospital corridors. It is going to be a number of hours before the doctors will let you see her. She is traumatised and in need of medical attention. We have a bit of business to do before we go to the hospital."

Fernando Alvés didn't like being told that he couldn't visit his own daughter but realised that what the inspector said made sense. However, he wasn't too sure about what 'business' they had and this made him feel uncomfortable.

"What are you up to, inspector?"

"That was the exact question that I wanted to ask you, Mr. Alvés. Why did you try to put us off the trail of the kidnapper at the railway station? You told us that you were going to the marina, did you not?"

"You must have misheard me."

"You clearly said the marina, sir, but were holding a brochure from the castle as you spoke to us."

Velasquez' astute observation had at least got the police to the location of the drop even though they could do little to prevent it happening. Fernando Alvés looked less comfortable now.

"I wanted to have sufficient time to make the drop. I didn't want the kidnapper getting spooked when he saw police everywhere. He might have killed my children."

"He had already killed one. Remember, Sergio was dead before you handed over the money. Did you have some kind of a deal with Oleg Petrov?"

"You know I did. I borrowed eight million Euros from him. I would call that a significant deal."

"You know what I mean. Did you agree to give his men an opportunity to catch the kidnapper before we found you?"

"Why would I do that?"

"You would do that so that you and Petrov would get your money back. That is a substantial loss, even for him."

Fernando Alvés couldn't deny the logic of the inspector's argument.

"I don't know how I am going to pay him back."

Carlos reflected on how little the difference would have been if Fernando Alvés had told them the whole truth. He could have had the complete complement of the Alicante police force in the castle and still have lost the money. Fernando Alvés was in a fix with the Russian and that was something that bothered the detective. This was all too easy for the gangster and

Carlos' thoughts returned to who was behind this whole thing.

It made sense that it was Oleg Petrov. He stood to gain two million Euros by kidnapping Sergio and Carmen. However, something as open as kidnapping wasn't his style. His business was always carried out behind closed doors and he avoided police interference at every opportunity. He knew that the police were involved before he lent the cash. Was this some kind elaborate money laundering operation? He would have a word with the Fraud Squad about the state of Oleg's financial health. Oleg was lying, but then he always lied.

Was Fernando Alvés telling the truth? Once again, the probability was that he was not. There were aspects of this case that didn't sit comfortably with Carlos Rico and he was determined to find out what they were.

At the Alicante Central Hospital, the doctor refused to let father or detective near to Carmen Alvés.

"She is in shock and poor physical condition. She has no obvious injuries other than skin ruptures where shotgun pellets were crudely removed, but it will be a while before anyone can speak to her."

The use of a shotgun took them by surprise. The ordeal faced by Sergio and Carmen was becoming more shocking as the facts were slowly uncovered. Fernando Alvés was lost for words, but this wasn't a luxury Carlos could afford.

"It is imperative that I interview her before too long. There are things I need to know in order to catch the man who was holding her. This man killed her brother."

The doctor eyed Carlos with suspicion over the top of his half-rimmed glasses.

"I realise that you have a job to do, inspector, but I wouldn't be doing mine if I were to let you loose on this poor girl one minute before she is ready to talk to you. She is in a fragile state and it would take very little to push her into a full nervous breakdown. She shows all the signs that she has already visited this dark place in the recent past."

Carlos knew he was right and had expected nothing else. The doctor turned to Fernando Alvés and stated the conditions under which he could see his daughter.

"You can sit by her bed, hold her hand, and do nothing else until I tell you. Speak only to comfort and not to extract information. Do you understand, Mr. Alvés?"

Fernando Alvés agreed to the passive role dictated by the doctor and was led into the private ward where his daughter lay. Carlos thought that he detected a look of victory in his eyes as they parted and wondered at the callousness of the man in such circumstances. His daughter lay in pieces in a hospital ward and he gloated at being allowed to see her before the investigators.

The buzzing of his phone in his pocket brought Carlos back to the case. It was Velasquez.

"Sir, we know who he is."

"How?"

"Army records."

"I'll be right back."

Carlos told Christiano of the development and their sense of excitement grew as they drove to the Commissary. On arrival, they saw Velasquez filling the incident board with details of Pedro Ribera. The enhanced CCTV photograph from the castle was mounted beside one of a much younger man, though they were undeniably the same man separated by several decades.

"Tell me about the Taker, Velasquez."

The constable thought that he had drawn the short straw the previous evening when he missed the stakeout, but on hearing the outcome, felt a sense of relief. He struck gold in army records and followed the suspect's varied and interesting life post service.

"Pedro Roberto Martin Ribera was born 1960 in Madrid. He achieved little in school and soon after notched up a series of convictions for petty offences. The magistrate gave him the option of joining the army or going to jail, and he chose the former. He joined the infantry in 1977 and was a natural. Soldiering suited him down to the grubby ground he stood on and he excelled so much that he was transferred after two years to the infamous Spanish Legion battalion 'the Grooms of Death'. He was stationed in Cuetta and became a specialist in SERE; Survival, Escape, Resistance, and Evasion. He had a history of disciplinary problems and this led to him being incarcerated in an army jail on more than one occasion. On his final release, he absconded and joined the French Foreign Legion. He served with distinction in Rwanda, Gabon, and Zaire before encountering his personal devils yet again. He was sent to military prison for threatening to shoot his commanding officer who had reprimanded him for exceeding the Geneva Convention and it seems just about every other convention. On release, he served in Brazzaville and Kosovo before disappearing.

"It was thought that he had been taken as a prisoner of war, or even killed, but indications are that he had enjoyed the thrill of the kill in Africa too much to walk away from it. It looks likely that he operated as a mercenary for several years and it is suspected that he worked for a PMC, or Private Military Company, for many years thereafter.

"The mercenaries are a very close-knit group of people, and it was difficult to find one who would to talk to me, but I succeeded. The ex-soldier, who refuses to be named, told me that Pedro was special. He was brave as a bull but with half the brains. His survival training had kept him alive on many occasions when the rest of his troop perished and he continued to fight on beyond the age when most would have called it a day. My informant tells me that Pedro would want to die in a fire fight, and to push him into this type of situation would result in the loss of many lives."

"Well done, Velasquez. I'm impressed. Does your informant have any idea of where Pedro Ribera might be now?"

"He said that he might be working for a man they call 'The Colonel'. This is Colonel Klaus Meerkerk, director of The Flying Dutchman PMC, based in London. This is a thinly disguised company of mercenaries. It is borderline legal and they pay their taxes. Pedro Ribera has allegedly worked on several contracts with this company."

"I will contact Scotland Yard and ask them what they know about The Flying Dutchman. Perhaps Colonel Meerkerk can throw some light on the whereabouts of Pedro Ribera."

Carlos knew that if he did, he wasn't likely to tell the police. Brotherhoods such as this survived on mutual trust that was held above all else. The Colonel would tell him nothing.

Pedro Ribera was actually back at the Agost Clinic for Mental Health and wondering why. He had called the Fixer several times and got no reply. He was sitting on ten million Euros and desperately wanting to be somewhere else. His training dictated that he did nothing until directed but his instincts screamed 'get out of here'.

He used his time to eradicate every sign that he and the Alvés kids had ever been there. The clinic was a mess, with paint peeling from the walls and the floors littered with debris, so hiding the evidence of recent occupation wasn't too difficult. He knew that it wouldn't withstand DNA analysis but on a superficial level, it was what he considered sterile. The wards where he had held Sergio and Carmen were returned to the unkempt state he had found them in, with fresh dirt replacing that which he had removed before the kidnapping.

The green room was dismantled and everything burnt on a large bonfire. Signs of recent use were removed from the Alternative Therapy Room and it was locked tightly, hopefully for ever, and the keys committed to the surrounding desert landscape. The access hatch in the corridor was covered with a grimy carpet that none would volunteer to touch without protective clothing. Only his quarters remained clean. He had all but returned to field conditions as he awaited his final instructions.

The Limousine stood out, even under the tarpaulin, and had to be disposed of. He waited for darkness and drove it two kilometres up the dirt track. He stopped, looked, and listened for a considerable time before releasing the handbrake and letting it roll down the hill into the waiting gully. It would never be found unless someone was seriously looking for it. His lone source of transport was now the trail bike and it was his intention to leave this at whichever air or seaport he chose as his point of departure.

Pedro was ready to go and had one last thing to do. He had to make sure that Sergio's grave was invisible. For the first time in his life, he feared a grave. He didn't know what the boy had done to get inside his head, but whatever it was, was having a profound effect on him. As he neared Sergio's last resting place, he started to sweat. It wasn't hot and he couldn't rationalise this to himself. It was as though there was a force field holding him back.

"Sergio, you bastard, you're haunting me."

The small mound under which Sergio rested was levelled and Pedro knew that he was just killing time; the job was done and the end was near, but somehow there was something else that bothered him. He knew this would be his last job; he had reached the end of the line.

His frustration was echoed by that of Carlos Rico. He knew that the key to catching the kidnapper lay with what Carmen could tell him, but the doctor continued to be protective of his patient. He watched as Fernando Alvés talked to his daughter and desperately tried to lip-read her responses, with no great success.

"We need to talk to her. She is the only person who can tell us where to find Pedro Ribera."

Christiano Marcos shared his angst, but could do nothing to better their lot. He pushed the team in the Commissary, urging them to have a 'eureka' moment with the other evidence, to no avail. The Taker's whereabouts remained unknown and, as far as they were concerned, he was in all probability very far away. The odds were that he took the ransom and put as many miles between himself and his pursuers as was possible, while casually spending an enormous amount of money. They couldn't count on him giving himself away and so had to concentrate on the only person who could tell them anything about him.

Carmen cracked when her mother arrived. Almu ignored Fernando Alvés as she was granted access to her daughter, and he stood back rather than be brushed aside. They hugged tightly and cried for several minutes before either uttered a word. Sergio's absence was not going to be high on their list of conversational topics, so Carlos observed with little hope of gaining anything positive from their interaction. What was of more interest was the lack of involvement of Fernando Alvés. He was clearly being excluded, and there was every indication that this wasn't an unusual occurrence.

"Their relationship is relevant to our case. There is something they are not telling us."

"It's not unusual for a child to favour one parent over the other. He's been a busy professional; his wife would have spent more time with them as children."

"No. I feel there is something more. Have we found anything to implicate Petrov in the disappearance of the money, sergeant?"

"He seems even more upset than we are. He is behaving as if he has just lost eight million Euros. The word is that his heavies are knocking on doors."

As they spoke, Christiano noted that Fernando Alvés was staring intently at the inspector, as though he were trying to read his thoughts. Perhaps Carlos was right and the father had concocted a plan with the Russian to recover the money. Or maybe he was reflecting on the loss of an only son. Whatever was happening, the sergeant knew he didn't want to get involved in a poker game with the man with the unreadable face.

Another playing a cagey game was the Fixer. When he eventually called, Pedro picked up after only two rings. He was getting very nervous and couldn't see the reason for the delay. He didn't like what the Fixer had to say one little bit.

"What do you mean 'wait'? When that girl starts to speak, the cops could be on top of me in no time. Remember that I have ten million reasons for you to want me safely out of here."

The distorted voice sounded unworried.

"The police are on a high state of alert at the moment. In addition, there are a lot of gentlemen from Eastern Europe charging around Alicante looking for you. We should give it a day or so before we terminate our business agreement, just to let the city calm down a little."

"You seem to be very well informed."

"It is in both of our better interests that I keep my ear to the ground. People tell me things."

Pedro pondered who these people might be. He was a pawn in a much bigger game and was uncomfortable in his ignorance.

"Who are you, Fixer?"

His question was ignored.

"I will call you tomorrow. As soon as it is safe to move the money, we will do so and you can make good your escape."

Pedro had no option but to accept what he had been told. He had been in far worse situations, with enemy troops closing in while he waited to be extracted. On this occasion, he merely had to relax and wait for his instructions. Relax, and wait. It sounded so easy.

*****

When the doctor finally relented and allowed Carlos to interview Carmen, what happened next astonished the Alvés family.

"I want you to go public. I would like to arrange a press conference and put the face of the kidnapper into the public domain. Carmen must tell them the full horror of what happened to her. People will have seen Pedro Ribera and we need their help to find him. This is the only way we will get justice for the death of your son and the rape of your daughter."

Carlos decided that the recovery of the money shouldn't be a factor in this decision, as he needed to win the support of the mother. Almu Alvés had the casting vote on this issue, and she was far from convinced that this was what she wanted. She looked at her husband and he didn't seem comfortable with the inspector's proposal.

"My daughter has lost her brother and been defiled by this awful man. Of course I would love to see him behind bars but not at the expense of what little dignity he has left her with. You must do what you have to in order to catch him, but she will have no part in it."

"I want to do it, father."

No one had heard Carmen enter the corridor outside her ward. She stood in a hospital issue nightdress and housecoat, accompanied by a nurse who seemed determined to get her back into bed.

"Come Miss Alvés. The doctor said that you can speak to the police, he said nothing about getting out of bed."

Carmen ignored her.

"I want this man caught and I will do everything in my power to help the inspector catch him."

Almu moved to support her daughter and Fernando Alvés followed suit. The nurse continued to protest, but was ignored by all. Carlos offered a compromise that he hoped would get the support he needed for the televised appeal.

"I understand that the personal nature of the attack is something you would want to keep from the press and public, and I see no reason to say anything more than that you were assaulted. After all, you were the victim and shouldn't be subjected to further distress. The nature of the assault shall remain secret."

"No inspector, I lived; Sergio is the victim. I want to do this for him. I want to tell them everything"

Her father objected vociferously, insisting that his little girl had gone through enough. Carlos began to regret this approach and waited for a lull in the proceedings to suggest a further compromise. However, it was Almu Alvés who saw the look in Carmen's eyes and cast her vote.

"Fernando. She wants to do this for Sergio, so we must respect her wishes. Inspector, she is to have complete protection from the press. I know how vicious they can be."

Both men agreed to Almu's terms. She held her daughter and guided her back into the ward. Carlos agreed to inform them when he had made the arrangements.

A televised appeal relating to a major crime made great television and was guaranteed airtime. The Alicante Police Media Officer, Luis Barreta, had little difficulty in persuading the major news channels to allocate whichever time he wanted, and the celebrity status of Inspector Carlos Rico added extra spice. His face was known all over the country after his encounter with the Alicante Assassin, and his impending appearance caused a wave of activity in the commercial departments of the media companies, as advertisers vied for an adjacent slot with guaranteed huge viewing figures.

Time was a critical parameter and Carlos had to strike fast. He told the Alvés family that they were to have Carmen ready for the appeal in two hours. The doctor was furious that his authority had been undermined, but Carmen insisted that it went ahead. She was taken home and dressed for the cameras. At Carlos suggestion, she wore no make-up; he wanted her gaunt appearance to be seen by everyone. This, above all else, showed the traumatic nature of what she gone through.

On arrival at the Commissary, the Alvés family entered by the side door in order to avoid the large press presence that had gathered in anticipation of the Carlos Rico show. In the media room, Ferdinand had projected a full screen shot of Pedro Ribera with the contact number for the appeal printed in large letters above and below. Four seats were positioned in a line in front of the screen, with microphones on the desk in front of two of them. Carlos led the Alvés family to their seats and briefed Fernando and Almu.

"This is going to be emotional and I want the public to concentrate their sympathy, and therefore their attention, on Carmen. The press will try to get you to say something controversial; that is what they do. Please refrain from saying anything other than what we have agreed. Support Carmen. Carmen, I want you to tell your story, omitting the bits we have discussed. Remember, the purpose of this appeal is to find the kidnapper."

All three nodded their intention of complying with Carlos' wishes, though experience told him this was unlikely. Emotions usually got the better of people on such occasions, making them answer questions best left alone. It was down to Carlos to try to keep control of the appeal.

The camera crews had scrambled for the best positions when the doors were opened, with the lighting teams requiring their own police presence as old rivalries came to the fore. The front men prominently positioned themselves amongst the hacks, microphones at the ready. On a nod from Carlos, an unseen voice counted down from three. Carlos read his rapidly prepared speech.

"Good afternoon. I am Inspector Carlos Rico of the Alicante Police. I would like to ask for your assistance to find this man." He pointed to the large face on the screen behind. "He is Pedro Ribera, aged fifty. He was born in Madrid, but has spent most of his adult life in the Army. We believe that he is responsible for the kidnapping of two young people from Alicante airport on the afternoon of June 13th. Carmen Alvés was subsequently seriously assaulted and we believe that her brother, Sergio, has been murdered while in his charge."

The sound level in the room went through the roof as every journalist shouted their question at the inspector. Carlos held his hands up in a gesture designed to silence the crowd, but had to use the advantage given by the microphone to regain control of the appeal.

"Gentlemen, please. We believe that he was driving a green Land Rover with a blue right-hand front wing, license plates A 2264 CD, in and around the city since June 13th, and are appealing for anyone who may have seen this man or a Land Rover fitting our description to contact us."

Another clamour of questions was ignored as Carlos introduced Fernando Alvés.

"Mr Fernando Alvés, father of Carmen and Sergio."

The mob hushed in order to hear what Fernando Alvés had to say. Carlos had asked, via Luis Barreta, that the cameras concentrated on Carmen. She looked weak, vulnerable, and distressed, and this was what would convince the public to engage with the police appeal. Fernando Alvés looked close to tears as he spoke, with Almu sobbing uncontrollably on the other side of Carmen.

"This man has done unspeakable things to my children, and I beg anyone who has seen him, or even think they might have seen him, to come forward and help the police."

"Did he rape Carmen?"

Fernando Alvés had a look of panic on his face as the journalist asked the insensitive question. He looked to Carlos for guidance, but it was Carmen who answered.

"Yes. He raped me."

Chaos broke out in the room as the press turned into an unruly mob, baying for answers to their ever more pointed questions. Carlos insisted on calm or he would clear the room.

"We cannot confirm the death of Sergio Alvés at this point ..."

"I can." Carmen now stood with the microphone in her hand.

"The kidnapper told me that Sergio is dead. He claims it was due to an accident when we escaped. He shot us with a double-barrelled shotgun, raped me, and killed my brother. I thought that he had left me to die too when he collected the ransom."

Kidnapping, rape, an escape, shooting and a ransom were all too much for the men from the media. Carlos delivered one last warning in order that Carmen might finish.

"I called to Sergio, but he didn't reply. We had called to each other every day from our cells. During the last day, there was no reply. I knew he was dead. The kidnapper seemed different after that, almost apologetic. I don't know if he killed Sergio in the torture chamber, but ..."

This time Carlos finished the proceedings. There were details emerging that he was unaware of, and the appeal had delivered its message in dramatic fashion.

"That is all for now. Thank you", he called as he shepherded the Alvés family through the door behind the platform they had sat on. The appeal had never been intended as a press conference as the police knew too little to expose themselves to the full barrage of inevitable questions they would face. However, they needed the help of the public and fast if they were to catch Pedro Ribera, and this was the only option that would deliver rapid results. Chief

Inspector Roberto Martinez, who had watched from the sidelines, gave his opinion on the outcome.

"That went well, Carlos", he chided sarcastically.

"As well as we could have hoped for under the circumstances, sir."

"Let's man the phone lines and hope that something good comes of this."

Sergeant Christiano Marcos had arranged for the extra manpower required to handle the information gathered as a result of the televised appeal to be in place and fully briefed.

"We are going to receive three types of call; cranks, those seeking attention, and those who genuinely think they know something. If Pedro was seen walking down the Paseo with Napoleon, thank them and move on. The crime fans and lonely souls of the city will try to help, and shouldn't be dismissed without a hearing. If in doubt, consult a supervisor."

Christiano indicated that the supervisors make themselves known.

"Finally, there are those that have seen something that will help us. If they sound genuine, inform me. What we are looking for is a pattern, perhaps where several people report seeing him in the same area at the same time. If they ask for Carlos' autograph, tell them he can't write."

All laughed at this comment except for Carlos himself, who had entered the room behind his sergeant. The laughter stopped so quickly that Christiano didn't have to turn around to know who had just come in. He blushed slightly as he spoke to his inspector.

"The team are fully briefed, sir."

"So I have just heard, sergeant. I am going to interview Carmen Alvés. Keep me informed of any developments."

The scowl on his face meant that Christiano couldn't meet his gaze and he mumbled compliance as Carlos made to leave the room. He stopped at the door and turned to address his sergeant.

"For your information, I can write. I can also count. However, I can't play the piano. You are an investigator, deal in facts, comedy is not your forte."

Christiano wasn't entirely sure if he had been rebuked for his throwaway comment or the inspector was pulling his leg, so produced a weak smile of acknowledgement. He had been warned that working for Carlos Rico would lead to such moments. Carlos closed the door behind him and smiled.

He wasn't smiling when he entered Interview Room Three. Fernando Alvés sat by Carmen's side. He was a big man with receding hair that gave away his age as being in his mid-fifties. His body language said that he was used to getting his own way and wasn't going to be pushed around by anyone. Carmen on the other hand, had her mother's slight built, and her long, dark hair framed a pretty, delicate face. Carlos had doubts about what the father could contribute to this interview but let him stay in order that he could observe their relationship. Something wasn't right and because he couldn't put his finger on it, this bothered him.

"Carmen, you can have a female officer present during the interview if you wish. You may also have a lawyer present, but you are giving evidence as the victim of this crime and are under no suspicion of any wrongdoing."

"Ask your questions please, inspector. I am tired and need rest, but I understand the urgency for information that will help you to catch this man."

Fernando Alvés made to speak, but Carmen stopped him. Carlos had been warned by the doctor that Carmen was suffering from post-traumatic stress disorder and may break down at any time, so knew that he had to extract as much relevant information as he could before she reached this point. If she did, he would be denied access to her until she made a complete recovery, by which time she would have forgotten important information and Pedro Ribera would be languishing in Brazil.

"Carmen, let's start with the abduction at the airport. We have video footage of the Limousine pulling up outside and the man meeting you and Sergio as you emerged from the arrival's lounge."

"He said that Juan was sick and that my father had sent him to collect us."

"Mr Alvés, can you confirm that your chauffeur arrived to meet the wrong plane?"

"Yes. He was at least an hour late. He had been told to meet the flight, but it had been delayed."

"How would the bogus chauffeur know that Juan wasn't going to turn up?"

"I really don't know, inspector. Perhaps he was the one who made the call informing me that the flight was delayed."

"You didn't mention this call before, Mr Alvés."

"I'm sure you are wrong, inspector."

Carlos made a point of writing something in his notebook and glancing at Fernando Alvés to make sure he saw this. He returned to Carmen.

"You must have noticed that you weren't heading in the right direction as you left the airport?"

"We noticed nothing. When we got into the back of the Limousine, he sprayed a vapour into our faces and we passed out. When we awoke, we were tied together by a clever knot. If I moved, it tightened the rope around Sergio's neck and vice versa. We travelled for around two hours before he stopped to make a phone call to my father."

"Did you have any idea of where you were?"

"None whatsoever. He kept the blindfolds on until we were inside the hospital."

Carlos could scarcely believe his ears. They had been snatched, gassed, bound, and taken to a hospital within two hours of arriving at Alicante airport. This was a much more elaborate kidnapping than he had ever suspected and he needed help to decipher the volume of information he was getting. He excused himself and called Christiano.

"Get down to Interview Room Three now. Carmen Alvés is telling me a story that even a piano player would struggle to comprehend."

Christiano re-allocated his duties in the call centre and accepted the olive branch offered by Carlos. The inspector continued his questioning while making copious notes of the growing number of potential lines of enquiry as Carmen told her story.

"What made you think you were taken to a hospital, Carmen?"

"The trolleys, the sort of bed with wheels on they use in hospitals. He strapped us to those trolleys overnight such that we couldn't move. It hurt like hell."

"They are referred to as gurneys. Were they new?"

"Nothing was new. The hospital looked like it had been abandoned and there was litter everywhere. Even the bed was dirty, but after the gurney, it felt luxurious."

"Can you tell me anything more about the hospital? Maybe the location or what type of hospital it was?"

"That's easy, it was a psychiatric hospital."

"What makes you say that, Carmen?"

She smiled at the stupidity of the question.

"Because the windows had bars and the doors were made of steel. This was no more than a prison."

Carlos thought of the evidence trail for the chair in the video and remembered the mention of their use in such establishments. He watched Carmen closely and saw that she seemed to be relaxing as she unburdened herself of this information.

"Did he torture you?"

"He didn't make full use of the facilities, if that is what you're asking. Even he seemed to recoil in the presence of the apparatus of evil that placed housed.

"He started by taking us to the room with the green wall and made us read statements and ransom demands. That was the first time he struck Sergio. Well, I say the first time but he cut his throat with a large knife during the trip from the airport. I think Sergio managed to hit him and he was punished. It became very clear from the start that they were never going to be friends."

She turned to her father.

"Sergio was so brave. He stood up to him and was beaten for it."

This was the first sign of tears and Carlos decided to move on before the trickle became a flood. They had the rape on video and so he skipped this incident as it was guaranteed to take her beyond her bearable limit.

"Tell me about the escape. How did you get away?"

"I'm not exactly sure. The kidnapper brought me my dinner on a trolley, left my cell, and locked the door. A few moments later, I heard an almighty crash and my cell door was unlocked. I cowered in a corner thinking it was him, and was surprised when Sergio opened my door. He had somehow overpowered the kidnapper, though we never got to discuss this. Sergio told me that we had to get away before he regained consciousness and we ran to try and find the keys to the Land Rover."

"Can you describe the building you were running through?"

"It wasn't large and probably had only eight or ten wards. There was a kitchen with one corner cleaned for use and a large reception area. We couldn't find the keys and decided to make a run for it in hope of flagging down a passing car."

"What did the landscape outside of the hospital look like?"

"It was how I imagine the moon to look. It was no more than a desert. There were hills and valleys all around. Everything was brown sand and rock, there was no green to be seen anywhere. As we ran up the dirt track that led away from the hospital, I noticed that the rocks on one side of the road had layers of brown, red, and yellow; I know it's not relevant but it reminded me of the German flag. In other circumstances, it would have been interesting but we were running for our lives."

Fernando Alvés asked her if she wanted to stop but she refused.

"We had run maybe a kilometre up the track when we heard the shots."

"Was this the shotgun?"

"No. We think he was wearing a pistol when he was jumped by Sergio. In the excitement of the escape, he didn't think to take it from him. He used it to shoot the lock from the cell door."

"Were you near the end of the track?"

"I don't know. It was getting dark and when we heard the Land Rover start, we decided to take cover off the road until he passed. He knew that we couldn't have gone far and toyed with us."

"How did he toy with you?"

"He drove past us very noisily, almost certainly to frighten us. It worked. He then came back down the dirt track with his engine switched off so that he made no noise. He had one of those things that soldiers and hunters wear to see in the dark. We were caught in the middle of the road with nowhere to go. We jumped to our left but he had already seen us. That was when he used the shotgun."

"Were you running away?"

"No. It was too dangerous to run in the dark. There were cliffs and chasms. He shot us as we lay face down in a ditch. It was no more than a punishment for trying to escape. Sergio took the majority of the pellets."

The tears had begun to well in her eyes once again and Carlos realised that he was now pushing his luck.

"What happened next, Carmen?"

"He carried me to the car and returned for Sergio. I heard some shouting before he returned alone. I asked where Sergio was and he told me that there had been an accident and that he would return in the daylight the following morning to rescue him. I never saw Sergio again."

She could no longer hold back the tears as she thought of her final moments together with her brother. Fernando Alvés insisted that they call the interview to a close and Carlos had to agree. To continue would have been an interrogation. As they stood to leave, Carlos thanked Carmen and commented on how brave she had been. This caught her attention and she offered one last piece of information before she left. It was difficult to comprehend what she was saying among the sobs, but both investigators agreed that she said, "He said that he called a doctor to look at Sergio."

Christiano instantly picked up on the relevance of the doctor and said that he would ask Velasquez to speak to his mercenary informant in hope of identifying a doctor or field medic that might have worked with Pedro Ribera.

"Check Army records too. His connection might have been in the distant past," Carlos offered. "I am going to the university to talk to a scientist. The rock formation described by Carmen is unusual, and probably would be of interest to geologists. Get Ferdinand to find the whereabouts of the chairs that didn't go the police or prison service, and you talk to the health services and identify every psychiatric hospital ever built in the Valencia and Murcia regions. Put these with the results of the appeal and we will be able to cross-refer and locate where they were held."

All of a sudden, the advantage was swinging in their direction. The televised appeal produced a number of sightings of the vehicle in the vicinity of the road where the calls had been traced to and this established time frames around the movements of the kidnapper. A lady called to say that she was his estranged wife who hadn't seen him for over twenty years, and although her relevance to their enquiry seemed tenuous, the local department in Madrid were asked to have a chat with her about her absent husband.

The Taker himself was aware of the televised appeal and knew that his face was now known the length and breadth of Spain. Any escape would now cost him a lot more money due to its illegitimate nature and he wasn't pleased that his profits were being eaten into by the Fixer's cautiousness. There would have to be further recompense for his inconvenience.

His calls to the Fixer went unanswered and he was getting very frustrated. It was something totally forbidden in his line of work, but he saw no alternative but to contact the Colonel directly.

The secretary at Flying Dutchman PMC answered his call in the cagy manner he expected. She said that she would ask if there was a consultant available to speak with him and said that he should state the nature of his call. He replied that he had a problem in completing a sub-contract and he went under the name of the Taker.

The Colonel was far from pleased to hear from Pedro. This wasn't procedure.

"Taker, I hear that you have been the subject of a great deal of local attention. That was quite unprofessional, don't you think?"

"This was none of my doing Colonel. The Fixer is messing me about. I want to finish the contract as agreed."

"There are shades of Barcelona re-emerging, Taker. I don't think that we will be able to do business in the future."

Pedro had resigned himself to this outcome but his concerns were more immediate.

"I need to be out of this situation but I still have something belonging to the Fixer. What do you suggest I do? I can't maintain my current position for much longer."

"Wait for orders, Taker, and don't call me again. Otherwise I may have to find another sub-contractor to terminate our relationship."

Pedro felt abandoned, isolated, and, not for the first time in his life, scared of the unknown that was his future.

*****

The appeal had the desired result, with over twenty people claiming to have seen Pedro Ribera or his Land Rover in the Vinalopó Valley during the time of the kidnapping. Pedro was tall for a Spaniard of his age, and his vehicle had the unusual blue wing repair, so their attempts at remaining unseen were inherently flawed. Sightings were also reported in Santa Pola and Alicante on the day of the drop, all pointing to the location where the Alvés siblings had been held being nearby.

Those caught up in the drop, wittingly or not, confirmed that the man in the photograph was the same man they had met for the only time that day. The bread deliveryman and café owner in Arenales, as well as the street dweller in Alicante had no hesitation in pointing to Pedro Ribera when presented with a group of photographs. The drug user who had delivered the package to the house said no different. Pedro Ribera was based somewhere between the town of Villena and the coast, with his detected phone calls indicating he was in the proximity of the main road between Alicante and Madrid. The results of the other lines of investigation would help to narrow this down.

Carlos Rico took the opportunity to go home on his way to the university. He didn't expect to find Marta there as it was a working day, but her presence was apparently his fault.

"It was just like after Raúl Berbegal. Everyone saw the televised appeal and it brought it all back."

"I'm sorry. That was never the intention."

"For God's sake Carlos, can't you see that you have just made it worse? The media hear 'Carlos

Rico' and know that there isn't going to be a dull moment. I was sent home because members of the press were trying to get me to comment on something that I know nothing about. They were bombarding my office with calls. My boss was livid."

"I don't know what to say. Do I apologise for doing my job?"

Marta held her bemused husband and remembered the number of days until his retirement.

"No, Carlos. Please do your job as you always have done. Maybe try to get involved in less controversial cases."

He had no acceptable answer to this request and therefore didn't attempt to reply. They held each other for a few minutes before she volunteered to iron him a fresh shirt while he showered.

"When did you last sleep?"

"On this type of case, I get more sleep than in a normal day. We spend most of our time waiting for someone else to do something."

She knew this wasn't true but accepted his lie.

"Where are you going now? Have you eaten?"

"I had breakfast at the Commissary. I'm going to the university. I need to know about rock strata."

Sometimes it was better not to ask.

On arrival at the university, Carlos discovered that the senior members of the Department of Geological Studies had departed for a conference in Madrid. He found a lone PhD student and thought his journey was destined to come to naught.

'Chico', as he insisted on being called, didn't inspire confidence. He was nearly two metres in height, though Carlos doubted that he weighed more than eighty kilos. His clothes said he wasn't doing his doctorate just to kill time and so Carlos was prepared to treat him as a serious academic.

"I need some help. I am involved in an enquiry that involves rocks."

"I saw the appeal, inspector; emotive stuff. How can I help?"

"The girl described the location where she was held as having layers of different coloured rock. The light was poor but she described them as black or brown, red, and yellow. Is this possible?"

"Yes. We are sitting on something we geologists call the Betic Cordillera. It is the result of the meeting of the African continent and the Iberian Peninsula, and it has produced some remarkable results.

"The black colour is the result of organic material crystallizing in igneous rock. The mineral magnetite, an iron oxide, is mostly responsible for this. Copper Sulphide causes the quartz in sandstone to appear yellowish in certain light, and another type of iron oxide, or rust, as you may know it, forms hematite, which has a distinctly reddish tinge.

"Black, red and yellow layers, or strata, occur very rarely together. This means that people like me are attracted to them as we can study many different aspects of our science in one field trip. I spent last summer on such an expedition, not twenty kilometres from here."

Carlos' heart skipped a beat at such at such positive feedback. He envisaged pulling teeth to get anything near as good, but Chico was coming through for him.

"Can you show me exactly where your expedition took place?"

Chico walked to a whiteboard and pulled on string that dangled on one side. A map appeared from above the board. Carlos recognised the Mediterranean coast of the Alicante region but the relief map was bereft of the features with which he was familiar. Chico produced a laser pointer from an unseen source and explained.

"We are here, and the Vinalopó Valley is here."

Carlos followed the red spot on the map and nodded.

"I gave this lecture to a group of undergrads yesterday. I am basing my final paper on this region so I got to know it very well over the past two years. The rock formation you are looking for is to be found in this area."

Another sweep of the red dot circumnavigated an area heavy in contour lines. Chico reached into a drawer and produced a driver's map. Carlos was now on familiar territory as he recognised roads and towns. The university man used the long, thin index finger of his right hand to point to the area around the small town of Agost.

"You may know this as the location for the filming of the western classic, 'The Magnificent Seven'. It was used because of its resemblance to the deserts of Mexico."

"Can you narrow it down any further?"

"I'm afraid not. The chaotic nature of the strata in this valley makes it unique. Without more information, anything I say would be guesswork."

"One last question and you don't have to answer it if you don't want to. If you wanted to hide in this valley, where would you choose?"

Chico thought for a moment and then pointed to a particular ridge on the east of the valley.

"This area is particularly barren. There is no reason for anyone other than geologists to go there. If I didn't want to be found, this is where I would hide."

Carlos thanked Chico and left for the Commissary, full of hope.

The large map in the incident room now had two distinct sets of markings; red crosses for reported sightings and blue triangles indicating the locations of psychiatric hospitals. The inspector took the green marker pen and, with an exaggerated sense of theatre, drew a circle around the area identified by his new geologist friend. Only one blue triangle lay within the circle. Everyone in the room froze as it dawned on them that they had found the location they had been looking for. For emphasis, Carlos stabbed it with a fat finger.

"This is where he held them."

In 'where he held them', Pedro pressed 'accept call' on his phone and hoped for good news. The Fixer's voice had an urgency previously missing. Pedro wondered if the Colonel had been in touch with him, but held back from asking. The only thing that was important was the termination of their business.

"The police are close. You must move."

"Where do you want me to deliver the money?"

"That isn't important at the moment. You must leave now. They know where you are."

"Every cop and customs official in Spain knows what I look like, it is going to cost me a large percentage of what you are paying me just to leave the country."

The Fixer was waiting for this opportunity to make his new proposal.

"I am prepared to double your fee if you do another little job for me."

"Two hundred thousand Euros? What little job?"

Pedro didn't like the sound of this development but an additional hundred thousand Euros couldn't be dismissed without being given serious consideration.

"I want you to go to another location. It isn't far. A young woman lives alone in a country house. She is potentially useful to us and must be kept locked away until I have struck a deal."

"I'm not going to kill anyone. I told you that the boy was an accident."

"I believe you and I don't want you to harm her. I need you to detain her and wait for me to tell you when it is safe to leave. This is purely a distraction that will allow the money to be delivered and then allow you to depart the country unseen."

Pedro's mind reeled at the thought of repeating the past week and his initial reaction was to say 'no'. He could take his share and leave with a relatively clear conscience. The Fixer read his thoughts and intervened in the mental struggle Pedro was experiencing.

"Pedro, remember that I am making this call primarily to warn you that the police are coming to the clinic. I am on your side and you have ten million reasons why I wouldn't want anything bad to happen to you. Think about it, but don't take too long; the cars have already left Alicante."

Pedro was once again sweating as he analysed what he had just been told. His flight instinct was fully engaged.

"I want two hundred thousand more."

The Fixer seemed to be thinking about this proposal but in reality was letting the clock run down in order to increase the pressure on his Taker.

"I said I would do it for two hundred thousand more, you will still get over nine and a half million."

Pedro couldn't do the simple sum to arrive at the correct figure because his mind was being affected by adrenalin. He started to put on his bike leathers as he waited for the Fixer's reply.

"Go to Hondon de las Nieves and call me when you are there."

The line went dead and Pedro wasted no time in hoisting his rucksack onto his back and clipping a large grip full of money onto the rack at the rear of the trail bike. He didn't bother locking the clinic; the police would knock the door down. He accelerated up the dirt track at a speed he knew was reckless but now was the time to take risks. He almost lost control at the bend in the road where he had caught Sergio and Carmen and once again cursed the spirit of the young man for this effect he had on him.

"No way, Sergio. Leave me alone," he said from within a cloud of dust.

As he reached the tarmac at the end of the track, he roughly pulled the bike to the left and skidded across the road. He stopped for a second to steady his jangling nerves and was alarmed to hear sirens. They were almost upon him. He accelerated so hard that his front wheel left the ground. It bounced twice, by which time he was doing over eighty kilometres an hour in the opposite direction to the approaching police cars. He cut the blind bends all the way to the dual carriageway and his luck held. Once on the main road, he put another ten kilometres on the odometer before stopping to find out exactly where he was meant to be going.

The GPS on the handlebars indicated two adjacent villages called Hondon de las Nieves and Hondon de los Frailes, and Pedro couldn't remember which he was meant to go to. He didn't want to sit at the side of the road in case the police were looking for his bike, so pulled in behind a deserted factory, and called the Fixer.

The Fixer, with his garbled tones, replied surprisingly quickly.

"You got away before they came then?"

"Only just. Whoever your source is needs to give us a bit more time to play with. Tell me the details of what you want me to do for an additional two hundred thousand Euros."

The Fixer didn't miss the declared cost of further dealings but it didn't seem to bother him.

"On the road between the two Hondon villages, heading east, there is a garden centre. Travel north from the garden centre and take the second road on the left. About one kilometre up this road there is a house. The name on the gate is 'Los Aves'. A woman called Anna-Maria lives there alone. I want you to gain access to the house and tie her up. No harm is to come to her. I will contact her on your phone. You are to let her speak to me and I will tell her what is happening. A few hours later, I will come and collect the money from you. Do you understand?"

Pedro Ribera could see the light at the end of the tunnel and this raised his spirits.

"North from the garden centre and second left. After one kilometre, a house called Los Aves. Secure the woman and wait for the call."

"Good. This will all be over in a matter of hours."

"Why is this woman so important? What does she know that can harm us?"

"She is merely a pawn, she knows nothing. It is almost as important to me as it is to you that you get out of the country quickly and quietly. You are the only person who can link me to the Alvés kidnapping and murder. I can use this woman as leverage to guarantee you safe passage. She has a relative who will not want her harmed. He will arrange your escape. However, I warn you, be careful with the woman. I have been informed that she can sometimes be a bit 'odd'."

"You said 'odd', what do you mean by 'odd'?"

"I have no more time to discuss this. Do as you are told and we will be done with this whole sordid affair very soon." The Fixer cut the conversation in his usual abrupt manner and Pedro followed the brief he had been given.

The lane leading up to Los Aves had no other houses, with vineyards on both sides of the road for as far as the eye could see. A clump of Mediterranean pine and false pepper trees gave away the location of the house, and Pedro stopped his bike one hundred metres short of it. He removed his helmet and leathers and produced a pair of binoculars from his rucksack. There didn't appear to be anyone moving in the house, so he closed to within the surrounding trees before looking again.

This time he saw her. She was a tall, dark-haired, attractive woman of around forty. She was simply dressed and busy mixing the contents of a baking bowl. The side door to the house was wide open so there was no need to force an entry. This seemed too easy to Pedro, so he waited another ten minutes in order to make sure all was as it looked. Anna-Maria continued to prepare her cakes for the oven and spoke to no one. The Fixer was right; she was alone.

When he grabbed her from behind, her shock was absolute. She jumped as her tranquil domestic afternoon suddenly took a frightening turn. Pedro used his superior strength to pin her to the wall as he told her what was happening.

"I'm not going to harm you. When I release you, I don't want you to scream. I am going to tie you up and we are going to wait for a phone call. The caller will talk to you, he will come here to collect something, and then I will leave. There is nothing to worry about, Anna-Maria."

She analysed his words before responding.

"How do you know my name?"

"I know a great deal about you Anna-Maria."

This was something he would later regret. She agreed that she would present no problems and when he removed his weight from her, offered her hands to be tied. He searched his pockets for the cable-ties he had used so often and discovered that he had dropped them somewhere between the bike and the house. He looked at the meek and frightened woman and thought that they were overkill.

"Do you have any rope?"

She pointed at the cupboard under the sink.

"There is a washing line in there."

Pedro retrieved the washing line and tied her hands together before knotting the other end around the arm of the nearby settee. She looked quite unbothered by what had just happened to her and Pedro thought this strange. He expected panic and worry, but maybe this was the 'odd' behaviour the Fixer had warned him about. How did the Fixer know about her?

His own thoughts were interrupted by the ringing of his phone.

"Is she ok? Is she panicking? She is sensitive."

"Don't worry. I haven't harmed a hair on her pretty head."

"I need to talk to her."

"Ok. Give me a minute."

He untied her wrists and handed her his mobile phone. Her face lit up when she heard the voice speaking to her and Pedro strained to hear what was being said, without success. Anna-Maria uttered a succession of 'yes' and 'no' responses, with one period in the middle of the call where she looked quite sad. She finished with an 'ok' and handed the phone back to Pedro.

Pedro listened in case the Fixer had something more to say to him, but the call had been ended. Anna-Maria offered her hands to be tied once again and Pedro asked what was happening.

"We wait."

"Wait for what?"

"It will all be over soon, Pedro."

Now, it was his turn to panic.

"How do you know my name?"

"I know a great deal about you, Pedro."

The sweating returned as the kidnapper felt he was being played with. He checked Anna-Maria's bindings one more time before he went to the kitchen to make himself a coffee. His nerves were jangling, causing him to spill more of the coffee powder over the worktop than into his cup. He needed this thing to come to an end.

The cloud of dust raised by the four police cars as they raced down the dirt track to the clinic didn't cause them to moderate their speed. The front car had barely stopped when Carlos and Christiano threw themselves out into the car park, closely followed by the rest of the investigative team and two cars of uniformed officers. Carlos stopped for a few seconds to take in what was in front of them.

The sign above the entrance had lost several letters to the elements, but for those who knew what they were looking for, this was the Agost Clinic for Mental Health. The front double doors were open and Carlos warned that they should proceed with caution.

"He might still be in the building. Revolvers in hand, I want a full search of every room in this hospital. Be careful not to damage potential evidence. Our first search will be to establish that we are alone. After that, we will identify which rooms have been used recently and carry out a more thorough search for anything that might tell us what went on here and where we might find Pedro Ribera. Mendez, find out where forensics are?"

Sergeant Christiano Marcos allocated search areas to the attending police and they gingerly entered the building. The reception area, dust notwithstanding, looked like the staff had just popped out for a few moments. Documents, and even a coffee mug, sat on the desk as if the secretary had gone to powder her nose. The main corridor had the expected ten doors leading off, five on either side. As they reached each door, Christiano allocated an officer to lead the entry procedure and declare it clear before the rest continued down the corridor, repeating the clearance process. After two nervous minutes, he announced that they were alone. Carlos then barked that they state whether there rooms had been used recently and five declared that there were signs of activity. A brief scan of these fitted what Carmen had told Carlos; a ward each for her and Sergio, Pedro's quarters, a kitchen and a common room that must have been the green room where the first video was made. There was no sign of the torture chamber seen in the video.

"For now, we ignore the wards. They were used to incarcerate Sergio and Carmen. We concentrate on the kidnapper's quarters, the kitchen, and the common room. That is where he spent most of his time and therefore that is where we are more likely to find something that will tell us where he has gone. Get someone to look at the car park and immediate dirt track area. They are looking for signs of what kind of transport he used to leave. The sand and dust in this area will have covered anything more than a few hours old, but I can feel that he was here not too long before we arrived."

Christiano knew better than to question the nose of an experienced detective and set the search in place awaiting the men in white. He returned to tell Carlos that his orders were being followed and found him in deep thought.

"Sir?"

Carlos slowly turned to his sergeant as though continuing an unfinished conversation.

"Why here, Christiano? Why this hell-hole?"

"Because of its remote location, sir."

"No, Christiano. That is not the reason. The geologist at the university knows this area like the back of his hand but he never mentioned this place. To know of the very existence of the Agost Clinic for Mental Health suggests that the kidnapper was a member of staff, a patient or someone involved in bringing supplies here.

"Get Ferdinand to find the complete history of this place from the day it was built to the discharge of the last patient. I want a list of every staff member who ever worked here and every patient. I need a list of suppliers and all of their employees. And tell him that I want these lists today. He has my full authority to cajole, bully, or threaten anyone who refuses to give full co-operation."

Christiano wasn't as convinced as his boss, but at least this would rule out a lot of dead-end leads in one fell swoop.

Velasquez had won the task of sweeping Pedro Ribera's quarters for preliminary evidence and had trouble containing himself as he approached the inspector with gifts in hand.

"What have you found, Velasquez?"

"I'm no medic, but I would bet from the smell that this syringe contained a painkiller like Novocaine. There are parts of a First-Aid kit all over the floor as though someone in a great deal of pain was looking for something."

"This could have been used on Sergio for whatever his injuries were" Christiano suggested.

"Or perhaps the kidnapper himself used it after being jumped by Sergio. Was there any blood on the floor?"

"Yes sir, though it looks like someone had half-heartedly tried to clean it."

"Leave it for forensics. What about the kitchen?"

"A kettle that had been boiled within the hour, I would say" a uniformed officer reported.

"So he's not far away. Tracks?"

Mendez said that a two-wheeled vehicle had left recent marks in the car park.

"That bloody trail bike again. So we can assume that he has abandoned the Land Rover and we are looking for the same trail bike he used when he gave us a cheery wave at the castle. Tell traffic to pull in every man over one metre eighty and fifty years old on a trail bike in the communities of Valencia and Murcia. He's not going to get away this time."

However, it wasn't traffic or Ferdinand who made the next breakthrough; it was Constable Ferrera. He had found the connection Carlos sought and he could barely contain himself as he half-ran, file in hand, towards his inspector. The crowd of officers around the inspector parted as though they knew what he held. They stood in silence as he spoke.

"You're not going to believe this, sir," he said.

Carlos was excited but tried to hide this.

"What won't I believe, constable," he said with poorly disguised hope.

"Fernando Alvés daughter was a patient in this hospital."

Pedro also had difficulty in believing what he saw on return from the kitchen. Anna-Maria was still tied to the settee, but she was completely naked. He froze in the doorway as he tried to make sense of what he saw and failed to do so.

"What's going on? How did you do that?"

Anna-Maria smiled at him and parted her legs, fully exposing herself to him.

"I love games. I especially love games when you tie me up. I'm so helpless, I can't defend myself."

She said these words in such a lascivious manner that it was impossible to believe she had ever been helpless. Pedro felt defenceless; she was in complete control. She tugged at the bindings on her wrists and they held tight.

"How did you get your clothes off with your hands tied? It's not possible."

She tugged again at the ropes as if to confirm what he had said. Her facial expression changed to one of mock panic.

"You're going to take advantage of me, aren't you? That's why you tied me up."

"No" he protested, "I mean you no harm. I'm waiting for the other man and then I will leave."

Pedro was well out of his comfort zone. Barcelona was bad, Sergio was even worse, and he had no idea of where this was leading but he knew that he didn't want to go there. She crossed her legs in a burlesque manner and smiled at him again.

"Am I not your sort, Pedro? Do you like little girls, or perhaps little boys? That's it; you're a paedophile. You can't handle a full-bodied woman. I frighten you. You can't do it."

"Stop this, you bitch. I'm not a paedophile and I don't like little boys."

He knew he sounded far too defensive and wished that he had just walked away. She once again pushed her legs apart and thrust her pubic region at him, smiling all the while.

"Too much for you, soldier? Would you be interested if I were black? You like African women, I hear."

How did she know all this about him? Now she was trying to lick her own breasts and he didn't know what to do to stop her.

"Is Mister Floppy in town, Pedro? Is the little soldier not standing to attention?"

Pedro hadn't thought about sex since the rape of Carmen, and even that was business. Only then did he realise that he was aroused by Anna-Maria and her teasing. He kicked off his boots, stepped out of his trousers and pants, and approached the temptress with his rampant penis in his hand. It may have been the result of the tensions of the past week or even attributed to the sexually arousing nature of Anna-Maria's floorshow, but either way he knew that he needed satisfaction, now. He would show this bitch that he was all red-blooded heterosexual male.

He stood in front of her and proudly displayed his erection. Her eyes were firmly focussed on it as she drew him towards her. She grasped his erection with her left hand and clamped her lips around it. He gasped with pleasure as she took it into her hot, wet mouth and closed his eyes as waves of pleasure shuddered through his body. The fact that she had held him with an untied hand suddenly dawned on him, but it was too late.

Anna-Maria had the rope around his neck. She had managed to do this with his penis still in her mouth, making sure that his attention was not on what her hands were doing. A variation on the classic distraction technique, she thought. As the washing line tightened around his windpipe, his hands instinctively rose in an attempt to remove it. The temptress stood as she thrust Pedro to the ground between her legs. His face was centimetres from what he had so desperately sought moments before, but his thoughts were on the rope tightening around his neck. He looked up at her and considered begging for his life. He had never before asked for mercy and instead asked a question.

"Why are you doing this?" he growled as his throat closed. "Who are you?"

The irony of the last thing that Pedro Roberto Martin Ribera would hear as his world became a kaleidoscope of coloured lights around the face of Anna-Maria almost made him smile. It was perfect.

"You killed my brother. My name is Anna-Maria Alvés."

At that moment, not twenty kilometres away, the words of Ferrera were being challenged by his comrades.

"Carmen was a patient in this clinic?" Christiano said in amazement.

"No. Fernando Alvés had another daughter. Anna-Maria, born 27 February 1975, Alicante. Father, Fernando Alvés, 18 years old, son of a rich

253

industrialist. Her mother was Anna Consuela Villa, 15 years old, daughter of a neighbouring farmer. It seems the families covered up the birth and the farmer and family moved away soon afterwards. She was spoiled and it seems that she was a wild child from a young age. Her file says that she became sexually promiscuous at twelve and had to be taken out of school for giving sexual favours to the boys. She was then tutored privately, with little more success as she tried to seduce her male tutors, and became aggressive with the female replacements when they rejected her less than subtle advances. The final straw was when she was found performing oral sex on the handyman at her grandfather's home."

"Pepe Baccaral?" Christiano asked.

"Yes" an amazed Ferrera answered. "How could you possibly know that?"

Christiano stated that he was the security guard at Alicante Airport who initially brought their attention to the kidnapping of Sergio and Carmen.

"This is all very neat" Carlos commented. "Carry on Ferrera."

"After biting a man who refused to have sex with her in a toilet in a shopping precinct, Anna-Maria was assessed as being violently unstable and a grave risk to the public. She was taken into care in the Agost Clinic for Mental Health, aged thirteen, in 1988. And here she remained until the clinic closed in September 2008. There are no records here of what happened to her after that date."

"Well done, Velasquez. Get onto the Department of Health and find out what happened to Anna-Maria Alvés. I also want to know why this clinic closed.

Mendez, get back to Alicante and bring Fernando Alvés into the Commissary. He has a lot of questions to answer."

"What do we do now, sir?" Christiano asked.

"We continue to look for Pedro Ribera and ten million Euros. Do you think that it is a coincidence that he left just before we got here? I, for one, do not. Coincidences should always be ruled out by detectives; they are put in place by those trying to misdirect us. If this is the case, then who warned the kidnapper we were coming?"

"No one outside of the team knew. We came directly from the brief, so no one had any time to let it slip. Surely you don't think we have a mole?"

Carlos didn't like to consider this as a possibility. He had personally recruited each and every member of his team and had complete confidence in all of them. However, the coincidence, and his confidence in his team pointed to a contradiction.

"We are missing something and it will become obvious in due course. In the meantime, let's see what Pedro Ribera has left behind."

Small fragments of green material confirmed that the common room had indeed been the studio in which the first video had been filmed. Chalk marks on the floor indicated that something had been set up with a great deal of precision and this supported Mendez' theory about the degree of skill required to superimpose a background on a video shoot. The kitchen produced no more than one would expect to find in a room built for cooking. They quickly dismissed this as a source of anything that would be of any use in finding their man.

The room identified as Pedro Ribera's quarters held many items that might give a clue to his whereabouts, and just as many red herrings. Abandoned maps were scrutinised and dismissed; they contained the same information as that plotted on their own incident board. Clothing and personal items would be used in evidence to prove he was the kidnapper but were of no help in finding him. The fact that he fled on a bike indicated that he would be carrying very little; after all, he had ten million Euros that would leave little room for anything else.

After an hour, Carlos made the decision that their best hope of finding Pedro Ribera was through Fernando Alvés. Forensics were left with the task of gathering and classifying whatever was left and putting it into a form that was presentable in a courtroom.

"One last thing, Felipe."

The Senior Forensics Officer hated Carlos' 'last things'. He turned with a resigned look and waited for the sucker punch.

"Sergio Alvés is buried somewhere around here. We need to find his grave, disinter him, and bring his body back to the mortuary. We need to know how he died and only he can tell us."

Felipe raised his eyebrows in acknowledgement and returned to the task in hand without uttering a word. This was the lot of a Forensics Officer.

"Oh, and as you know, there is a dungeon-type room that doubles up as a torture chamber in or around this building somewhere. I'd like to see it, if you don't mind, Felipe."

"If I find the Golden Fleece in my search, do I tell you or Jason and his Argonauts?"

"Thank you, Felipe."

On return to the Commissary, they found Fernando Alvés waiting in the interview room and he was far from pleased at being there. Both he and his lawyer jumped to their feet and protested, and Carlos dismissed both with a bored look. They saw that their protests were falling on deaf ears and the lawyer eventually asked his client to sit down.

"What is the meaning of this outrage, inspector? It is totally insensitive to drag my client away from his family when they need him most."

"We have found where Sergio and Carmen were held."

"My God, where is it?"

Fernando Alvés had a look a shock on his face as he asked the question.

"It is somewhere you know very well, Mr Alvés; the Agost Clinic for Mental Health. Why didn't you tell us about Anna-Maria?"

The lawyer became very animated as he spoke into Fernando Alvés' ear. They had a heated argument expressed totally in hisses and exchanged glances that initially indicated that the lawyer felt betrayed, and then that Fernando Alvés was paying his wages.

"My client fails to see the relevance of his first daughter to what has happened to his other two children."

"Sergio and Carmen were held in the same remote institution where Anna-Maria was detained for twenty years and you don't see this as being rather peculiar?

This clinic was located in a place that was chosen for its obscurity. Would you like to tell me about Anna-Maria?"

Another discussion between lawyer and client resulted in Fernando Alvés nodding in agreement with whatever his brief had said. He straightened himself into a self-righteous posture before he spoke.

"I know how precious your time is inspector, so if you tell me what you know, I won't delay you by revealing facts that are of no interest to you."

Carlos had seen this ploy too often to be fooled. Fernando Alvés wanted to give away as little information as he had to, but Carlos wasn't prepared to play his game.

"Just take it from the very start, Mr Alvés." He referred to his notes. "I have taken you away from your family when they need you most. The least I can do is let you tell the full story."

Fernando Alvés' smile was forced as he continued.

"We were young and exploring life, Anna Consuela was the daughter of a local farmer and I got her pregnant. My father's money made the shame that would have fallen on both families go away, and when the baby was born, she came to live at my father's house. She always knew that I was her father, and we told her that her mother died in childbirth. Her early life was as perfect as any child could have wished for, and everything seemed to be idyllic until the calls started to come in from the school.

"Anna-Maria had developed tendencies that were proving disruptive in school, so we brought her home and hired private tutors to look after her education.

None of these teachers managed to communicate with her and I think this is when she started having problems integrating socially."

Carlos allowed Fernando Alvés to paint his sanitised picture of Anna-Maria's early life, as it bore little relevance to what followed.

"Then, there was an incident in a shopping precinct. No one is quite sure what exactly happened, but the result was Anna-Maria bit a man and the police were called. She was subjected to psychiatric assessment and the recommendation was that she be taken to a clinic for further assessment and a short period of treatment."

"This clinic was none other than the Agost Clinic for Mental Health, Mr Alvés?"

In response to Carlos' question, the lawyer's nod to Fernando Alvés indicated that there was little point in lying about something the police already knew.

"Yes."

"What happened to Anna-Maria in the clinic?"

"She was a young girl in a mental institution full of people with real problems. She was scared and she lashed out at the system that thought it perfectly acceptable to put a thirteen year old girl into the same place as adults who had been mad all their lives."

The political incorrectness of his words made him stop for a minute, during which no one spoke. After a few deep breaths, he continued.

"She was declared an incompatible patient after she apparently attacked other inmates, and was removed into a separation ward. The separation ward didn't just keep her away from the other patients; it also left her in one-on-one situations with unscrupulous members of staff. I believe that they are now uncovering a culture of malpractice, common among members of staff in such places, but this is of little consolation to Anna-Maria."

"Do you mean she was abused in the clinic?"

"Abused? She was raped on a daily basis by nurses who were being paid a lot of money to protect her. She was so afraid that she ran away several times."

"Her records show that she was complicit in her own abuse. In fact it is documented that she instigated most of it."

"She was thirteen and mentally ill. She didn't know what she was doing."

Fernando Alvés was on his feet and shouting. He realised that he had said the words he had been dancing around, hoping not to have to admit that she was the real problem. It was too late, and obvious by the file on the desk in front of the inspector that he knew the recorded facts.

"They attributed her actions to a number of unpronounceable conditions and stabilised her using medication. She had become so violent that they enforced what they called a six-man door opening procedure. This involved three strong men holding her down while another administered her medication, with a doctor and a psychiatrist on hand to assess any complications. When the medical staff were satisfied all was well, they evacuated her cell and the nurses holding her did so in a regimented fashion; releasing legs, arms and then head in that order as they bolted for the door.

She wasn't allowed shoes due to her tendency to kick anyone who came within range. For nearly two years, she was nothing more than a zombie. I visited every week until she left the clinic."

"Where is she now?"

"When the clinic closed, the system wanted nothing to do with her, so I bought her a house. It is in a quiet location and she has a full-time private nurse. I still visit her every week, and she is unrecognisable from the angst-ridden teenager she once was. She is living a happy, balanced life, and the nurse ensures that she takes the medication required to make this so. She was mentally ill, not stupid."

At Los Aves, Anna-Maria admired the fruits of her labours. Pedro Ribera lay on her living room floor, having died in a manner he could never have predicted. His face was blue, his eyes were bulging, and his tongue hung from his mouth, but the look on his face wasn't one of unhappiness. He had faced death many times but never expected it would come at the hands of a naked woman. Anna-Maria fondled the penis so recently ready to penetrate her, before throwing his discarded trousers over his exposed parts.

"Shame" she said aloud. "I could have had some fun with him if he hadn't murdered my Sergio."

She kicked the body at her feet, returned to the kitchen, and draped her apron over her otherwise naked body. The wooden spatula lay on the worktop where it fell when Pedro surprised her. She inspected it for cleanliness and, satisfied that it hadn't been tainted by what had occurred since being dropped, returned to mixing her cakes as though the past hour had never happened.

Once she was happy that the oven was at the correct temperature, she placed the cake on the second shelf, put her clothes back on, and undid the rope from around Pedro's neck. She admired the converted washing line, as she recalled many such tethers. She had been tied up so many times in her life that she had become an expert in extracting herself from anything other than the very best the market had to offer. The nurses often referred to her as 'Houdini', though she never knew who he or she was. She saw the opportunity for some fun with Pedro and took it. Did that make her mad?

In the Commissary, Carlos was being reminded of Fernando Alvés' rights by his lawyer.

"I must insist that you either charge my client with a crime or release him this instant."

Christiano referred to his watch and raised his eyebrows at his inspector indicating that they had exceeded the time limit for a 'voluntary' interview. Carlos had one last request.

"Mr Alvés, I need to know where Anna-Maria is and the name of her nurse."

"Anna-Maria and her nurse are currently in Portugal. The nurse has family there and they go to visit two or three times a year. The smell of the ocean invigorates Anna-Maria."

"I still need a contact number."

"I can give you the home number of the nurse, but as I said, she isn't there."

"You don't have an emergency contact number?"

"If there were to be an emergency, inspector, I wouldn't be calling my mentally ill daughter to tell her, would I?"

Carlos knew he was being toyed with but was unable to force the issue any further at this time. He pushed a notepad and pencil in front of Fernando Alvés and indicated that he wanted a number. Fernando Alvés referred to the mobile phone that he was now familiar with and copied a number. As he stood to leave, Carlos gave him some advice.

"Mr Alvés, don't leave town. We will be speaking again very soon."

Fernando Alvés looked as though he were about to say something but his brief grasped his upper arm and led him from the room.

"What's he hiding, sir?"

"That's exactly what we are going to find out, Christiano."

Ferdinand had followed the brief from his inspector and produced a comprehensive list of former employees, patients and service suppliers to the clinic. He also had the short but very dark history of the Agost Clinic for Mental Health.

"It was opened in 1940, just after the civil war. It was initially used to house ex-prisoners from both Republican and Nationalist jails who had been subjected to systematic abuse and torture, some for as long as three years. The suspicion is that they were 'the unheard'; people who could implicate others now in power as having carried out atrocities during the civil war, and had to be removed from society. They were locked up and medicated into oblivion until they had no memory of what they once knew. Some died, and others survived, at least physically.

"By the nineteen fifties, it had become a mainstream clinic for mental health, though some of the practices were distinctly nineteenth century. Electric shock treatment was common, and there were rumours, unsubstantiated of course, that the performance of lobotomies continued into the nineteen seventies. As the press become less restricted after the death of Franco, it was getting ever more difficult to perpetuate the old ways as questions were beginning to be asked.

"Regardless, it survived until 2008, when it was closed, not because of horrific malpractice, but on financial grounds.

"There is no one on any of the personnel lists that has done anything to merit our attention. The institution may have abused Anna-Maria Alvés for twenty years, but not for the last seven."

Carlos thanked Ferdinand for eliminating a strong line of enquiry. Felipe and his Forensics team had returned an initial report, and once again, it told the investigators nothing that they didn't already know. What they could confirm is that Pedro Ribera was the same man who botched the Barcelona kidnapping five years before.

"Partial prints are a match, and I'm sure that when the DNA samples are returned, they will eliminate any doubts. We found your torture chamber and I'm not too sure that you, or anyone else, would really want to see it. I can confirm that it has been used recently."

Carlos shuddered and tasked Ferdinand with liaising with the team in the north to ascertain if they might have anything that could indicate where Pedro Ribera might retreat. The Advanced Treatment Room was at the mercy of the men in white, and Velasquez's mercenary informant refused to co-operate on the subject of a possible doctor, the old-boys network closing ranks on this occasion. However, a lead about the missing medic came from an unlikely source. When Carlos was told that he had a call from Scotland Yard, he was expecting a nil return.

"Inspector Rico, I'm Detective Sergeant Rowlings from the Serious Crime Squad at Scotland Yard. I've been told that you were making enquiries about the Flying Dutchman PMC."

"Yes, sergeant; Do you have something for me?"

"A number of their ex-employees have made themselves known to us from time to time, usually after the Flying Dutchman has disposed of their services. They are mostly ex-Army types who are seeking a new career using the only skills they know. We have formed a dossier on them and we have four men of Spanish origin who have been involved with Colonel Meerkerk's organisation in recent years. I'll fax you through the details."

Carlos thanked the man in London and made his way to the fax machine, coffee in hand. Within ten minutes, an eight-page fax with the promised details sat on the desk in front of the grateful inspector.

Pedro Ribera wasn't one of the four men whose details Carlos had, but Alejandro Basseta was. A former career soldier, he trained as a paramedic and served the Spanish army with distinction. After retiring from the official military, he worked with at least two different Private Military Companies, and the indications were that he could have served alongside Pedro Ribera. What made him extra interesting was that he lived only ninety kilometres away in Albacete.

"Get the car, Christiano. We're going to Albacete."

Before he left the office, he shouted to Ferrera.

"Find me the nurse who is looking after Anna-Maria Alvés. If they're in Portugal, I'm the Queen of Sheba. Before you do that, find Ferdinand and tell him I want to know all about Fernando Alvés recent finances. Tell him I said to use every means at his disposal."

The drive to Albacete helped to clear the heads of the investigators and allow Carlos to conveniently forget that he had virtually ordered one of his DCs to hack into Alvés bank details. Sometimes it was easy to get too close to a case and this clouded judgement. The rolling roads of the Spanish interior gave them time to reflect on what they knew.

"Do you think the clinic was chosen by someone who wanted to get at Fernando Alvés in a personal way? Someone who knew about Anna-Maria?"

"Are you referring to ex-business partner Jorge?"

"They were partners when they were very young and I don't imagine for a moment that he doesn't know about her. I was also thinking about his wife, Almu. How much does she know?"

"Fernando Alvés met Almu the year after Anna-Maria was committed. It is possible that she knows nothing of her. He is a man well capable of keeping a secret, as we know."

Their conversation was interrupted by the satellite navigation system telling them to turn off the main road. Ten minutes of a winding country lane led them to the last known address of Alejandro Basseta. They saw the curtain twitch as they pulled up in the drive of the quiet country property. Carlos indicated that they waited in the car to see if someone acknowledged their arrival. A few seconds later, a tall, upright man in his late fifties approached. The police officers got out of the car and identified themselves. The man reciprocated without smiling and invited them into the garden. He asked his wife to prepare coffee and sat his guests around a wooden table.

"You know why we've come, Alejandro?"

"Yes, and I'm not going to lie to you. Ask your questions and I will answer them, but I will not surrender any information that you do not directly ask for. Those are my conditions."

The detectives exchanged a look. His frankness surprised them as much as his openness. Alejandro was a soldier under interrogation.

"Did you attend to a young man in the Agost Clinic for Mental Health last week?"

"I attended to a young man last week. I asked not to be informed of the location."

"Who brought you to the clinic?"

"Fusilier Pedro."

"Pedro Ribera?"

"In our line of work, surnames were an unnecessary complication."

"What condition was the young man in?"

The conversation stalled while Alejandro's wife placed a tray of coffee on the table. When she returned indoors, he continued.

"He was a mess. Both legs were broken and his arm needed attention of someone more skilled than me. He was riddled with shotgun pellets and I was unable to ascertain the extent of the damage he sustained to his internal organs. His fractured skull was the least of his worries."

"What did you do?"

"I patched him up as best I could and left medication that would help to stabilise him until he got proper medical help."

"He died."

"I thought he would. I told Pedro that he needed proper attention. When he brought me back, I told him that I didn't want to hear from him ever again."

"What condition was he in?"

"Physically, he was tip top, but he was trying to hide the fact that his jaw had been recently broken and not reset properly."

"Thank you Alejandro" Carlos said as he placed his cup on the table.

"One last question; Do you know where Pedro might have gone?"

"No. I specifically asked him to tell me nothing. Will I be called to testify?"

"Do you want to testify?"

"I haven't always been proud of what I have been involved in, but on this occasion I would like to think that my actions were of the humanitarian kind. If my testimony will make a difference, I will. If not, I would prefer to disappear into anonymity."

The men shook hands and the detectives departed, closer to Pedro the man, but not to his whereabouts.

On the return trip to the Commissary in Alicante, Carlos received a call telling him that the team had unearthed some very important information. He urged Christiano to drive faster, but one hundred and forty kilometres per hour was his absolute limit. As they approached the city, curiosity got the better of the sergeant.

"Did Ferrera indicate what these developments were, boss?"

The inspector wondered how long it would take Christiano to ask.

"They have found the nurse."

"So we know where Anna-Maria Alvés is? How does this bring us any closer to Pedro Ribera?"

"No sergeant, we know where the nurse is, and she isn't in Portugal with Anna-Maria".

"So Fernando Alvés is lying to us?"

"No, sergeant; Fernando Alvés is lying to us again, and he isn't the only one."

Christiano left that statement hanging in the air. He could wait another ten minutes to hear the full story. Inspector Carlos Rico wasn't the only one who could play mind games.

Ferrera was the cat who got the cream. He smiled widely when he saw his superiors arrive, and could barely contain himself while they removed their jackets. Carlos gathered the whole team round and nodded at Ferrera to proceed.

"The number given to us by Fernando Alvés for the nurse is registered as yet another temporary SIM, the sort people pick up at the airport when on holiday. Of course, there was no reply, so I contacted the health services and they have no record of Anna-Maria's whereabouts after the closure of the clinic. However, a trawl of the private nursing agencies produced a result. Nurse Delphina Salud Gomes isn't in Portugal, but she thinks that Anna-Maria Alvés is, with her father. She received a call from Fernando Alvés three days ago when he told her that he was taking his daughter to Lisbon for a week and that her services would not be needed."

"Are the father and daughter holidays a regular occurrence?" Christiano asked.

"Delphina says that she has tended Anna-Maria for the past four years and this is the first time her father has taken her away. She is at home, here in Alicante."

"Did you get an address for the daughter?"

"She lives in the countryside and has no recognisable address, but she says she is happy to take us to where Anna-Maria lives. It is near a small town called Hondon de las Nieves.

"There is one more thing, sir. The nurse says that Anna-Maria needs to take strong anti-psychotic drugs every day. If she misses her medication, she can become unstable and very unpredictable."

"Shall I get the car, sir?" Christiano suggested.

"Not yet. If this woman has been institutionalised for most of her life, she won't be able to drive and therefore is going nowhere fast. Bring Fernando Alvés back in. I want to know why he is doing everything in his power to mislead us."

Constable Ferdinand stood up and waved a sheet of paper at his inspector.

"Sir, there's something else you should know before you do that."

"Are you going to tell me what is so important, Ferdinand, or should I guess?"

The young detective blushed slightly but carried on with his revelation.

"Fernando Alvés is broke. His business is in tatters and he owes a lot of money."

"He managed to rustle up two million Euros for the ransom. That doesn't sound like a man with no money to me, constable."

"This is where it gets interesting, sir. Alvés.com was sold for two million Euros to a Jorge Bocanegra over two weeks ago."

"Fernando Alvés sold his business to his ex-partner? They hate each other with a passion."

For once Carlos sounded astonished.

"So Jorge Bocanegra had already bought Fernando Alvés' business before we interviewed him and he didn't think to mention this to us? I knew there were things people weren't telling us, and now I want to know why. Bring them both in."

"But Bocanegra is in a wheelchair, sir" Christiano protested.

"I don't care if he is building sandcastles on the bloody moon. I want him in my interview room in one hour's time. I want to sit these two 'gentlemen', side by side and find out exactly what is going on."

His tone indicated that anyone still in the briefing room in ten seconds time would have their head bitten off. Because of his familiarity with the location, Christiano took Ferdinand to Denia to detain the disabled storyteller, while Velasquez and Ferrera went to pick up Fernando Alvés, yet again. Mendez made himself scarce until the inspector had brooded back to his office before amending the incident board. Things were happening fast, and woe betides anyone who missed something important now.

Carlos sat at his desk and tried to conjure up a scenario that would explain the string of facts he had to work with, the kidnapping, the death, the mercenary connection, and the extraordinary behaviour of the former best friends and business partners. They were all connected in some way. How deeply involved were the Russians? Fernando Alvés would be occupying a watery grave in no time if he crossed them, and Oleg Petrov knew more than he would ever tell.

He thought about the potential mole in his department and mentally assessed each member of his team as a possible culprit, though none seemed likely. He went back into the briefing room and stared at the photographs on the board for a long time before returning to his office. It was there in front of him but he wasn't seeing it. Think, Carlos, he said to himself. The solution to this whole sordid affair is there for the taking. Take it Carlos. Look at what you have. Deeply absorbed in his thoughts, he nodded off. He was awoken with a start.

"When was the last time you got any proper sleep?" The enquiry from Chief Inspector Roberto Martinez was based on the genuine concern of a friend. "Or any of your team, come to that?"

"I'm sorry. I was thinking and just dropped off. We are getting very close to whatever's happening in this case. When I wrap it up, I'll sleep for a week, but until then I'll push on."

"I hear there have been developments."

Carlos pointed to the chair on the other side of his desk and brought his boss up to date with the case. Roberto was surprised when he heard Carlos' report.

"What do you think is going on, Carlos? I've seen that look on your face before and it usually means that you have reached a conclusion. Spill the beans."

"You have also known me too long to ask such a foolish question. You know that I only work on facts and, at the moment, I don't have all of them. Anything I tell you now would be merely guesswork."

"You know who's behind all of this, don't you?"

"Roberto, if I am right, you will have the kidnapper behind bars before the day is out, but on the chance that I am wrong, I reserve the right to not make a fool of myself."

Roberto Martinez knew that pushing his old friend any further would bear no fruit. Carlos Rico had his own peculiar ways of working, but his results over the years spoke for themselves.

"I'll leave you to it. Let me know when I can call the mayor's office and take the credit."

"I'll do that, Chief Inspector," Carlos said in jest.

As Roberto left, Christiano Marcos waved to indicate that the required candidates were now present in the interview room.

"I want you in there with me, Christiano. They are going to play games and your young mind is more agile than mine."

The sergeant investigator knew this was unlikely, but was flattered by the vote of confidence he was being given. Carlos was the most adept player of mind games he had ever met, and he had a determined look on his face. There was going to be no hiding in interview room two today.

The austere room was busier than normal, with four men seated on the side of the table facing the one-way glass observation panel. The decor was deliberately drab and uninspiring, so Carlos got straight down to business. Fernando Alvés sat on the left, Jorge Bocanegra in his wheelchair on the right, with Fernando's lawyer and Jorge's carer occupying the two chairs in between. No one was speaking as Carlos and Christiano entered. They had watched the unhappy foursome from the other side of the unsettling mirrored window for a full five minutes to ascertain the chemistry in the room before entering, and there was none. Jorge broke the silence.

"What's the meaning of this? It's an absolute disgrace?"

Carlos ignored Jorge and addressed David Campo, his carer.

"Has he rested today? You said that he is likely to get irritable if he hasn't rested, Mr Campo."

"I'm crippled, I'm not deaf. You can speak to me, inspector."

"I will most certainly be speaking to you, Mr Bocanegra, all in good time. Mr Campo?"

"Yes he has rested and had his medication, but he tires easily."

"Well perhaps I should get straight to the point."

"What exactly is your point, inspector?" Jorge Bocanegra snapped.

Carlos didn't like being talked to in such a manner, especially in his own station, and he wasn't going to make any concessions based on Jorge Bocanegra's disability.

"My point is that when we last spoke, I asked you about your relationship with Fernando Alvés, and you failed to mention that only days before, you bought his company for two million Euros, the exact amount that you, Mr Alvés, contributed towards the ransom."

Fernando Alvés and Jorge Bocanegra exchanged a cold glance. Carlos looked directly at the man in the wheelchair and waited for an answer.

"I may be in a chair, but I am still capable of running a business. At the time we spoke, I knew nothing about the kidnapping. The television appeal was the first I heard of it."

"Why did you buy Fernando Alvés' business?"

"Because he was giving it away. The man is an idiot. He has always been incompetent in business dealings, and this was a way in which I could hurt him. I took the only thing he had."

"What do you know about Anna-Maria, Mr Bocanegra?" Christiano asked.

Jorge Bocanegra appeared surprised at the question. He looked to the other end of the table as if seeking a lead from the man he supposedly despised, and none was given.

"I knew that she existed, and I met her on two occasions when I took Fernando to the clinic."

"So you knew about the clinic?"

"Yes. That doesn't make me a kidnapper."

"You also knew Sergio and Carmen, did you not?

"Of course I did. We were almost one family at the time."

"You never married?"

"No. What's that got to do with anything?"

"You and Mr Alvés parted ways after the birth of Carmen. Why?"

"I told you before; we wanted to take the business in different directions."

"Do you agree with that, Mr Alvés?"

Fernando Alvés consulted his brief before confirming the cause of their rift.

"And there was no other reason?"

"No. We split because we wanted different things."

Carlos decided the time was right to drop the bombshell.

"Was it perhaps for quite the opposite reason; you both wanted the same thing; Almu. Your wife and your lover," he said pointing at Fernando Alvés and then Jorge Bocanegra in turn.

As he pointed, each protested loudly. Carlos had hit the nerve was hoping to. Christiano was as shocked as the others.

"What are you talking about, sir?"

"When you were collecting our friends here, I had a long, hard look at the pictures on the incident board. Sergio and Carmen don't look remotely like Fernando Alvés. He is a large, barrel-chested man with blue eyes. They do, however, bear a striking resemblance to the slightly-built, brown-eyed Jorge Bocanegra. Look at what Mister Alvés described as Carmen's 'pixie ears'."

The sergeant looked at the man in the wheelchair and couldn't disagree that he had the same ears as Carmen Alvés.

"What took me so long to see was all too clear to you a long time ago, Mr Alvés. Your parting was based on the fact that Jorge Bocanegra fathered your children, and that was something you couldn't ignore."

It was Jorge Bocanegra who responded defensively.

"I threatened to take Almu and the children away after he found out, but he made sure that would never happen. He took nothing to do with Sergio and Carmen at home and shipped them out to boarding schools at the first available opportunity. Almu has been a virtual prisoner for the last twenty years. Fernando Alvés has been playing judge, jury, and executioner, and enjoying every minute of it."

"I loved Almu" Fernando Alvés butted in "and in my own way, I still do. But every time I looked at the children, I saw him."

"You may have loved her but you loved the money the business was bringing in even more. She was no more than a trophy to you."

Jorge's comment had Fernando Alvés on his feet, charging towards him, his face full of hate. Only Christiano's well-timed lunge across the table prevented the man in the wheelchair from feeling the weight of his ex-partner's fists. Mendez and Ferrera came charging in from the observation room and removed Fernando Alvés, with his faithful brief following close behind.

"I think this is a good time to take a break, sergeant."

Christiano straightened his jacket, turned to the observation window, and directed Velasquez to arrange coffee for Jorge Bocancgra and David Campo. The constable pressed the transmit button on the desk,

"Got it, sergeant."

When Christiano entered the detective's office, Roberto was shouting at Carlos. He turned about and listened from outside the door.

"That was one hell of a risky stunt you pulled in there. What if you were wrong? You would have looked a fool."

"I have been a fool all along. The family resemblance is undeniable and none of us saw it. It is all beginning to fall into place. I want to interview Bocanegra first and let Alvés sweat for an hour. I don't know if Bocanegra can give us anything more, but Alvés doesn't necessarily know this."

Roberto Martinez couldn't argue with the success of his inspector's gamble and decided to let him continue.

"Be very careful with Fernando Alvés. His lawycr is waiting for any slip up that will get him out of here. Bocanegra is guilty of nothing more than adultery."

"Withholding evidence?"

"If he had no part in the kidnapping, get him back to wherever you found him. Prosecuting invalids for petty offences isn't good for our image."

Carlos agreed and poured himself a coffee. Christiano almost fell in the door as the chief inspector opened it, leaving none in any doubt about his eavesdropping.

"Not a good trait, sergeant" Roberto fired as he passed in an ugly mood.

Carlos smiled at Christiano's embarrassment.

"No need to brief you on the way ahead, you've already heard it all."

"The CI wasn't too pleased."

"On the contrary, the CI is very pleased. He just shows it differently to most people. Grab a quick coffee. I don't want Bocanegra's medical condition interfering with our investigation. We are close, very close. We need to scare these people into telling the truth."

Predictably, David Campo's opening gambit was to state that his patient needed to rest, and Carlos shallowly promised that they would be taken home shortly.

"How did Fernando Alvés know he wasn't the father of the children? They were no more than a baby and an infant when you had your separation. Did he have a blood test?"

"No, the doctor had told him he was sterile after an industrial accident. He told me everything in those days. When Sergio was born, he was elated. He told me that the doctor must have got it wrong. When Carmen appeared, he went for a check and the doctor arrived at the same conclusion as before. That was when he confronted us. We had become careless and he started to recognise the signs. We didn't deny it; I loved Almu and blurted out the truth. All hell let loose, as you can imagine. You've seen his temper."

"He arranged for your factory to be torched and for two attempts on your life. Is he owing to Oleg Petrov for these deeds?"

"I don't know anything about the Russian."

"Why did you buy his company? In spite of what you tell me, you clearly aren't in a suitable condition to deal with the demands of a business."

"I heard through the grapevine that he was in financial trouble. I bought the business to support the children that he never let me see. I intended that Sergio did the day-to-day dealings. I wanted to tell them I was their father."

"One last question; do you think it is possible that Fernando Alvés arranged the kidnapping of Sergio and Carmen?"

Jorge Bocanegra stared at the table for what seemed a long time before answering. Carlos looked at David Campo, his eyes asking if the patient was well. The carer gave a slight nod, indicating that he was all right. Eventually, he answered.

"Fernando Alvés is capable of anything. I am no doctor, but in my opinion Anna-Maria's insanity was inherited."

Carlos thanked Jorge and David, and asked Christiano to arrange for them to be taken back to Denia.

"Now for Mr Fernando Alvés" Carlos said as he rubbed his hands in anticipation.

Christiano was unsure of his boss's intentions. He was still uncomfortable with his unconventional approach, having had little opportunity to experience the modus operandi of this unusual yet enigmatic detective. 'By the book' had been his education, but

Detective Inspector Carlos Rico read from a different tome.

"Do we push his temper, sir?"

"Not unless we have to. The chief inspector was right about his brief. He will call harassment and bullying at the first opportunity. It is better if we let them think we know more than we do."

"Is there anything you would like to let me in on before we start, sir?"

"Not this time, sergeant. We are flying by the seat of our pants."

Fernando Alvés had been well coached by his lawyer. They began the interview with an apology for his outburst.

"I'm sure you will understand, inspector. I trusted Jorge Bocanegra completely and he abused this by sleeping with my wife. It was a long time ago and I would prefer to forget about it."

"What happened twenty years ago is of no interest to me, Mr Alvés. I am investigating the kidnapping of Sergio and Carmen, the subsequent rape and murder, and your involvement."

"What makes you think I am involved? I may not have been their biological father, but I loved those kids."

"You are in financial difficulty, I believe?"

"I don't see what my finances have to do with this."

"You tried to lose the police when you were handing over the ransom. It was almost as though you wanted the money to be paid."

"That's ridiculous. I told you, I was worried that the kidnapper would harm them if he saw the police."

Velasquez knocked and entered. He passed a note to Carlos, who read it before passing it on to Christiano. The look that passed between them had Fernando Alvés worried. Carlos went on the attack.

"You warned Pedro Ribera that we were going to the clinic in Agost, didn't you?"

"No I didn't. How would I have known?"

"The over-enthusiastic Family Liaison Officer told you as we left the station. Her intentions were good, but you abused them. However, your information gave Pedro Ribera just enough time to get away before we arrived."

The conversation between lawyer and client told the investigators that they were right.

"No comment" wasn't an admission of guilt, but it indicated Fernando Alvés was rattled.

"Why did you lie about the nurse, Mr Alvés?"

"I don't know what you mean."

"She isn't in Portugal with Anna-Maria. She is very definitely in Alicante and waiting to take us to where Anna-Maria lives."

There was another whispered conversation before the lawyer asked for ten minutes to consult with his client.

"I'd like to do it in a room with no microphones, if you please, inspector."

They were cracking, and the panic was clear to the detectives.

When they reconvened, Fernando Alvés had changed his mind and wanted to talk.

"None of this was meant to work out this way. Yes, I am in big trouble financially. I owed Oleg Petrov over a million and saw this as a way out of a very bad situation. Petrov is not the kind of man you want to owe money to; his business associates tend to end up hurt."

"Take it from the beginning," Carlos said.

"I previously had dealings with Petrov."

"This was the intimidation of Jorge Bocanegra?"

The shake of the head from the lawyer produced a 'no comment' response from Fernando Alvés.

"My client has agreed to speak about the kidnapping and nothing else."

Carlos knew he could return to the Bocanegra situation at a later date and came back to the kidnapping.

"How was Petrov involved in the kidnapping?"

"It was one of his men who told me about the Flying Dutchman Private Military Company. Russians speak a lot when you pour a bottle of good vodka down their uneducated throats, and they remember little the following day.

"I contacted a man who called himself 'the Colonel'. I paid him my last twenty thousand Euros for the name and loyalty of a man called Pedro. I never met him. I was instructed to call myself 'the Fixer' and remain at the end of a telephone. He sent me a voice scrambler and insisted that I used it. I asked about the necessity for such a degree of personal security, and he told me that it would be better for all concerned if I remained anonymous."

"When did you first contact Pedro Ribera?"

"Two weeks before the kidnapping. Before the clinic closed, I took advantage of their slack security and stole a set of keys from the reception desk. The staff knew they had lost their jobs and didn't make any effort to find them. I don't know why I did it, but seven years later, they were the perfect solution to my problem of where to take Sergio and Carmen. I wanted them to be safe. I sent the keys to Ribera and told him to prepare for the kidnapping."

"And the chauffeur at the airport?"

"I told him the wrong time to ensure that Ribera was well clear of the airport when he arrived. I scolded him when he returned without them and he accepted that his overworked boss had made a mistake. I wasn't pleased when your sergeant turned up on my doorstep."

Fernando Alvés' openness was almost disarming. Was he admitting to one crime in order to hide another more serious? Carlos tried to read his face, but Fernando Alvés was proving to be a consummate actor.

"So you were calling Pedro Ribera when we were sitting in the next room?"

"I was playing the two roles, father, and Fixer. As Fixer, I was directing Ribera and telling him what to say to me as the father. It seemed all too easy. Then, it started to go wrong. I was enjoying the game, and underestimated how much pressure I was putting the kidnapper under. The rape was never meant to happen. I was genuinely shocked."

"Why did you delay paying?"

"My two million was merely bait. I intended to take Petrov's eight million along with my money and flee to Argentina. I had it all planned. Petrov, on the other hand, wanted to take my two million for catching the kidnapper and rescuing the children. He held back on his delivery in order to show me who was running the show."

"Will you testify against him?"

"It makes little difference to me. Whichever way this ends, I'm dead. If I get as far as prison, he will have me killed. Even in protective custody, he will get to me, one way or another. The betrayal is enough to guarantee this, let alone the eight million other reasons he has.

"The escape of Sergio and Carmen was carelessness on Pedro Ribera's part. Sergio had more balls than I ever gave him credit for. Ribera told me that his death was an accident and that he brought a doctor to try to save him."

"What about the handover. Was that your idea?"

"I knew nothing about it. Ribera held his cards close to his chest. I found the whole thing very exciting, as I had no idea what was coming next. Yes, I tried to lose you so that he could get away with the money; my money."

"It was you who warned him that we were on to him, was it not?"

"Yes. He had already released Carmen and I wanted to wait until the dust died down before collecting my prize and leaving the country. It was important that he, and the money, got away."

"Do you know where he is now?"

"Yes. I sent him to kidnap Anna-Maria."

"You did what?" This was turning out to be a day of many surprises, and Christiano could barely believe what Fernando Alvés had just said.

"I told him that I, as the Fixer, would talk to her and arrange safe passage. I told him a relative would co-operate if he knew that Anna-Maria was being held by a dangerous fugitive. The fictional relative was to be told he was the same man who kidnapped the Alvés brother and sister."

"You really did enjoy this game, didn't you? Anna-Maria needs regular care. Did you take this into consideration before misleading the nurse?"

Carlos was sensing that Fernando Alvés was holding something back.

"Have you talked to Pedro Ribera since he has taken your daughter as a hostage?"

"Yes."

"As the Fixer, or the father?"

"Pedro Ribera thought I was doing it as the Fixer but Anna-Maria knew I was her father. I told her what he had done."

*****

"How did Anna-Maria respond when you told her about Sergio and Carmen?"

"She was very calm. Then, she always is when the dark side of her personality takes control. She can be two very different people at the same time."

Fernando Alvés allowed himself a wry smile. His lawyer had long since given up on any potential salvation and was warming to the increasingly bizarre revelations that were unfolding. Fernando Alvés looked directly at Carlos as he spoke. He felt no guilt.

"Anna-Maria knew it was me. She hasn't been exposed to too many voices in her very limited world. Pedro Ribera, on the other hand, heard what he expected to hear."

"Was this meant as a safe house for Pedro Ribera and the money?"

"It was meant as a safe house for the money."

"And Pedro?"

Fernando Alvés looked uncomfortable, and this echoed across the table. Carlos saw the look of deceit and quickly ran through the possible outcomes.

"Is Pedro Ribera safe?"

"I don't know."

Carlos and Christiano looked at each other and knew that their priority no longer lay in the interview room. They now had not only the chance of catching the kidnapper, but potentially saving him. There was something about Fernando Alvés demeanour that made them feel uncomfortable, though neither dared to put their thoughts into words. Carlos needed to act.

"We have to go and find your daughter and Pedro Ribera. Will you take us or do we have to ask the nurse that you tried very hard to hide?"

Fernando Alvés ignored his lawyer completely.

"It would be better if I were there, inspector. Anna-Maria hasn't had her medication for three or four days. She could be dangerous. My worry is that your men may be over-vigorous in restraining her, and someone will get hurt."

Carlos didn't know if he was being played, and looked deep into Fernando Alvés' eyes to find the answer. He knew the situation at Anna-Maria's house, as reported, but Fernando Alvés was holding something back. What was it? There weren't too many possibilities and none seemed relevant to anyone or anything outside of this case. Carlos wanted an end to this web of lies, and made his call.

"Get the cars, sergeant. Mr Alvés will travel with us. Assume Pedro Ribera is armed and dangerous, and that Anna-Maria Alvés is vulnerable, but also potentially dangerous."

"I will be accompanying my client, inspector," the lawyer instructed.

"Remove this tedious man from the premises," Carlos said to his officers behind the glass. "We have work to do, and he isn't helping."

The drive to the countryside near Hondon de los Nieves was done in complete silence. Sergeant Christiano Marcos drove, with Inspector Carlos Rico occupying the other front seat. Fernando Alvés had the back seat all to himself, and only spoke when they were in the vicinity of Anna-Maria's house.

"Take the next left. The house is just up the lane."

His matter of fact attitude told the detectives that he knew what awaited them and was enjoying the realisation of his final act. Technically, he was only guilty of conspiring to abduct, but the Russian involvement meant an inevitable death sentence would be meted out, in due course. Fernando Alvés had been caught red-handed, and making no attempt to hide from the ugliness of his current situation.

"Just pull in at the side of the drive, sergeant. If we are lucky, Anna-Maria will have baked us a cake. If she has, please do her the courtesy of eating it and saying that you like it. I don't know where her future lies after I am incarcerated and that above all else is what bothers me about this affair."

Carlos Rico's thoughts were on things other than cakes and familial sensibilities. In the next few moments, he was going to apprehend a kidnapper, rapist, and perhaps even a murderer. Pedro Ribera was the target, but Anna-Maria Alvés was an obstacle that had to be overcome. Fernando Alvés was given one last chance to make things easier for everyone.

"Is there anything that you haven't told us about what we are about to encounter?"

"What do you mean, inspector?"

"I don't like surprises, Mr Alvés. Is your employee, Pedro Ribera, likely to try to shoot himself out of a corner?"

"No inspector."

"You sound very sure about that, Mr Alvés."

"I know my daughter. He may have been a professional killer, but she is a natural."

Carlos and Christiano shuddered collectively on hearing this. Bad people, they could handle, mad people were different.

"How many people are in this house, Mr Alvés?"

"I really don't know, inspector. I set something in motion and I have no idea of how it worked out. I would guess a maximum of two people."

"What have you done?"

Carlos almost didn't want to know. Christiano held the car door closed such that Fernando Alvés had no option but to answer the inspector.

"Pedro Ribera thought that I was Anna-Maria's relation when I called, but she knew who I was. Despite her problems, we are very close and I am her only relative. Sergio and Carmen were unfulfilled promises of family that would probably never happen. This was my doing, based on their impurity."

"What has this to do with what we might find here?"

Christiano was struggling to join the dots. Fernando Alvés recognised the futility of lying, and chose to release the truth in a slow, cryptic fashion. Carlos was not a fan of cryptic.

"I repeat, Mr Alvés, what have you done?"

Fernando Alvés looked straight at Carlos, probably for the first time, and spoke in an unmistakably clear voice. This was his final declaration.

"I told Anna-Maria that this man had killed her brother. She knows what she must do."

The words hung heavily, unchallenged, in the air before Fernando Alvés continued.

"She has never seen Sergio or Carmen, though she has followed their lives in detail from a distance. I promised they would meet, but the time was never right. I have always been conscious of Sergio's parentage, and was loath to introduce him to my real daughter. I know this may sound petty to you, but put yourself in my position. What would you have done?"

"Is the timing relevant?"

Carlos had been considering the nurse's three days absence. If Anna-Maria elected not to take her medication, what state of mind would she be in? Was Fernando Alvés clever enough to have planned something so intricate and impersonal? The scenario Carlos was painting in his mind was one where a man, in order to avenge a festering sore, had used two of his children to steal money from a Russian gangster and then manipulated his eldest child to destroy the evidence.

"Did you take the nurse out of the equation in order to make Anna-Maria miss the drugs she needs to keep her 'normal'?"

"That wouldn't be a nice thing to do. I told her about Sergio because I didn't want any secrets."

"You felt the need to tell her on the very day that you sent the man you deemed responsible for the murder of her brother to her house. After removing her medical care and knowing that she was likely to be psychotic, you presented Pedro Ribera to her on a plate."

Carlos had now had enough of the theoretical; he needed to know exactly what was happening in Los Aves. The armed back up was in place, and there was no way anyone was going to escape.

"Stay here" he ordered Fernando Alvés. "I will call you if I want you. Sergeant, come with me."

The singing of the birds in the false pepper trees almost mocked the gravity of the situation faced by the police officers. Were they facing an experienced and highly trained killer, an unstable woman with a propensity to violence, or both? There was only one way to find out.

As they approached the front door of the house, Christiano followed the procedure to the letter. He dashed, turned, and postured in grand television fashion while his bemused boss watched in astonishment.

"Stop pissing about and open the door, sergeant."

A somewhat hurt Christiano obliged.

The door opened directly into the kitchen, where Anna-Maria Alvés stood, apron-clad and face painted.

"Hello. Have you come to tie me up too?"

Christiano looked at Carlos, hoping for guidance. For him, this was like a nineteen fifties television advertisement gone bad. The pretty lady dressed like a model American mother held a large cake knife in her hand as she spoke in a matter of fact fashion.

"Carrot cake?" she offered as she sliced her product fresh from the oven.

"Yes please" Carlos replied. "And my sergeant would like some too."

"Are you police officers?"

"Yes Miss Alvés. Were you expecting us?"

"Delphina tells me not to let strangers into the house, but when they come, I always have such fun."

"Have you had any visitors this week?"

"O yes. The soldier. He liked games. He liked to tie me up. Are you going to tie me up?"

"That wasn't my intention, Miss Alvés."

Christiano was beginning to enjoy the interchange between his ultra-conservative superior and the overtly sexual Anna-Maria Alvés

"Where is the soldier?"

"He's in the garden."

Anna-Maria undid a few more buttons on her dress, revealing more thigh than was suitable to accompany carrot cake. She smiled at Carlos as she did this and asked if he would like to see more. The inspector's glare was enough to stifle Christiano's urge to snigger.

"I'd like to see the soldier, Miss Alvés."

"He's not much fun anymore. He's dead."

Christiano signalled for the armed officers to stay back as Carlos continued his subtle handling of Anna-Maria Alvés. With Pedro Ribera declared dead, there seemed little threat if they could persuade Anna-Maria to put the large kitchen knife down.

"Can you take me to the soldier?"

"He really is dead. He had an accident with a washing line."

Anna-Maria placed the knife on the worktop and led the detectives through the living room and out of the patio doors into the neat garden. Pedro Ribera's body was propped on a wooden bench. The ligature marks on his neck confirmed Anna-Maria's comment about an accident with a washing line. His trousers were on back to front.

"What happened to him, Anna-Maria?"

"I strangled him. He killed my brother."

"What happened with his trousers?"

"He wasn't wearing them when he died. He was fun, but he had to die. Father said so. I put his trousers on him but he is very heavy. I got it wrong but he isn't complaining. Not anymore."

"Did he have anything with him when he came here?"

"You mean the money?"

"Yes, the money. Where is the money?"

Anna-Maria's facial expression started to change. Her smile twisted into something quite different, something Carlos Rico found disturbing.

"I took care of the money."

"Where is the money, Anna-Maria?"

She ignored Carlos' question.

"He had something else."

She moved with incredible stealth to where Pedro Ribera lay and removed something from his jacket pocket. The pistol was pointing at the policemen before they had an opportunity to move.

"I've never had a gun before. It's real, you know."

As if to prove what she said, she fired at the wall above their heads. Both men instinctively threw themselves to the ground as shattered brick and plaster rained down on them.

"Where is my father? I want to speak to my father. He will know what to do."

Carlos slowly picked himself up and brushed the dust from his jacket. He looked to see that Christiano was all right and indicated that they remained calm, though his heart was racing.

"Guns are very dangerous, Anna-Maria. Can you put it down, please?"

She raised the pistol once again and fired another round, this time only inches above their heads. They knew that a third shot would not miss them. Carlos held his hands up in a conciliatory gesture.

"Your father is outside, in the car. I will get him for you."

She seemed to be trying to work out if this was a trick. She pointed the gun at Christiano. He closed his eyes, fearing the worst.

"You go and get my father. If you aren't back here with my father in two minutes, I will shoot your friend."

Christiano looked at Carlos.

"Go and get Fernando Alvés and bring him here. Tell the others to stay back."

Christiano turned slowly such as not to spook the woman with the gun and made his way back to the car. This was the first time he had been shot at and his shaking legs could only just take his weight. He stopped in the kitchen, out of sight of the pistol and steadied his breathing before emerging into the driveway. He hadn't stopped to consider how the shots might have affected the behaviour of the accompanying officers and was frightened yet again as the cocking of multiple weapons greeted his appearance.

"Put your weapons down. I am alone. No one has been injured. The inspector wants you to keep your distance."

Fernando Alvés dashed from the car towards Christiano.

"Is she alright? Is Anna-Maria safe?"

"Yes, she is unharmed. She is the one doing the shooting."

"She doesn't have a gun. How could she?"

"She may not have had, but your former friend, Pedro Ribera did."

"Former friend?"

"She did as you asked her. You didn't lay a finger on him but his murder is very much your doing. She wants to talk with you. You must get her to put the gun down."

Christiano opened the door to the kitchen and indicated that Fernando Alvés entered. As they reached the garden, they saw that Anna-Maria was now sat on the bench next to the very dead Pedro. She kept the gun pointing at Carlos, who looked justifiably nervous.

She smiled when she saw her father. He walked directly to her and she threw her arms around him, gun still held tightly in her hand. The sergeant took his place next to his inspector. Somehow, this didn't make Carlos feel a whole lot better.

Fernando Alvés looked over his daughter's shoulder at the sorry figure of the former mercenary. He was a big man and it was a remarkable feat that Anna-Maria managed to kill him. He knew how this would end when he directed Pedro to tie his daughter up. She had a special talent when it came to ropes. The reversed trousers indicated that her other special talent was still being practised too.

"Am I in trouble, father?"

"I don't think that is going to happen. You are not a responsible person, my darling. You are certified mentally ill and you haven't been taking your medication. They can't touch a hair on your head. Diminished responsibility, I believe it's called."

The watching detectives knew that what Fernando Alvés had said was true. If he had gone undiscovered for one more day, he would have been on the plane to Argentina with ten million Euros. By manipulating Anna-Maria, he had eliminated Pedro, and with him, anything linking Fernando to the kidnapping. It was almost the perfect crime. His mistake was lying about the nurse.

"Where do we go from here, inspector?"

"I would like to have this conversation without the gun, Mr Alvés."

Fernando Alvés reached across Anna-Maria and took the gun from her hand. She smiled at her father as she released it. Father makes everything right, he always did. As Carlos stepped towards him to retrieve the gun, Fernando Alvés raised the pistol and made it quite clear that he had no intention of handing it over.

"Not so fast, inspector."

Carlos froze where he stood.

"This isn't helping anyone, Mr Alvés. Give me the pistol before anyone else gets hurt."

Fernando Alvés ignored the inspector and turned to his daughter.

"Did you do the other thing I asked, Anna-Maria?"

"Yes, father."

"What other thing did you ask Anna-Maria to do?" Carlos asked, dreading the reply.

"I asked her to take care of the money. Where is it darling?"

Anna-Maria smiled at her father, proud of having done as he asked. She pointed to the smouldering fire in the corner of the garden.

"The money was what caused the soldier to kill my Sergio. It is evil. I took care of it as you told me, once and for all."

The three men turned to look at what they had assumed was garden rubbish being burned.

"Oh my God" was the best that Christiano could muster. "That's what ten million Euros smells like?"

"Oleg Petrov isn't going to be very pleased," Carlos said with a sardonic smile.

Fernando Alvés had turned white with shock as he realised what his daughter had done.

"Please tell me that you are joking, Anna-Maria?"

"No father. The evil money has been destroyed. You have got lots of money, father, you don't need any more."

Fernando Alvés had tears in his eyes as he turned back to his daughter.

"Do you know what you have done, you stupid girl? You really are barking mad."

"Father? Why are you saying these things? You have always told me that I'm not that word."

Fernando Alvés had strictly forbidden the use of 'mad' in her presence. The denial had been perpetuated for thirty years, but no more.

"We have no money. You won't be able to stay here any longer. They will send you back to an institution, just like the clinic in Agost, back with the strange people."

"No, please father. Don't send me back."

Fernando Alvés pointed the gun at the detectives, urging them to step further back towards the wall with the very obvious bullet holes. He then hugged Anna-Maria very tightly.

The policemen knew what was about to happen and were helpless to stop it.

"I'm sorry I shouted at you. Goodbye darling" he said with tears running down his face.

"Goodbye, father" she replied. She also knew what was coming and accepted her father's will with a smile.

He raised the gun to her head and pulled the trigger. She jolted with the impact of the bullet and was dead before she hit the floor at the feet of Pedro Ribera.

Carlos and Christiano made to rush Fernando Alvés but he fired a shot in their direction that had them throwing themselves to the ground yet again.

"She would have had a miserable existence without me around. She is better off dead than back inside an institution."

"Fernando, you need to put the gun down. You know that you are surrounded by armed officers who are itching to shoot someone."

"You really can't see it, inspector, can you?"

"I can see that you are very upset, Fernando."

"I was Mr Alvés before. Put a gun in my hand and I become your friend, Fernando."

"The inspector is right, Fernando. There has been enough death. Please put the gun down."

"When I came here today, I expected to say goodbye to my daughter and tell her to use the money to make herself comfortable. I knew that I was going to go to jail for a long time and wouldn't be around to help her.

"When I saw that she had burnt the money, It was clear that the game was up. Oleg Petrov will have me dead within days. I don't want to spend the final days of my life wondering when the bullet is going to come. I have decided that I will go with my daughter."

Before Carlos and Christiano could protest, Fernando Alvés placed barrel of the pistol to the side of his head and pulled the trigger. Oleg Petrov would not get his revenge. The detectives looked in silence at the three bodies lying in front of them. They formed a strange, silent mosaic of death, shrouded in the blue smoke from the pistol and the smell of cordite, so loved by Pedro Ribera. Blood, lust, madness and greed, all wrapped up in deceit.

"This has been a tragic loss of life, sergeant."

"We are lucky that we aren't lying there with them."

"Faced with this, Christiano, I don't feel lucky. Let's make our survival known to the others and get forensics in to clean up. This is going to be one hell of a report to write up."

"Did anybody benefit from this sorry saga, sir?"

"The three people here definitely lost everything, as did Sergio Alvés. Carmen will recover but will have to live with her experiences. Almu has had her family torn apart and will have to rebuild her life. Petrov has lost his fortune and the crippled Jorge Bocanegra is hardly what you could describe as a winner."

"Could we have done anything different, sir?"

"We do our best sergeant. People can ask for no more. I'd better get back to the Commissary and let the chief inspector know that we aren't going to be putting any pressure on the prison system."

"I was told to expect surprises working for you, and you don't disappoint, sir. Three murders and a suicide on my first big case, it doesn't get any more surprising."

Carlos considered his sergeant's words and briefly reflected on other eventful moments in his long career.

"Surprises are vastly overrated. I would like nothing more than a long spell of tedium. No more surprises, sergeant. Give me good, honest boredom every time."

Carlos now had the job of informing the family of the death of Fernando Alvés.

*****

Almu Alvés wasn't prepared for what Carlos had to tell her. She thought that her husband might have perhaps been involved in some kind of underhand dealings; this was what he did on a daily basis. She wouldn't have been surprised by yet another cruel swipe at Jorge Bocanegra, as he had done so at unpredictable intervals in the past. However, to have been behind the kidnapping of his own children was far beyond what she thought him capable.

"You are telling me, inspector, that Fernando paid someone to kidnap Sergio and Carmen?"

Carlos considered sensitivities and arrived at the conclusion that he could spend his time more constructively elsewhere. Almu may have been yet another victim of Fernando Alvés' particularly strange spin on life, but her lot was far from bad.

"He hired a man from a Private Military Company. He paid him to collect your children from the airport and take them to a location few knew existed. What do you know about Anna-Maria?"

Almu studied Carlos for a moment, wondering if his question was set to trick her. The detective's expression gave nothing away. She chose to answer.

"At first, nothing. Fernando never mentioned her. Shortly after we married, he disappeared every weekend for several hours giving no explanation and I thought that he might be having an affair, so I hired a private investigator to follow him. He reported back that Fernando was visiting a clinic for people with mental problems and I asked the advice of a friend. He told me that I had nothing to worry about."

303

"This was Jorge Bocanegra, the man you had an affair with for over three years and fathered your children?"

Almu turned white on hearing Carlos' direct approach.

"How do you know this? Only Jorge, Fernando, and me knew."

"I saw the similarities between Sergio, Carmen and Jorge and the lack of the same with Fernando and called their bluffs. Fernando was no happier when I confronted him with this sordid truth than he probably was when he first found out. How did he find out about you and Jorge?"

"Is it relevant, inspector?"

"Not in the slightest. This, madam, is for no purpose other than appeasing my own curiosity about the human condition. You don't have to tell me anything, if that is what you choose."

Almu was disarmed by Carlos' frankness and needed a few seconds to think about how to respond. She walked to the table on the far side of the expensively carpeted room and poured herself a brandy. She looked back at Carlos and waved the decanter. Carlos smiled.

"Why not. I need to relax."

Almu poured the second drink and brought it to her guest. They chinked their glasses in acknowledgement of their mutual plight and sipped the ice-cooled liquor.

"Fernando was obsessed with his job. He lived for the company and his love for me was as second best. Even then, it was obvious that Jorge was the brains behind the business. Fernando's family supplied the money for them to get started, and if it weren't for this, Fernando wouldn't have been involved at all. Jorge was brilliant; he could handle the business effortlessly while arriving at innovative solutions to the customer's problems. The world was Jorge Bocanegra's oyster for the eating."

"And you?"

"It started as a rather patronising attempt to get me involved. Fernando actually loved me in those days and felt guilty about leaving me alone in this big house for as much as eighteen hours a day. He and Jorge encouraged me to get involved with the marketing side of the company, though I always knew that what eventually hit the market bore little resemblance to anything I conjured up. Jorge was intelligent and amusing. I don't know how it happened, but it did. We became lovers and it was so easy to manufacture time together when we knew that Fernando was elsewhere. Getting pregnant with Sergio was a shock, but Fernando claimed parentage and the problem went away."

Carlos sipped his brandy and indicated that Almu continued.

"After Carmen was born, Fernando began to question the incompetence of the doctor who diagnosed him as being infertile. When a second, independent doctor confirmed the findings of the first, it became all too obvious who had been spending more time in my bed than their shared office. All hell broke loose."

"Did you want to leave with Jorge?"

"Yes, but Fernando said that he wouldn't allow his children to live with a whore and her pimp, as he called us. The business broke up acrimoniously and Fernando made it quite clear that if I wanted my children, it was to be on his terms. I loved my children more than anything in the world and accepted his conditions. I asked Jorge to stop calling me for the sake of the children."

Carlos returned the conversation to his original question.

"And Anna-Maria?"

"Jorge told me about her, though he himself knew very little. The Alvés family closed ranks when they had a secret to hide. I never confronted Fernando with the fact that I knew, I thought it better to let it carry on as it had always done, long before my arrival on the scene."

"And now, what will you do?"

Almu had obviously been considering this question herself, but hesitated before replying. Carlos saw a determination in her large, expressive eyes that had previously been missing.

"You think that I will go back to Jorge but I'm afraid that that ship sailed a long time ago, inspector. Fernando's finances are a mess. He didn't leave me as a rich woman. I do however, have this house, which I will sell and use the proceeds to buy something more realistic. Carmen and I will move on. If Fernando left us anything, it was the ability to survive without him."

The news of her husband's recent suicide hadn't affected Almu as much as Carlos expected. She actually seemed more saddened by Anna-Maria's murder, even though she had never met her. Surprisingly, she showed no pleasure in Pedro

Ribera's passing, and chose to pass the news to Carmen herself.

"Does he have family, inspector?"

"An ex-wife is all we know of."

"Pcrhaps he is luckier than some. What will happen to the money?"

"Anna-Maria burnt it. Ten million Euros were smouldering in a barbeque when we arrived. She thought that the money was the reason Sergio died."

"She may have been mad but maybe she saw something Fernando missed. If it weren't for the money, Sergio would still be with us. If his plan had succeeded, my husband would now be in Argentina. One way or another, I was going to be alone today. I will shed no tears for the passing of Fernando Alvés."

Carlos had done his job and passed on the news of a death to a next of kin. Compared to most, this was easy. Almu seemed calmer now than at any other time since he met her. Fernando's death, regardless of the circumstances, had given her a long awaited release that she couldn't have expected. She excused herself saying that she should tell Carmen of her father's death.

"Would you prefer me to do it, Almu?"

"No, inspector, this family has taken up quite enough of your time, thank you."

With the hard part of his job over, Carlos called Christiano and invited him to join him at the café Avenida. His sparring partner, Enrique, was sat in his usual place at the bar when he arrived. The welcome was as warm as it ever was.

"Carlos, you useless waste of taxpayer's money, how are you? I haven't seen you for a week. Have you been asleep in your office?"

Carlos ignored the words of his friend and raised two fingers in the direction of Juanvi the barman. He produced a glass, which he filled with red wine before topping up Enrique's.

"I have been busy enforcing the law."

"To what end?"

"I could have answered that question as a younger man, but now, I'm not so sure. Two hours ago, I was standing in a garden. The birds were singing and I had three people lying dead at my feet."

"Were you responsible for their deaths?"

"I'd like to think not. It's not my job to apportion blame. I do my best to sort out the problems people create, but sometimes they are too far gone by the time they come to our attention."

Christiano's arrival was acknowledged by Enrique.

"We can sleep soundly in our beds. Sherlock Holmes is here."

"And a merry Christmas to you too Enrique. Get me a glass of wine."

Enrique obliged and Carlos was impressed by the manner in which his sergeant had dealt with the most obnoxious man in the city.

"You're fat and stupid, but I think I'm going to like you," Enrique said grudgingly.

Christiano grinned and saw something similar crossing Enrique's face.

"How did it go with Almu Alvés, sir?"

"Surprisingly easy. She is a beautiful lady but she has an internal strength that will carry her through her loss and on to a better future. Have there been any developments at the Commissary?"

"Felipe has confirmed that the barbeque tray contained the cremated remains of ten million Euros."

"Fucking hell," Enrique gasped.

"You didn't hear that, Enrique," Carlos said firmly.

"Someone burned Ten million Euros. They must have been mad."

"You are closer to the truth than you will ever know. That is why I called you here, Christiano. I would like to take the opportunity to introduce you to the former owner of the majority of that money. He doesn't give interviews, and we usually need a warrant to get near his office, but I think he will be very interested in hearing what we have to tell him."

Christiano Marcos smiled in anticipation of the forthcoming meeting with Oleg Petrov. Even though he had no idea who the investigators were speaking about, Enrique smiled as the schadenfruede flowed around the bar.

"Three more wines before these officers leave to mete out justice, Juanvi."

Inspector Carlos Rico wasn't sure about justice, but this wasn't going to get in the way of passing on such a piece of bad news to his Russian adversary. As the three amigos sipped from their recharged glasses, there was a party atmosphere bubbling under the surface. Carlos burst the bubble and announced the need to move on.

"Enough of this gay banter. Sergeant Marcos and I have work to do. We'll see you when you learn how to behave like a normal member of society, Enrique."

"And fuck you too, coppers" was not an unexpected reply.

Oleg Petrov's office was guarded like a fortress so he knew that police officers were approaching long before they reached the front gate. As expected, he wanted them, and Carlos Rico in particular, to come and inform him of the whereabouts of his eight, or ten million Euros. His army had been actively seeking Pedro Ribera, with no success, and Oleg was getting agitated. He ordered that the detectives be sent directly to his office. Carlos expected no less.

This was the first time Carlos had gained access to the inner sanctum of the Russian mafia in Alicante and he intended to enjoy the moment.

"Keep your hands in your pockets and your mouth shut, Christiano. Do not react to any provocation. This is a golden opportunity for you to see the workings of one of our most formidable opponents. Petrov has established his kingdom over the past twenty years by a process of eliminating the opposition, one by one. He has used all of the expected tricks and some imported from his homeland. His legal front is construction and haulage, but it is a badly kept secret that he really makes his money through the usual avenues of the sex and drug trades. Money lending and laundering are also part of his portfolio and his heavily muscled henchmen make sure that everyone pays on time."

"Have we pulled him?"

"He has been in custody several times but his personal lawyer, Paulo Benitez, always gets him off. Others stick their hands in the air and confess to his sins. Three years in jail and all of your debts go away. We're not going to get Petrov today but I thought that this was an opportunity for you to make his acquaintance. Call it an investment."

Christiano knew that he was being primed for something that would probably happen after Carlos Rico had retired and felt flattered that he was being groomed to take down the man that his boss never managed to nail.

"Look and learn, sergeant."

The shake down came as a surprise to Christiano and only the recent words of his inspector resonating in his head stopped him reacting to the overly rough search techniques applied. Danny the doorman enjoyed his moment, and Christiano now owed him a testicle rattling that would be repaid in due course.

Oleg Petrov's office was as vulgarly offensive as they had expected. The paintings that adorned the oak panelled walls were authentic but crude. The highly polished desk was twice as large as it needed to be, and Petrov's throne bordered on the ridiculous. He had prepared for their arrival, and was suitably posed when they were escorted in. He looked up from a quickly closed document and settled back into his luxurious chair.

He pointed a lazy finger at the two carefully prepared chairs, deliberately set at a height lower than his own. Carlos and Christiano sat and waited for Oleg to speak.

"I believe that you have something to tell me, inspector?"

"Are you expecting good news, Mr Petrov?"

"Do the police ever bring good news?"

Carlos' expression gave nothing away. He wanted to get as much out of his time with the Russian as he possibly could. He responded with an obviously forced smile.

"I have come to tell you about events that occurred today relating to Fernando Alvés. You lent Fernando Alvés a considerable amount of money, I believe?"

"Whatever transaction passed between Mr Alvés and myself is not the business of the Alicante police."

"Fernando Alvés is dead."

For the first time, Oleg Petrov's reaction was genuine. His face froze. As much as he tried to hide his shock, his eyes betrayed him.

"Was it an accident?"

"He shot himself."

Carlos was toying with the Russian and Christiano was enjoying every minute.

"Why? He had already paid for the release of Sergio and Carmen."

"He was worried that you would have him killed."

"Why would I do that, inspector? The man owed me eight million Euros."

"The money has gone, Mr Petrov."

Carlos now had his complete and undivided attention. Oleg Petrov sat bolt upright in his chair and his hands grasped the edge of the desk.

"What do you mean, gone?"

"Did you know about his other daughter, Anna-Maria?"

"No. Is this relevant?"

"She was, shall we say, unstable. She burnt the money."

Oleg Petrov looked hard at the inspector as though waiting for the punch line to a bad joke, but no punch line came.

"No one would burn ten million Euros.

"She thought the money was evil. The money was why her brother, Sergio, died. She thought that her father was a rich man and the money was irrelevant. Your eight million Euros and two million of the former Fernando Alvés have been reduced to ash. I assume that you were insured, Mr Petrov?"

Oleg Petrov tried, unsuccessfully, to look unfazed. He lied.

"Of course. The money isn't an issue. Please send my condolences to his widow."

Carlos was happy; he had had his fun. Oleg Petrov was struggling to contain his rage and the inspector wanted to land one last blow before he left.

"Off the record, Mr Petrov, I know that you are embarrassingly out of pocket and no insurance agent is going to recompense you. Now that we aren't running around chasing kidnappers, the investigative branch of the Alicante Commissary will be concentrating on organised crime. We will be watching you and your band of thugs very closely."

Oleg Petrov's white knuckles now clenched the armrests of his chair. His smile was more of a facial contortion as he watched Carlos and Christiano leave his office.

"Good day, Mr Petrov. It's always a pleasure to spend time with you. Perhaps next time we will do it at the Commissary?"

Oleg Petrov snapped his fingers at Danny the doorman to escort his guests from the premises. The detectives left with a renewed levity in their step.

"Was that necessary, sir?" Christiano asked.

"Not at all, sergeant. But it was fun."

Christiano smiled and he saw that his inspector was struggling to contain his own smugness. Sometimes a coppers lot was a happy one.

The Verdict

An Asian girl is seriously assaulted, and a young black man stands accused. He claims they were lovers, but there is nothing to support this, as the victim lies in a coma. At his trial, the jury are directed to return a unanimous verdict, but prejudices and personal confrontations result in a very dysfunctional group who look unlikely to reach a harmonious conclusion. Alliances form, but discord prevails. Is it feasible that a jury can reach a decision based entirely on what is heard in the courtroom? *The Verdict* asks this question.

fiVe

New telecom company, 'fiVe', wants its name on everyone's lips and top ad agency Collards is commissioned. The 'fiVe' Show is born and Saturday night television would never be the same again, with its million pound prize making the show essential viewing. As customers flock to participate, human nature throws up a colourful array of complications. Redtop Journalist Rip Heggity thrusts himself into the chaotic, ensuing melee, but what he uncovers is not what he expected. This is not just a simple game with winners and losers. There is a lot more at stake, and the involvement of sinister entities means finding the truth is far from easy.

Clean Sweep

In the first of the DI Jim Bennett series, he faces the perpetual challenge of keeping two warring families apart in Welford, a dysfunctional town in the heart of England. A community of travelling gypsies stop to rest, and the daughter of their leader is viciously beaten, with every low life in town a suspect. When a young boy goes missing, everyone blames the gypsies, making the town a powder keg. Fire bombings of the homes of the Marston and Connelly families point to the gypsies taking matters into their own hands, and DI Jim Bennett knows the pressure is on him to stop an all-out war in Welford. When things seem at their darkest, a mysterious benefactor steps in to help.

Hunted

In the second DI Jim Bennett novel, he faces professional and emotional challenges as Welford descends once again into chaos. An ex-soldier becomes a one-man crime wave, quickly graduating from ram raiding to armed robbery and worse. A wave of metal thefts and pick pocketing drain police resources, while out of town, sheep rustling and violence surrounding a local foxhunt spiral out of control. As Jim tries to resolve these issues, his job is complicated further by the arrival of a new and difficult DCI. Jim is forced to use all of his experience in an attempt to swing the odds in his favour.

The Oubliette

In the third novel in the DI Jim Bennett series, a moneylender wakens in a dark hole, puzzled as to how he got there. 'The oubliette' is being used to address perceived injustices, with its master depriving his captives of everything until they confess their sins. Simultaneously, an art theft leaves CID puzzled due to the thief's ineptitude, and the death of two young men confirms the presence of crack cocaine on the streets of Welford. A confidence trickster, a geriatric thief, and a man with no memory add to the police workload forcing Jim Bennett to resort to a commodity that his DCI doesn't condone; a copper's instinct.

Alicante

Alicante in fiesta season is the backdrop to the story of Raúl Berbegal's transition from obsessive sociopath to sexually deviant psychopath. As he slays with apparent impunity, Inspector Carlos Rico must interpret the symbols left at the crime scenes to end a horrific killing spree. As the body count rises, so does the personal nature of their relationship.

Assumption

In the third novel in the DI Carlos Rico series, a cruise ship is hijacked and a city depositary robbed in sensational fashion on the same fiesta weekend. The motives appear to be the presence of a VIP passenger for the former and €30 million for the latter, but all is not as it seems. Two local criminal entities are involved, but to what extent? With the pressure on, Carlos Rico is assisted by the unconventional DI 'Tasty' McManus from New Scotland Yard, as they investigate a criminal world littered with dark characters.

Camden Lock Down

A number of seemingly unrelated events culminate in an explosion in London's Camden Lock on one of the busiest days of the year. The number of dead and injured is almost as high as the list of possible culprits, with the initial evidence showing that the police aren't without their share of the blame. Detective Inspector Bill 'Tasty' McManus is the controversial choice to investigate what actually happened in the vicinity of the Stables Market, and with a tapestry of lies and deceit waiting around every corner, he soon finds that he has few allies in his unpopular quest.

Phoenix

In the fourth novel in the DI Carlos Rico series, Oscar Sanchez breaks his brother out of a burning psychiatric hospital with one thought in mind: to kill. As police investigate, the uncertain body count rises. When the undisclosed modus operandi of the infamous Silk Tie Killer, a man thought long dead, is found at the scene of subsequent fires, the detectives fear they may have made a mistake. With fire and death raining down on the city, Carlos Rico must catch a ghost to end a nightmare, but it's never that simple in Alicante.

Printed in Great Britain
by Amazon

42642839R00183